HIS TOUCH

It was a simple matter, really, to move his hand to cup her head and bring her forward. With her height, there was an easy fit, and no long delay to the meeting of their mouths.

Lydia kissed with innocence that shifted to eagerness and her essence swirled on his tongue. Her willing participation was like ambrosia to a starving man. Need throbbed through him as Victor pulled her closer and deepened his kiss. One persuasive touch loosened her hold on the slit nightshirt.

He wanted to touch every inch of her skin, to trace the lines of her every curve, to taste her flesh. The material slipped from her shoulder and offered him a tantalizing glimpse of heaven.

BOOK YOUR PLACE ON OUR WEBSITE AND MAKE THE READING CONNECTION!

We've created a customized website just for our very special readers, where you can get the inside scoop on everything that's going on with Zebra, Pinnacle and Kensington books.

When you come online, you'll have the exciting opportunity to:

- View covers of upcoming books
- Read sample chapters
- Learn about our future publishing schedule (listed by publication month *and author*)
- Find out when your favorite authors will be visiting a city near you
- Search for and order backlist books from our online catalog
- Check out author bios and background information
- Send e-mail to your favorite authors
- Meet the Kensington staff online
- Join us in weekly chats with authors, readers and other guests
- Get writing guidelines
- AND MUCH MORE!

**Visit our website at
http://www.kensingtonbooks.com**

THE WEDDING RUNAWAY

KAREN L. KING

ZEBRA BOOKS
Kensington Publishing Corp.
www.kensingtonbooks.com

CHAPTER 1

November, 1818, Southern England

Lydia Margaret Hamilton ran up the stairs two at a time and burst into the private sitting room at the Cock and Bull Inn. "I bought two tickets for the mail coach and no one even looked at me!"

Her mouth pursed in disapproval, Jenny tossed a handful of Lydia's newly shorn blond curls into the small blaze behind the grate. Initially, the maid had refused to cut Lydia's hair. So Lydia had hacked off a big chunk with her sewing scissors. Once she had a big hole in her hair, Jenny had to even it up.

"Oh, that smells awful." Draping one leg over the chair arm, Lydia sprawled in her seat the way her brothers would. "By the way, I am to ride on the outside on the coachman's box."

Jenny put her hands on her slim hips and said as sternly as a girl of her diminutive stature could manage, "Miss Hamilton, you cannot ride on the outside."

"Don't be such a fusspot, Jenny. You are my maid, not my minder, and I refuse to let you ruin my last moments of freedom."

"Hardly freedom to be dressed in trousers and riding on a carriage box with the coachman, Miss."

On the contrary, for the first time in her life, Lydia was making all her own decisions. She had never experienced greater liberty and she lived in the freest country in the world. "I had to take an outside seat for one of us. There was only one inside seat left, or we'd have to wait for the next mail coach. It's not as if the weather is inclement, and I won't miss a bit of the countryside." Lydia smiled brightly. Snow probably covered Boston.

Lydia bounced out of the chair, too excited by her adventure to sit still, even if pantaloons allowed her to sprawl with unfettered abandon. "You'll have to stop calling me miss, or we'll get stares. Besides, riding on top is what a young man would do."

Jenny folded her arms. "But you're not a young man, and pretending to be one will get us both in a peck of trouble."

"I pass, don't I? No one looked twice at me." Lydia spun around.

She'd registered in the mail coach logbook as Mr. Leonard M. Hall, from Boston, Massachusetts, America. She didn't want her brothers, father, or abandoned fiancé to easily chase after her if they followed her across the ocean.

"From Plymouth Rock to Plymouth, England," she joked to the clerk. He had given her one of those absent smiles as if he were trying to appear amused by the young American, but really hadn't paid her any mind.

Jenny stared at Lydia's front, specifically at the juncture at the top of her thighs. "You don't quite look a man."

The two pads strapped around her waist straightened her midsection, hiding her curved-in sides. She didn't have much to bind down on top, but she planned to wear her coat and waistcoat at all times. The towering concoction of her cravat hid her lack of an Adam's apple. While pretending to be a young man, her ungainly height became a blessing. Yet Jenny frowned.

"What is it?"

Jenny blushed. "Well, a man is . . . has other parts."

Lydia twisted her lips to the side and looked down. Jenny at sixteen had more experience with male parts than Lydia had at twenty-one, even though she had five older brothers and had a fairly good idea of the differences in their anatomy.

"Should we roll up a sock? I suppose I could sew up and stuff, ah . . . er . . . a male appendage, but you'll have to help me design it." Lydia opened her trunk and retrieved her sewing supplies.

"Oh, no!"

"We've got a few hours, until the mail coach leaves this evening."

"I'm not going. You never said anything about pretending to be a young man when you said we were going to London."

Lydia sighed. She supposed she should have anticipated this outburst from Jenny. When the maid had opened the trunk and found Trevor's—Lydia's youngest older brother—outgrown shirts, jackets and waistcoats along with James's—Lydia's oldest and largest brother—breeches and pantaloons, Jenny had gasped and fallen on her backside. It was the final clue that this trip, despite Lydia's insinuations, was not sanctioned by Lydia's father or fiancé.

"Jenny, I am determined to spend time in London and you can go with me or you can find your own way back to Boston." Lydia hated to be mean, but she needed Jenny's help. "Might I remind you that you would not even have employment if I hadn't interceded on your behalf after you were caught in the bushes with the neighbor's groom."

Jenny blushed. "Well, I won't likely have employment when I get back after helping you with this nonsense, will I?"

"When we go back, I will tell Papa I left you no choice in the matter and you did your best to protect me from my worst impulses. Fair enough?" Lydia grimaced. "Or if I end up marrying Mr. Sullivan, I will have fits until he finds you a position in my new household."

"Should have married him and been done with it. I don't know what you hope to gain delaying the marriage."

Well, there was a way to take the wind out of her sails. Until recently, Lydia had been anticipating her impending nuptials with, if not enthusiasm, at least a little joy. "I overheard him talking about me. He called me mannish. Would you want to marry a man who called you mannish?"

Jenny, who was petite and perfectly rounded in all the right places, would never have to worry about being called mannish. Her brown eyes filled with sympathy nonetheless.

That statement had been bad enough. While Lydia didn't think herself particularly vain, her fiancé's opinion of her had stung. But it didn't end there.

Her betrothed had confided in his friend that he
meant to take over her father's shipping company
and oust her brothers from control . . . and that marrying Lydia was the means and the price of taking
over the lucrative enterprise.

Shaken, Lydia had tried to tell her father, but
he'd been firm. She was to marry Oscar Sullivan
and that was that. He thought she was just trying to
worm out of another proposal.

If her father's business was her main attraction
for Mr. Sullivan, then she could act so outrageously
that she was disowned. If he thought she was mannish, then she would become a man. Coupled with
her desire to have a European tour like all her
brothers, the solution to run away to England and
masquerade as a young man struck her as the only
way to go.

Besides, the only way she could get into the gambling hells and increase her modest amount of
money to see them through was as a young man.

Northern England

The smell of smoke and ash hung heavy in the
air. Even after a week, pockets of Victor John
Bartlett's home still smoldered. A wisp of gray
curled in the air above what had been the west wing
of his estate. The only part that remained standing
was the menacing thirteenth-century keep that
loomed sentinel over the river and the road. It pro-
claimed that the earls of Wedmont owned this land
and would repel all interlopers.

But the destruction had come from the inside.

Eleven of the previous twelve earls of Wedmont were probably rolling in their graves, and blaming Victor for bringing in one not of their kind, one who finally finished the destruction. His own father, no doubt, moldered silently in his crypt. After his wild, wicked, wastrel life, nothing was likely to disturb his eternal rest. He had started the ruin of the long and noble earldom, and he had never particularly cared what happened to his son, much less the family estate.

Victor kicked a pile of coals in the keep's storage room entrance, dispersing their nearly spent heat. He climbed over the blackened remains of a roof beam and crossed into the hollow shell of blackened stone. The once mighty rafters were now jagged black spikes of charred timber on the ash-coated stone floor. Five years ago he'd been praying for this to happen. The fates, as ever, got the timing wrong.

The heat radiating from the scorched stones irritated the burn on his forehead. Picking up a piece of twisted metal that must have been the blade of a medieval battle lance that once hung on the wall, Victor climbed back out to the lawn. The neatly kept expanse contrasted oddly with the ruins behind him.

Servants had piled salvaged pewter plates and cups in the middle of the drive. Not that there was much. The valuable plate and antiques had been sold off long ago, before he'd married to restore wealth to the estate.

A well-appointed traveling coach swayed up the drive. No markings or crest adorned the mahogany paneled doors. His father-in-law.

Dread poured through Victor's veins. Dread, guilt, and regret. The fire followed the argument he'd had with his wife. The last argument he'd ever have with his wife. Victor clenched his hand. The lance's edges cut into his palm and reminded him how badly he'd failed her.

Now he had to face his father-in-law and tell him his daughter was dead, and Victor hadn't been able to save her. He'd carried her kicking and screaming from the blazing rooms, once. She'd dashed back in, and he hadn't succeeded in pulling her out a second time.

His portly father-in-law descended from the carriage. "What a disaster." He shook his head, took a surveying look, and pronounced, "We'll rebuild, grander than before."

"I should rather not." Still affected by the smoke he'd swallowed, Victor's voice rasped. "It is done. I have no good memories of this place." *And no heirs for which to preserve it.*

Victor would be the last Earl of Wedmont, unless a distant cousin was found after his demise. His father had littered plenty of by-blows across England, but he couldn't be bothered to sire more legitimate children. Victor would never marry again. He'd failed grandly enough the first time.

He dropped the twisted piece of metal, wiped his sooty palms against his thighs, and crossed to his wife's father. As he neared him, he saw the swollen red eyes of a man who'd been crying. Did he know? Suspect?

As Victor drew up close, the older man threw his arms around him and clapped him on the back.

"I know, I know. I stopped by the church and spoke with the vicar. I know you tried to get her out."

Victor had tried. Tried to make his marriage work, tried to love his wife, tried to stave off the madness that made her crazed. One out of three wasn't a raving success.

"You were a good husband to my gel. I didn't think you'd be, what with your gambling and you needing my money and all to save your bacon. You toffs aren't expected to keep to your wives, but you did."

His father-in-law clapped him on the back and held him in his arms, while sniffling and singing qualified praises. Victor wanted to sink through the ground. Using his wife's money to pay for whores or a mistress had been beyond even his limited moral code. And he'd supported himself with his gambling too many years to find much pleasure in it these days.

Although he found himself longing for his bachelor days, with a bottle of madeira at his elbow and a flush of cards in his hand. He wanted simpler times and simpler pleasures and to return to his old haunts.

Victor bit his tongue so hard it bled. His main vice these days was spitting out whatever caustic thought entered his head. Would that he had bit his tongue off a week ago rather than say what he'd said to Mary Frances.

"I know you brought in the best doctors to work with her," the older man said.

"Should have had them work with me." If he had any inkling that she would burn the place down, he never would have provoked her. But then his mouth had always been his downfall.

"There there. I know you're blue-deviled now."
Mr. Chandler released him but continued to pat his
shoulder affectionately. "Time heals all wounds."

Victor shook his head. "Not all wounds. What . . ."
he let his voice trail off. Whatever had brought on
Mary Frances's madness, whatever past injury
turned her into a clawing, biting demon at the
most inopportune moments didn't need to be dis-
cussed now . . . or ever. It wouldn't bring her back.
It wouldn't help him to help her. She was beyond
help now, beyond wounding now. His destruction
of her was complete.

"I hoped you and Mary Frances might have given
me grandchildren—"

Victor snorted. His wounds were still fresh.

"—but you're a young man still and you can
marry again and get children."

"I have a daughter." That he could not claim.

"You need sons. Sons to take over my businesses,
a son to carry on your title."

Victor winced. His wife wasn't in her grave yet. Of
course, if she'd lived he would never have had any
children by her. A wave of guilt swept over him. His
father-in-law apparently still thought of him as his
heir. "You are not so old." Victor told his father-in-
law. "You should remarry and sire your own sons."

Harold Chandler shook his head. "No, no. Mary
Frances never told you, did she?"

"What?" Was there something Victor should have
known? A clue that would have explained his wife's
insanity? A bit of information that would help him
make sense of it all?

"My wife Mary is still alive. Gave me five children,

she did, but Mary Frances is the only one what lived to be full grown. Good woman, my wife."

Where was she now? In almost four years of marriage to Mary Frances, Victor had never heard mention of her mother. He'd assumed she'd passed away, but was she chained to a wall in an asylum somewhere? Bedlam? Was that where Mary Frances got her madness? Victor stared at his father-in-law.

"She's in Newgate Prison."

"For arson?" Victor inquired. Perhaps starting fires ran in the family.

Lydia's head thrummed and her stomach churned as she tried to reach through the throng of male bodies and get her markers down in a hedge bet. She had her main bet down, but hazard was one of the few games where smart betting and hedging guaranteed winning.

A few of the men crowding the gaming hell could have done with a little better hygiene. She edged away from a short man wearing a stained shirt. By the time she repositioned herself, it was too late to get down her hedge bet.

Too much wine clouded her head. Laying her bets was hard enough, let alone remembering the odds and how to play the dice throws.

The thrower crabbed out and the dice were thrust in her hand as her large bet disappeared off the table. Fiddlesticks!

Her heart in her throat, she pitched the dice on the table. Throwing the dice made her the center of very rowdy attention. She had been in disguise for nearly three months now and the crowds in

London had grown until this hell on a Friday evening was stuffed beyond capacity. But then London thronged with houses, shops, museums, churches and manufactories. People, carriages, horses and carts crowded the streets, while a gray haze of coal smoke hung over it all.

In this exclusively male environment, the men jostled and shouldered and smacked each other like a pack of puppies. She expected that at any second one of them would reach over and nip her on the ear.

Lydia had done a credible job of disguising herself. She had the walk, her voice was naturally low, and she and Jenny had giggled all the way through the construction of a stuffed male member, now sewn to her drawers. But she couldn't quite manage to force her way through a crowd and it hampered her ability to bet effectively. She desperately needed more money to continue to live in London as a carefree young man. Unlike her brothers, she couldn't apply to her father for more blunt to see her through.

The hard drinking required of all young men on the town left her brain muzzy. She never wanted to stand out from the crowd, so she drank along with her cohorts.

Finally, she passed the dice. Lydia concentrated on the throw. A main of six. She reached to place her markers on the table and was jostled out of the way. "Excuse me," she muttered.

The other side of the table looked just as crowded. She swallowed and ducked under an arm. An elegant hand with long tapered fingers placed the bets she had tried to make as she watched with dismay. An elbow clipped her in the chin, and she reared back. The croupier called the bets and the dice were thrown.

Twelve. Double sixes. She knew exactly what to bet for a sure win. She ducked and squiggled her way to the table and her hand collided with the hand placing the same bets. She followed the line of the hand, up a black sleeve, to a stare at a man taller than she.

He gave her a mocking smile, if you could call it that. More just the slightest lift of his lips in a face she would call handsome, but for the slight air of wickedness in the lift of his winged eyebrows. His too-long walnut hair waved and curled in a studied disorder.

And she forgot to get her hedge bet down. Damn. He pulled his winnings from the table and met her stare with a slight furrowing of his brow, then a wink.

Heat flooded her face. Had he guessed she was female? Why the wink?

She stared at the green baize-covered table. Should she leave? But she had made good money in nights past here, and she needed to pay for the new lodgings tomorrow or she and Jenny would be out on the streets.

London proved more expensive than she expected, and she hadn't gotten a good exchange rate on her American dollars. Then they had been robbed.

While Lydia had been bathing, a thief had broken into their lodgings and stolen her main cache of six-teen hundred pounds. Lydia had dived sopping wet into her trunk. Hiding in the confined darkness, she had been as much afraid of being exposed as a girl as being caught naked, and she had not even tried to stop the robber.

New lodgings at a better address were necessary or Jenny's mutiny would be complete and Lydia might as well go home. There had been a second hidey-hole of money, but Lydia had spent the evening watching it disappear off the table. Why was her luck turning bad now?

All right, it wasn't so much luck. Gambling had risks, but she minimized them. What she couldn't do was compensate for failing to lay the necessary bets on the table. With the right wagers, chance determined whether she won big or won small. Frankly, she'd be happy with small wins.

Lydia elbowed her way back to the hazard table. She ended up next to the man in black, the man who had placed the same bets as she did. The dice rolled up seven. She reached out with her markers. Mr. Stained Shirt shoved her away from the table.

This was growing ridiculous. As she tried to move forward, two burly men snagged her elbows with theirs and moved in a lockstep toward the door, not the front door, but the back door that led to a dark alley.

What was happening? Where were they taking her?

Scream! She thought, but bit her tongue instead. Men don't scream.

"Let me go!" she managed in a gulped whisper.

The men, one of which was the man in the stained shirt, didn't falter.

She planted her boots, but they just dragged her backward as if she were the merest boy. She twisted her hips and planted her boots sideways. The two men lifted her. Mr. Stained Shirt flashed her a surprised glance as if he expected her to weigh more.

Lord, she was about to be tossed out into the alley like refuse onto a dung heap.

"Thinks you need a lesson, boy," said the smelly one. He leaned close to her and his fetid breath washed across her face. "I 'ave a 'ankering to rearrange that pretty face of yours."

"No, that's not necessary." The door loomed in front of her. And just being tossed out seemed like a good idea now. If she threw her feet up on either side of the doorframe, how long she could hang on?

"Quite necessary, boy. We got to teach young upstarts like you," said Mr. Stained Shirt.

"Don't know your proper place," said Mr. Bad Breath.

No, she didn't and Lydia couldn't decide for the life of her if screaming would make the situation worse or better, so they just dragged her along like a reluctant puppy fighting a leash.

"Where are you taking my friend?" came a voice from behind her. A lazy, almost bored voice.

She didn't care who he was, but friend, most definitely. Thank the stars he'd spoken up before she screamed.

The two men released her arms and stepped to the side, looking for all the world as if they'd only been standing beside her. "This chap is a friend of yours, you say, guv?" Mr. Stained Shirt sounded doubtful.

"Yes, my American friend—and I would like a private room to play piquet. I'm bored with hazard. Have your master supply us a room, clean cards and a couple of bottles of your best madeira."

The two thugs drifted away from Lydia as though they had never noticed her.

She had to play piquet with this newly acquired *friend*? But as she turned, the gentleman in black stood with his feet planted and his arms folded menacingly across his chest. His dark gaze swept over her and he looked nothing like a friend. In fact, his expression reflected disgust. Being thrown in a pile of dung after a couple of facers might be preferable to spending time in a private room with him.

Interceding on the impertinent colonial's behalf was the last thing Victor wanted. The boy bothered Victor. Exactly what bothered him, he couldn't quite say.

The youth's clothes were atrocious, outdated and ill-fitting, even if they were made of quality cloth. The blond mop of curls would benefit immensely from the attentions of a good barber. While the chap seemed to have gained his height and his legs were nicely turned, his shoulders were as puny as a twelve-year-old's. His wide, blue-eyed stare marked him as far too innocent to be on the town.

"They're on to you, you know. I take it you've beaten the house a bit too often for their liking," Victor said.

"I've won some," said the youth while digging his toe into the carpet.

His black riding boots were well made, but no gentleman wore boots after dark. It just wasn't the thing.

Pink swept over the boy's high cheekbones. He blushed too much, thought Victor.

Victor wanted to enjoy his freedom from responsibilities, not to take on a protégé. And an American?

Damn rebel would probably fail to be suitably impressed by Victor's title, although it was saving his hide right now.

That moment when their hands had touched and Victor had felt . . . what, he didn't know. A reluctant admiration for the boy's betting ability?

The boy tugged down his jacket and stared at the floor. "Uh, thank you, sir," he mumbled in a too-girlish voice. It was low enough to be a male's voice, but his inflections were off. Or perhaps the harsh cadence of an American accent just grated.

Victor rubbed his hand against his forehead. "Come on, then. See if you can beat me and take my money."

The youth's head came up sharply. "I don't mean to take your money, uh . . . sir."

"Why not? I have plenty. I can afford to lose, even if the house cannot. If you win fairly, you are welcome to my largess." Victor bowed. "You may call me Wedmont."

The unmannerly youth stared and didn't return a leg. Rude young thing. Didn't he know he should bow to his betters?

Victor turned and strode toward the room he'd requested. He held the door to the private parlor until the cub ducked inside. "You have a name, do you not?"

"Yes," said the boy with that wide-eyed stare that made Victor uneasy. "L-Leonard Hall, from Massachusetts. That's in America."

"Yes, I am aware of where that is. Do you have family here?"

"No, not at present, sir."

Victor gritted his teeth. *My lord* was the correct

form of address. Not *sir.* He was an earl, not a shop-
keeper. "Call me Wedmont, Lenny."

"Leonard, sir."

"I like Lenny better. You are still wet behind the
ears, cub. And it is customary to bow when introduced."

"In America we usually shake hands."

"I daresay you realize we are not in America."

"No, I guess not." Leonard looked around as if
just becoming aware of his surroundings.

Victor stepped forward, and Leonard jerked
back.

"Have a seat." Victor gestured toward the table.

"I think I should go now," Leonard backed toward the door.

Victor sat and picked up the deck. "Very well, but
I can guarantee that you shall be rewarded with a
thorough thrashing. The proprietor of this hell is
obviously dissatisfied with your person." Victor removed the low cards. "Cannot say I blame him, with
the fit of your coat."

Leonard took a desperate look at the door as if it
were barred and locked.

"Sit. I shall give you a chance to win whatever you
could have taken from the house. If you prove your
mettle, I might take you to a respectable club where
they don't discourage the winners with beatings."

Leonard stepped forward with a hint of a wry
smile on his face. "How do they discourage them?"

Victor glanced up. A frisson of unease coursed
through him. "Plenty of drink, usually. Or black-
balling. Or in the gaming hells that don't require
membership, lightskirts."

Damn, if Leonard didn't blush again. He gripped

the back of his chair. "I'm afraid I don't have the stakes. I did rather poorly tonight."

Either the youth was smart enough to realize he had a tough opponent in Victor or he really was short of funds. "I'll happily take your vowels, Mr. Hall. No need for me to relieve you of the last of your funds." Victor tossed the cards across the table at Leonard. "Check the deck and tell me if it's marked." He leaned back, draping one arm over the back of his chair and reaching out to hold the chair back beside him.

Leonard looked down at the cards. "Vowels?"

The boy was really too young for the lesson he was about to receive. Victor intended to show him what matching wits with a man who had made his living from gambling for years was like. Maybe if the cub got in deep enough, Victor could exchange the cub's promise to avoid gambling for his debts.

"I.O.U.s," explained Victor. Any schoolboy in England would have known that. "Have you never had blunt with which to play?"

"I've never played more than I could afford to lose." Leonard gulped air. "Before now."

He sat and gathered the cards, then looked through them carefully. The cub shuffled and dealt.

"Five pounds a point?" Victor asked.

The lad's sure dealing faltered and he flipped a card face up. Was the cub actually *sensible* about gambling? Or was it just that he hadn't learned to cover his debts in the time-honored method of getting a loan from a cent-per-center?

Of course not. Impossible that this youth was of the age of majority. Victor would bet he was barely sixteen. "What brings you all the way across the pond from the Colonies to London?"

"Just here for a tour, like my brothers."

Victor studied the boy. Not like his brothers. And he'd yet to meet an American who didn't take exception to their fledgling country being called a colony. "I should imagine your brothers were older when they took a tour."

"Only James, because the war was on."

Victor picked up his hand and arranged his cards. "And did they supply you with reference letters to friends so that you might be properly introduced to society?"

Lenny dropped his chin and shook his head.

"Surely, your family had some acquaintance here in London to look out for you?"

Lenny stared at his cards as if they were engrossing. He blew out a stiff breath of air before answering. "No, my family has been in America for several generations. We don't know anyone in England."

His older brothers had failed to make any friends during their stays? "So you are sent out in the world at the tender age of a dozen years? Your parents must be anxious to be rid of you."

"I'm one and twenty," Leonard said, and then looked unsure.

"You do not shave. You are not of age."

Leonard swallowed hard. "Indian blood. They don't shave, you know. My grandfather's mother." He shrugged. "Guess I got it from there."

Victor rolled his eyes. As a lie it was almost plausible, were it not for the blue eyes and blond hair. No doubt, Leonard was a sharp one. A bit too handy with his prevarications, which normally would have made Victor want to wash his hands of the youth. But an odd urge to protect the cub overrode Victor's usual dislike of dishonesty. With his newfound penchant for caretaking, that worried him almost as much as the strangeness of the feeling.

Should have retrieved the boy from the beating he was about to receive, driven him home, and vowed never to see the wastrel-in-training ever again.

CHAPTER 2

Lydia couldn't believe that she had a thousand pounds tucked into her pockets. In one night she'd gained back over half of the fortune it had taken weeks to amass.

As Mr. Wedmont's carriage rattled through the cobbled streets of London, fog grayed the air. The pink dawn strained to bleed through. Lydia folded her arms across her chest. She feared the full light of day might make her attire less concealing of her gender. He already was suspicious of her background.

"I shall call on you at one and take you to my tailor, cub," said Mr. Wedmont.

The idea of a tailor measuring her chased gratification right out of her body. Fear and fascination battled within her. Lydia squirmed in her seat. His dark-eyed stare made her nervous on more than one occasion this night. She kept wanting to clamp her knees together, but gentlemen, boys especially, didn't sit like that. "That's not necessary."

"Yes, it is. I cannot take you to my gentlemen's club if you dress like that."

His dark eyes roved over her with a freedom she found far too familiar, but he thought he looked at a young man. "I don't need a gentlemen's club. I just need a place to play hazard."

"You need to go where the players were born into their wealth and only shrug their shoulders when they lose a few thousand pounds. Men who have had to work hard to earn their money are less forgiving when they part with it."

Mr. Wedmont leaned over and caught a piece of Lydia's sleeve in his fingers. "The material is adequate quality, but I can only assume the tailors in Boston leave much to be desired. Be ready for me when I call."

Lydia panicked. Then she tried to relax and sprawl in the seat. "If you would just give me his direction. I'm sure I won't be awake at one."

"Then I shall have to rouse you."

The idea of this man shaking her awake in her bed provoked a truly awful image in her head. Heat swirled under her skin. Wayward thoughts about her rescuer invaded her mind. "I really don't need new clothes."

"Yes, I assure you, you do. When one is making one's living at gambling, then one must do everything one can to not appear shabby." Wedmont lifted an eyebrow. "You must ever look as if you are not in need of winning."

Lydia took a stiff breath. He looked wicked and very much a person who knew all about less-than-savory aspects of living, but managed to do it with a refined air. "Still, I have enough clothes to see me through my visit." If she could avoid him, maybe he'd forget about her.

Wedmont glanced to her burgeoning pockets. "You have enough money for a few decent outfits."

"Not today." She needed to move to new lodgings now that she could afford more rent. "I have prior commitments, you see."

"Fine, I'll come for you tomorrow at one, then. We shall see my barber, too. That is, if you promise to stay out of the hells this evening."

Lydia blanched. He would discover her identity if he kept this up. Would she have to insult him to get him to leave her alone? "I'm mindful of the debt I owe you, but really, sir. You have no need to immerse yourself in my affairs."

Mr. Wedmont folded his arms. "Really?"

Lydia folded her arms too and gave a short nod.

"You have no family or connections for protection. You have men ready to beat you into a bloody pulp if you so much as walk past that gaming establishment again. You likely have no means of support other than your winnings. You are as lost as a babe in the woods. Without a bit of guidance, you shall likely turn up floating in the Thames, boy."

Resentment welled up in Lydia. He might very well be right, but she could not risk exposure as a girl. "Why do you want to help me?"

"Bloody hell if I know."

Shocked by the swear words that normally would be kept from her ears, Lydia glared at him.

He glared back. "What are you, a minister's son?"

Oh, Lordy, a boy would not have been shocked. "No, my father owns a large shipping enterprise. My grandfather started the business years ago."

One side of his mouth came up in a lopsided smile. "So, well-to-do by colonial standards."

"We are not colonists anymore. How many times

do we have to whip you Brits in a war, before you recognize our country?"

"Mayhap a dozen or more times. Mayhap never."

He grinned, and her heart flip-flopped. Oh, he was an attractive man. More attractive than her supposed fiancé, even if Mr. Wedmont was older than she by perhaps a decade.

Her anger melted into panic that she would not be rid of this man. Doubt edged in. Perhaps she had made mistakes. Perhaps a young man did need an older man's guidance. And perhaps she really wanted to see him again, because his dark eyes and wry sarcasm curled her toes. Which was all for naught, because she needed him to think of her as a young man.

"Damned if I can figure out why I have decided to tutor you. I cannot say I like you much."

Or maybe she only liked him because he wasn't treating her as a weak, inconsequential woman. Fiddlesticks—he disliked her?

That was best, she told herself.

She could move to different lodgings today and lie low and surely he would forget about her. A misplaced sense of obligation was unlikely to prompt great efforts to find her. A sharp pang of regret stabbed under her breastbone.

She blinked back a sudden wash of sentiment that clouded her eyes. For a moment she missed being female. She would have liked to flirt with this man, but then again she really liked his frank roughness with her.

The carriage drew to a stop, and Lydia ducked toward the door. "I thank you very much for your assistance last night, and the pleasure of your gaming."

"We shall make a gentleman of you yet, cub."

Not expecting him to follow, she stopped close to the step and turned around to bid him good night. He shoved her upper arm, pushing her out of his way.

Lydia stumbled, although he hadn't shoved hard enough to cause harm. Would he follow her all the way into her lodgings? She had to stop him, before Jenny gave her real identity away.

Lydia faced him and gave a ridiculous bow, more like a servant than a gentleman. She intended to end things here on the sidewalk. "A pleasure to make your acquaintance, Mr. Wedmont."

"Just Wedmont," he muttered.

"Should you like me to walk the horses, milord?" asked the coachman from the box.

As she raised up from her near-genuflection, she saw clearly for the first time the crest on the carriage door. Good heavens, he was some sort of royalty.

"No, I'll just be a minute," he said to his coachman.

"My lord?" echoed Lydia weakly.

He leaned back against his carriage and cocked one heel up on the step. "And I thought from the way you nearly scraped your forehead on the pavement while making a leg, you might have realized the error of your ways."

"What are you?"

"A gentleman. However, I daresay there are those who would disagree with that appellation."

"I mean, you have some kind of title?"

"Yes, I am the Earl of Wedmont." He looked

amused. "Why, I am surprised to find you in awe. I thought you Americans had decided titles are passé and that all men are equal."

Lydia straightened. "We are equal."

"Not yet, cub. You have too much to learn. Although you might be my equal in piquet."

"I'm your superior in piquet." She had, after all, won three of their four games. "I'd say we were equal in hazard."

She almost melted into a pool of frayed nerves as she stared at him. She had to get away from him and stay away from him. Deceiving a lord was probably a crime. And what had she done, telling him her family was in shipping? Weren't all noblemen part of the government in England? He probably wielded enough power to learn who she was.

She stepped backward. "Well, good-bye, Mist . . . er, my lord."

"Wedmont will do, Lenny. Or if you can't manage that, you might just call me Victor. Although, I daresay as young as you are, my friends shall think you impudent. But far be it from me to offend your American views of equality."

Lydia took another step backward and resisted the urge to turn tail and run. Victor, oh my word, now she would think of him by his given name. Best if she didn't call him anything. "Yes, good night."

He looked around. "You need better lodgings."

Realizing how rundown the neighborhood looked, Lydia cringed. She'd been concerned about cost when she arrived, and she had not known if her gambling would be successful. "Yes, I agree. I'll see to it right away." Today, even.

"Perhaps, you'd better get your things and come stay with me."

"No!"

Victor swung around to stare at her. Lydia cursed her vehement objection. Would a young man from America turn down the opportunity to stay with an English peer? Probably not.

"Ah well, as an American, we value liberty above all else."

"Very well, cub. If independence means so much to you." He withdrew a card from his pocket. "Should you change your mind, here is my direction. I bid you good morning then, sir."

He turned and in one fluid motion opened the carriage door and stepped up into it.

Lydia stared at the nether side he'd presented to her. She had never particularly noticed a man's lower portions before, but Victor's seemed particularly fine. Long legs, slender hips, and perhaps she was thinking of a male's special appendages, because there was no way a tailor could mistake her for a male. Not that she had looked *there*. She shut her eyes.

Her thoughts raced down a road she couldn't travel dressed as a man. *Face it, Lydia, you are just perverse.* Just as her brothers and father said. In all the years since her eighteenth birthday when she'd been told to find a man to marry, she'd never come across one that interested her the way Victor did, despite his grudging rescue. She could never see him again.

Now, she had to remove to different lodgings, and that left her sad and empty.

* * *

Exhaustion made Lydia's eyes scratchy and her limbs heavy. She traveled to three advertised places before she found furnished lodgings in a better neighborhood, just off Bond Street. She paid the exorbitant rent, signed a lease for six months, and she and Jenny wrestled her trunks up the narrow outside stairs.

The lease worried her, but if she had to leave her lodgings, Mr. Hall would disappear into the ether and Miss Hamilton would reappear and return to America. Jenny wasn't happy, so Lydia thrust a five-pound note into her hand and told her to go buy a pretty for herself.

A heavy melancholy overshadowed her satisfaction that Lord Wedmont would not be able to locate her on the morrow for his self-appointed duty of improving her wardrobe. She told herself her tearfulness was brought on by a lack of sleep. Pretending to be someone else meant she could not let anyone get close, no matter what. Besides, if she bought new clothes, she wanted lace and ribbons. She wanted dresses.

Lydia struggled to remove her jacket, waistcoat and shirt, then unwrap the bindings that squished down her chest. She had been dressed as a man for over twenty hours, and her bound breasts ached. The freedom of movement trousers allowed came with a price.

She collapsed on her bed and must have dozed for a bit. A tap on the door brought her upright. Fiddlesticks, she didn't even have on a shirt.

The tapping rapped louder.

Oh, what if it was the landlord? He had a key. Lydia scrabbled off the side of the bed for her shirt.

She calmed as she drew the material over her head. It was probably Jenny.

Lydia slid to the door in her stockinged feet. "I told you to take the key," she said as she swung open the door.

A man stood there.

She slammed the door.

The tapping politely resumed. "Mr. Hall?"

"Fiddlesticks!" muttered Lydia. Had he seen that she had breasts? She ran across the room, grabbed her waistcoat and jacket and stuffed her arms into them. She put her hand to her throat. Her neck was too feminine looking to be seen bare. "Just a minute," she called.

She lacked the time to tie on a cravat. She grabbed a handkerchief and sloppily looped it around her neck. For God's sake, she'd never sleep without her shirt on again.

"Mr. Hall, I didn't mean to startle you. I am here at my lord's request. My name is Millars. I'm Lord Wedmont's valet."

She yanked open the door and folded her arms across her chest. "What?"

The man gave her an odd look, and Lydia prayed her lack of binding wasn't obvious. Oh my goodness, she'd forgotten the pads she wore around her waist to disguise the inward curves of her female form.

He bowed. Lydia froze. Was she supposed to bow in return? These English rules were so bizarre. She decided to be a rude American. She wasn't that sure of all the rules for proper male behavior in the United States. The last thing she needed to do was draw attention to her figure, so she held herself as stiff as a board. Boards did not bend easily, and she might splinter if she tried to do so.

"The Earl of Wedmont requests your presence at dinner tonight. He will send his carriage for you at half past seven."

How had he found out where she lived so fast? Shocked, she stared at the man.

"Dinner will be served at eight."

"I can't," Lydia finally managed and realized her mouth hung open. She snapped her jaw shut.

"I had the liberty of passing through the kitchen earlier, retrieving my lord's laundry, you see. I assure you, the smells made one quite delirious with pleasure. Cook is preparing a beef ragout with sherry sauce, also stuffed partridges with apricot fritters. There shall be apple tarts and plum pudding. Surely you will not eat so well here."

Her mouth watered. "I really cannot. Do tell his lordship that I am most grateful for his offer."

"He will not be happy if I return with a refusal."

Lydia blinked. "I have other plans."

"They cannot be delayed until after you dine . . . sir?"

The servant pursed his lips to the side and gave her a long look.

Lydia could not bear his scrutiny any longer. That Victor wouldn't leave her alone was bad enough. What would he do if he knew she was female? "Very well. I'll attend."

She shut the door before the man finished his bow. She felt awful and exhausted.

"Half past seven . . . sir."

"Yes, I heard you," she returned through the door. Good heavens, the door was thin.

"Very good . . . sir."

The long pauses before the *sirs* bothered her. Did he suspect? She raced over and opened the small shaving stand. The looking glass was only a four-inch circle and try as she might, she couldn't tell if her gender was obvious.

Either way, she didn't know whether to be exhilarated or alarmed. She suspected she was both. And for heaven's sake, how did Victor discover her new address within a day?

Victor woke in the early afternoon feeling rather peevish. He'd had a dream in which Leonard figured most prominently. A bizarre dream, but then one couldn't control dreams. Perhaps his dreaming mind had chosen to focus on Leonard rather than face the demons of his life.

His valet entered his room on tiptoe, whispered, "My lord?" and stood waiting expectantly.

"What is it, Millars?"

"It appears you are about to have guests. The butler would like to know if you are at home?"

Victor's first inclination was to say no, but company had to be preferable to ruminating on the dream he'd had. He rolled out of bed and moved to the window overlooking the square. As he looked down and saw blond curls, his first thought was of Leonard. Although Leonard wouldn't be wearing a dress or holding a squirming toddler.

At least Victor didn't think so. His dream had been rather muddled on that point.

No, the curls were in a froth of haute couture, pinned on top of the woman's head.

"I believe it is the Davieses and their children."

Ah, it was Sophie, his best friend and worst enemy's wife. But they only had one child.

"You could have told me before . . ." but he stopped breathing as Keene stood beside the carriage step. A small girl took Keene's extended right hand and stepped down, both her feet daintily stopping on each of the two steps.

Victor's heart pounded as he watched the tiny girl, her white pinafore neat and smudge-free, her ruffled pantaloons brushing the tops of her black patent-leather shoes. Long, dark sausage curls flowed down her back, held away from her face with a large blue ribbon. She looked up at his window, her dark eyes wide and wary, and Victor thought her the most beautiful child in the world. Yet she clung to Keene's hand as if frightened.

"Yes, tell them I'm at home and shall be with them shortly. Have cook prepare a nuncheon."

Could she see him standing in the window?

Victor raced through his ablutions and dressed in record time. He lost no time matching his morning coat to his unmentionables; everything he wore was black right now. His valet returned in time to help him into his coat.

As he dragged a comb through his hair, he realized he needed to see the barber as much as Leonard did.

"Victor!" Sophie squealed and raced across his drawing room.

She hugged him tight, while Victor looked across to see if Keene cast dark looks in his direction. But Keene was focused on holding his squirming son.

Victor allowed himself the pleasure of Sophie's

hug for a moment before he gently disengaged, but she was having none of it.

She put her hands on either side of his face and looked deeply into his eyes. Keene would have his hide.

"How are you?" she asked, the seriousness of her tone not allowing anything less than an honest answer.

"Well enough. I am alive, after all."

"Oh no, you have a scar," she said, her cool fingertips brushing against the red mark near his hairline.

"Yes, I suppose all the men you know must sooner or later wear the sign of the beast on their foreheads."

Keene stood and crossed the room. Victor hoped it wasn't to shoot him. Again. Instead Keene shoved back his hair with one hand and gave a mocking look. He adjusted his thrashing son, Richard, in his arm.

Victor felt mixed relief at Keene's disregard of his wife's manhandling. A few years back, an interested look in Sophie's animated direction earned Victor a threat to be boiled in oil. But having a son had perhaps cooled Keene's blood.

Instead, Keene looked him over. His dark gaze, so similar to Victor's, landed on the scar. "What happened?"

"Got brained by a falling beam when I went in after her."

Sophie's blue eyes filled with moisture. "We are so very sorry."

"Yes, well, it is done. The estate was nothing but an albatross anyway. There were too many days when I wished for its destruction."

Sophie had been a good friend of his wife's, although distance and madness made them grow apart. Yet her welling tears dismayed him. Uncomfortable, he cast a pleading glance in Keene's direction and stepped back.

The little girl sat primly on one of his sofas. Her shoes hung suspended above the floor, but she didn't swing her dangling feet. She sat very sedately, just as her mother would. She would have to be watched closely, when she became a young lady.

Keene leaned close to his wife, offering the unspoken comfort of long familiarity.

Sophie followed the direction of Victor's gaze. "We brought Reggie. We thought she might cheer you a little."

Cheer him? Remind him that his bloodline would go on, even though he no longer had a wife to produce a legitimate child? Regina was his daughter, but he could never claim her. To society, she was the daughter of his former friend George Keeting and his wife Amelia, and Victor had to leave it so. Was that supposed to be comfort?

Victor would have probably done the world a favor by never reproducing.

Although Keene had no such qualms about continuing their father's black pedigree. But he, too, had once thought to end the bloodline with his death.

The toddler let out a frustrated howl and squirmed devilishly in his father's arms. He, too, was just like *his* mother.

Suddenly, Keene pulled Sophie back and Richard was thrust unceremoniously into Victor's arms, "Take your godson," said Keene, equally as unceremoniously.

Victor took the youngster, who promptly threw his head back and kicked. He wanted to lift up the girl, but now she scowled in response to his nephew's distrust. With everything that had happened, a few months had passed since he had last seen her, but she should know she had no reason to fear him.

Keene wrapped his now free arm around Sophie. "Oh, let him down, do. He has been confined too many hours. Where are his leading strings?" Sophie said as she leaned into her husband, but her watering eyes danced over the children. "We've had Regina visiting with us this past fortnight. Amelia is to retrieve her as soon as she and George arrive in town."

Before going deaf, Victor leaned over and set down the howling toddler. The youngster tore around the drawing room. Victor winced.

Sophie and Keene, with the obvious ease of long practice, moved breakables to higher ground. Victor reached for the bellpull and opened the connecting door to the rear drawing room, so the little terror could run the length of the house.

"Please sit. I'll have a maid take care of that and we should have sandwiches momentarily." He walked over in front of the little girl and bent down. "What kind of sandwich would you like?"

Regina looked at Keene for guidance before answering. Her uncertainty tore at Victor.

Sophie plopped down beside Regina. "Don't be scared, darling. You remember Lord Wedmont. Did you know that your middle name, Victoria, is for him? I suppose you may call him—"

The drawing room door opened at that moment and a stylish woman with dark hair wound on top of her head in a loose, yet elegant fashion entered the room. "No, don't say it!"

"—Uncle Victor," finished Sophie, rolling her eyes at the newcomer.

"Mama," cried the little girl and she slid off the sofa and then waited with far too much patience to be told she could approach her mother.

Amelia glided into the room, as slender as ever, as beautiful as ever, and Victor shuddered as if a sudden draft had left him cold. His attraction to this woman had nearly cost him his life four years earlier. It had certainly cost him one of his best friends, almost two of them.

The room became a flurry of activity as the butler and a footman arrived with trays from the kitchen and Amelia pressed a kiss on her daughter's cheek, then greeted Sophie and Keene.

"I came up early," she said to their surprised faces.

Keene grabbed his running son on one of his passes and urged him with a sweetmeat to sit.

"Oh, do give him a sandwich first, Keene," said Sophie, her attention shifting to the children's needs.

Amelia removed her gloves and laid her hand on Victor's sleeve. "Might I have a brief word with you?" she whispered and inclined her head ever so slightly toward the rear drawing room.

As soon as they entered the room, she stepped behind the door, out of sight of the main drawing room.

"Amelia," he protested.

She glided toward him and slid her arms around his neck. "I was so horrified when I heard your news."

Victor resisted the urge to run. "So you expressed in your most kind letter."

She leaned up on tiptoes and threaded her bare fingers through his hair. "Are you all right? I have been so worried about you. I . . ." She closed her dark blue eyes, then opened them awash with tears.

Not again. He was the one who needed sympathy, especially with all these crying women. He thought of Leonard, who had maddeningly seemed to tear up when he told the cub he didn't like him. What was it about people becoming watering spouts around him lately? Even his father-in-law had blubbered for a good half-hour on Victor's new black silk jacket.

"I have thought of you so often, and well, George shall be in the country another month before he comes to town."

Amelia wasn't going to offer . . . was she?

"I don't want you to be lonely." She pressed herself against him from tip to toe, and he felt tips. He felt too much. Her lips curled up ever so slightly with that infamous sort of Mona Lisa smile. "I think of that night in the carriage often."

She was offering to become his mistress . . . again.

"You're married to George now," he blurted.

She made a moue of distaste. "We've been married a long time, and we bore each other."

Distaste curled through him and repulsed him. He put his hands on her shoulders. "Amelia, I shall ever be fond of you, but loving you just that once nearly cost me everything."

She trailed her hand down his shoulder. "I just want you to know, if you need me for *anything*, I will come to you."

He was shocked. He was dismayed. He shoved Amelia away. He'd rather sleep with Leonard. Oh God.

He pulled Amelia back, kissed her and felt . . . nothing.

She smiled. His insides were shriveling. She patted his arm, then stepped back while pulling on her gloves. "We should return before our absence is noted."

"I have gone to the kitchen to request more food," he said.

She continued to smile and nod, while he stared in horror. Leonard's big blue eyes swam before his mind's eye. His dream had muddled his mind, or Mary Frances's madness had been contagious.

Christ, he had sworn off wives, not women.

So why the hell did kissing Amelia do nothing to stir his blood, but the thought of Leonard—

Bloody hell and the blaring bells of Satan, he needed a drink.

CHAPTER 3

Victor's valet stood with a fresh neck cloth draped across his arm and a silly smile on his face.

"What are you so happy about?" asked Victor, rather peevishly, he noted. He was unhappy that his dinner invitation to Sophie and Keene had been automatically extended to include Amelia. Then again, Victor rather regretted his forceful invitation to Leonard.

"Nothing, milord," said his valet. He erased the smile from his face. "Just glad to see you back among friends."

Friends, family, his female offspring, who was obviously scared of him. On the whole it had been a rather distressing morning. Regina had refused to let him close to her while daintily eating his biscuits.

Not that Regina wasn't perfectly well-mannered for a five-year-old. Just that every time he approached, she would lean into Sophie or Keene or her mother, with her quivering chin ducked down.

He'd felt like shouting at her, *I'm your father, you darling girl. I adore every precious hair on your beautiful head, why in God's name are you scared of me?* Which made him cross that anyone should think of yelling at her, let alone himself. And doubly cross that he could not claim her as his daughter.

Bloody hell, she was likely the only child he would ever have, and she reminded him of his childhood fear of his own father. A fear that hadn't been so misplaced, or had it? Victor couldn't really remember his father paying him any mind. He had just known that the previous earl had wounded his mother in both visible and invisible ways. He'd been helpless to save her or prevent her death from a broken heart.

A lesson that seemed to be repeated in his life. He'd ruined Amelia, yet his financial situation at the time had made it impossible for him to set things right for her. He hadn't broken her heart, but her husband George's. He'd been unable to rescue his own wife from her madness and broken her heart with his demands. Whatever made him think he could be of any use to an inexperienced American lad? He was more likely to destroy him.

"Have any of my guests arrived yet?"

"I don't believe so, milord. As soon as you are finished with me, I am off with the carriage to retrieve your young friend."

Victor turned and looked at his man. Had he told him to go with the carriage? "Did you find anything odd about Mr. Hall?"

"In what way, milord?" His valet fussed with Victor's discarded morning clothes.

Victor loosened the knot he'd just tied on his cravat. It felt too tight and his face heated. He yanked the neck cloth out from under his collar. "Bloody hell, I need another."

How could he explain his unease about Leonard, without giving away his obscene interest?

"Here you are, milord." His valet handed him a fresh neck cloth and stood at the ready with a third.

Victor hadn't needed a third attempt at tying a cravat since his shoulder had healed over four years ago. Damn, if Millars was whistling.

"Lenny, Mr. Hall, that is, he just seems a little . . . off, don't you think?" said Victor.

"I'm sure I don't know what you mean, sir."

"Is it necessary that you retrieve him? Perhaps I should just send the coachman and carriage." Good grief, had he just asked his valet's advice about instructing his own servants? Had he lost his mind? "I wonder if I shouldn't go myself."

"You may trust me to bring the youth, milord. I am sure you should remain behind to greet the Davieses and Mrs. Keeting when they arrive. I am sure my attention to the matter shall bring favorable results."

Victor wasn't sure what would be favorable anymore. "He did not wish to dine with me, did he?" Was Leonard aware of Victor's unhealthy prurient interest?

His valet turned to put away the spare neck cloth, but not before Victor had seen the smile. "Yes, there was some reluctance, but we quite overcame that. A previous engagement, I believe."

"You find my interest in this boy amusing?"

"Lord Wedmont, I am most pleased to see you taking an interest in the welfare of another. If I may be so bold, I find the present circumstances of your state of mind much more encouraging than those of a month ago. So please forgive me if my joy at seeing you taking an interest in life's matters overrides my usual forbearance. If we are done, milord, I shall see to my other duties?"

Victor nodded. Had he been so maudlin that at the first spark of life, his valet was practically falling over with glee? It was true that after the funeral and the well-wishers had gone back to their own lives, and his father-in-law's interest had turned to the rebuilding Victor wished wasn't happening, he had sunk into despair.

He moved his household to his London house, the only house he owned now that was habitable, besides the dower house on his estate where he'd installed his father-in-law.

Once alone in his townhouse, Victor spent many afternoons alone in his bedroom, staring at the walls, wondering what he could have done differently to save his wife. Only knowing he could not inflict his grief on his friends and family had brought Victor out of his stupor.

Bloody hell, he needed his company to jerk him out of his black mood, even if Leonard's presence was likely to sit foul with him.

As he made his way into the drawing room, he heard the knocker on the front door. He stood in front of the fireplace as his guests were announced.

Sophie was first into the room. Amelia followed sedately, and Keene stood with his hands clasped behind his back until the doorway was clear. He nodded to Victor's butler as he entered the room.

"You know, you look rather good in all black," said Sophie as she skipped across the room, then leaned her cheek against his in greeting.

Victor swallowed. Please not let her say anything untoward.

"Might I speak to you tête-à-tête?" she whispered in his ear, while still close. She tugged on his arm.

Oh, hell, this day was going from bad to worse. Victor looked at Keene. Sophie cast a speculative glance in his direction. Then Amelia glided up to him and pressed her cool cheek against his.

He gestured toward the sofa. "Won't you both have a seat? My American friend shall arrive soon."

Amelia looked at him with just the faintest crease of puzzlement in her smooth brow. He took her elbow and guided her to a chair.

"Oh, Victor has taken on a protégé," Sophie told Amelia. "We are to meet him this evening." She flounced into a chair, her skirts whooshing around her. "I am ever so curious."

"Really, shall we be uneven?" said Amelia with her normal reserve. She sank gracefully onto the sofa, sitting on the edge with her legs turned sideways. Always a perfect lady in company.

That she had a deep streak of passion she hid from the world had fascinated him for the longest time, but now he watched her with the interest of an entomologist for an insect specimen pinned to a board.

Keene watched Victor watching her.

"It's just an informal dinner," said Sophie. "Victor is in mourning, he cannot entertain."

Never mind that he actually was entertaining, and that he had the audacity to not have an even number of people at the table.

"Whatever made you take an interest in this gentleman?" asked Amelia.

"His skill with the dice," Victor answered.

Sophie stood and crossed to the window. "Will

your friend travel in a hack? I hope he is to arrive soon. I confess I could fair eat a horse."

"I sent my carriage for him."

"Is that it?" She pulled back the curtain and pressed her nose against the glass.

Sophie beckoned in Victor's direction. At least Sophie was direct. If she were about to offer to *console* him, then she would be blunt about it.

He rather liked Sophie. And he didn't want to hurt her feelings. He tried to rehearse a gentle refusal in his mind, but the words sounded more like a missish marriage refusal. He crossed to the window and looked down at an empty street.

"There's no carr—"

"Shhhh," hissed Sophie. She wrapped her arm in his, cast one quick glance over her shoulder. "I want to ask you a tiny favor."

"Sophie," he protested. He tried to disengage his arm from hers.

His carriage turned the corner and rumbled up the street. Relief flooded through him. "There he is. His name is Leonard Hall."

"What part of America is he from?" asked Amelia politely, as if she had decided to be interested in this young man, since Victor was. Although there was a hint of question in her tone, as if she wasn't quite sure Victor had all his faculties in place.

"Boston," answered Victor, now caught in watching his valet descend from the carriage and then turn back as if he would hand down the other occupant. How very odd. "He tells me his family is in shipping."

Then Leonard bounced unassisted down the

steps, wearing his boots again. Irritation and relief surged through Victor.

Sophie nudged him. But Keene chose that moment to walk over to the window and look down on the blond-haired youth. Whatever Sophie intended to say to him would be postponed.

Lydia looked up at the imposing façade of the Grosvenor Square town home. In America most of the houses were constructed with wood or brick, but in London a lot of the houses had a stone exterior, or at the very least plaster covering brick, as if plain houses were too bourgeois. The façade of Victor's house fairly glowed with gray-veined white marble. An air of permanence and prestige hung about the square. A reminder that England was centuries old, settled and matured, with a patina of grace covering all.

There was a certain appeal to the eternalness, although Lydia liked America's ideals better. Here one had to be born to privilege and to govern; in America any man could advance himself to the highest position in the land, merely by the sweat of his brow.

Any *man*, that is. A woman's options in both countries were limited to marriage or what little she could earn in drudgery or an illicit vocation.

Lydia sighed as she was led through the impressive house to the drawing room. Tired of pretending to be a man, yet unwilling to return home, she felt trapped. She would have to be insufferably rude to Victor. She could think of no other way to repulse him.

She should just return to Boston and marry Mr.
Sullivan. But that was just as bad. She could travel
on to France or Italy, but she was hindered by not
knowing even a smattering of the language.

Her education had centered around learning to
play the spinet and the fine art of embroidery. Oh,
she had been taught enough arithmetic to manage
a household, but algebra had been deemed to be
beyond her female brain. No, instead she had been
taught to sew.

The butler opened the drawing room door, and
he announced, "Mr. Leonard Hall."

Good gracious, the aristocracy could be so formal,
thought Lydia as she stepped into the room and realized there were other people there. Oh!

As he introduced her to his other guests, Victor's guiding hand at her shoulder shot tingles
through her.

How could she be rude in front of these other
people? As she made a leg to the two women introduced to her, dismay tied her tongue. She had a
whole string of insulting comments on English val-
ues, but she hadn't been raised to be rude to a host
in front of guests. As much as she needed to get
away from Victor's patronage, she didn't want all of
London thinking Americans were boorish louts.

Perhaps she could get Victor alone later. No—
she didn't want be alone with him. Then the butler
announced dinner and she trailed after the others
to the dining room like a barely tolerated child.

She concentrated on eating and almost keeled
over in embarrassment when at one point Victor
gently told her to carve the dish of partridges
placed beside her.

Normally, her table manners were impeccable. As the sole female in her house, it had fallen to her to be in charge of such matters around the dinner table, but she had forgotten that in her role as a male she had different responsibilities.

That should have been enough reminder, but when everyone stood and she started to trail out behind Sophie and Amelia, Victor had been more impatient.

"Sit, cub. Do the gentlemen in America not linger over their port after the ladies withdraw?"

She shook her head, mortified at her gaffe. A footman placed three glasses on the table, poured a dark red liquid into them, and left the bottle on the table.

"Now, that it's just us . . . men, Lenny. Perhaps it is time you told me why you have run away from home."

Lydia didn't know which distressed her more, that long pause before he called them all men, or that he had guessed she had run away.

Two pairs of dark eyes bored into her. But Victor's bothered her more. They made her want to squirm. "I'm sure I don't know what you are talking about."

She grabbed for her glass of wine and sloshed it on her sleeve. She stared at the growing stain on her arm, and steeled herself to be insulting.

"Come now, Lenny. You do not expect me to believe that. You are here without friends, family or even a tutor. Now why have you run away from Boston?"

Victor folded his arms and leaned back in his chair. His dark clothes and the dim candlelight flickering over his face made him appear sinister. She was at his mercy.

Then again, as she stared at the sensual angles of his lips, being at his mercy might not be so bad.

Victor wanted to shake the boy seated at his table. Between the wide-eyed innocence and the reluctance to talk, Leonard exasperated Victor.

"I'm sure I don't know what you mean, sir," said Leonard. He fiddled with his glass of port on the dining room table. "I didn't run away from home."

Keene pushed back from the table. "Such delicacy in your questions, Victor. Perhaps Mr. Hall would be more comfortable answering without my presence. I shall rejoin the ladies and make sure my wife has not found her way onto a rooftop." He bowed, then left the room.

Victor leaned forward, hoping to intimidate Leonard, and instead caught the sweet smell of soap. The urge to lean closer and inhale Lenny's scent forced Victor to rear back. "I do not believe you."

Leonard stared down at his wine-soaked cuff. Which was much better than his blue-eyed stare of a minute earlier. "Very well, then. I'd rather not say."

"Would you like Millars to take care of your shirt? I could loan you one of mine while the stain is rinsed."

Leonard pulled his hands off the table and down into his lap. "I'm sure that's not necessary. I'm just clumsy."

The boy struck Victor as anything but graceless. In fact, Victor's eye was drawn to the smooth way Lenny moved. Bloody hell, he was not having these thoughts. He was not thinking of pressing the boy up to his bedroom so he could watch him remove his shirt. "Yes, I am sure you are so cow-handed you shall ruin my linen too."

Victor knocked back his port then stared at his empty glass. If he were to join the cult of Hyacinthus, the drinking would probably speed the process. Never in all his life had he experienced an urge like this toward any other male.

Or it may be that only a pretty boy, like Hyacinthus who drew the god Apollo's affection, was likely to stir anything unnatural in Victor's blood.

He could not stay alone with Lenny. But the thought of abandoning him to a fate of possible beatings bothered Victor. Clearly, he was too young to be alone.

Why would a young man of Leonard's age run away, not only from home, but across a vast ocean to another country? "Were you beaten by your father? Mistreated in some way?"

Leonard shook his bowed head, his blond hair catching the glints from the candlelight and making Victor feel as if he were chastising an innocent cherub.

Was there a more personal reason he had run away? Was it Leonard's own predilections that made Victor uncomfortable around him? Rather that his attraction to the boy sprang from the boy's own affinity for men? One could only hope.

"Is there something you feel you cannot tell your father? A trait or inclination you possess that he will find . . . objectionable?"

Leonard stood up. "I am grateful for your hospitality, but I think it would be best if I called it a night."

"Sit down, Lenny." Victor swallowed his second glass of port in one gulp. And he'd thought his question remarkably discreet, for him anyway. "You'll leave when I call for the carriage for you."

What was wrong with him? The lad wanted to leave, let him. Victor knew he could not. And he was mindful that Lenny had not answered.

"I am not quite sure what I should do with you. The more I look at you, the more I fear you will find yourself in harm's way. You are too green to be on your own. I should send you home, or at the least notify your parents that you are under my care."

"Parent. I only have a father."

A sudden wave of sympathy irritated Victor. The urge to comfort Leonard connected in his mind with the manner of comfort Amelia offered. A shudder of fascinated distaste rippled under his skin.

Victor hooked his foot behind Leonard's ankles and yanked his feet out from under him, while pushing his shoulder so Leonard fell back in his chair with a thump.

Leonard stared at him as if he'd never been handled so roughly. The lad had claimed older brothers; how could he be so squeamish of being shoved? He'd been so reluctant to push forward at the gaming hell that Victor truly wondered at his puniness. "Told you to sit down. Have some respect."

Tears filled Leonard's blue eyes.

"Bloody hell, you are not going to cry, are you?" blurted Victor. The temptation to throw an arm around Leonard's shoulder warred with the desire to shake him.

Leonard looked down and pulled his cuffs of his jacket down as if to hide his delicate wrist bones or the wine stain on his white linen shirt. The boy had very long, delicate fingers too. Fascinating hands. Victor shook off the thought of how those hands might feel against his skin . . .

against . . . No! Just because the boy had unnatural inclinations did not mean that Victor would participate in such debauchery.

"Never fear, we shall get you properly outfitted tomorrow."

"I'd rather not."

Victor breathed in a sigh of impatience. "Look, either go home to your father, or allow me to guide you about London. I have had enough death about me, that I cannot allow you to roam into danger with a clear conscience. You very nearly got yourself killed the other night."

Leonard blinked and shrugged his shoulders. Victor rubbed his scar on his forehead. He supposed he felt some of the perturbation of a parent dealing with an almost grown child. If only his feelings toward Leonard were fatherly. He could not figure out why was he signing on for the torture of having this tempting creature underfoot.

"I don't want you deciding what I should do."

"I have no intention of making your decisions for you, but for God's sake, allow me to guide you in your choices. You cannot have any idea of the dangers of this city, and how much you are making yourself a target for harm."

With the boy's inclinations and innocence and odd beauty, without protection he would surely be slaughtered.

Leonard rolled his eyes. "In what way?"

"Well, you stand out like a sore thumb. Only a knobskull would wear boots in the evening. Did you choose London because you can support yourself with your winnings from gaming?"

Leonard met his eyes and seemed caught in

between admitting the truth and continuing to hold his cards close to his chest.

Again Victor resisted the urge to reach out and pet his hand, to soothe the tortured boy. Bloody hell, he should not have invited him here, but the more time Victor spent with Leonard, the stronger the conviction grew that the cub needed protection.

"Supporting yourself with gambling is not an unusual path for a young man in this town. Many a dandy has lived by his wits and the turn of a card. Lord knows that I lived that way for several years in my youth. You could not find a more sympathetic guide."

"But, you're . . ." Leonard shook his head.

Victor winced. He was rich, thanks to his wife. "Yes, but it wasn't always so."

Leonard sucked in a deep breath and looked down. "You represent everything my country has fought against."

Victor leaned back in his chair. "My title offends you?"

Leonard nodded.

"Chance of birth and not always such an easy burden. But my family name is Bartlett; you may use that if you prefer it to Wedmont or Victor." The cub had yet to use a moniker with him. "By all means, drop the 'my lords' if they disturb your spleen."

"That hardly changes what you are."

Victor leaned forward. "And what am I, besides a man?"

"Insufferable, overbearing, interfering . . ." Leonard appeared to be searching his brain box for another insult to hurl.

"Don't forget rude. I too often speak my mind."

Leonard stole a glance at him.

"You sound like a fishwife," Victor told him.

Leonard's mouth gaped, rather like a fish out of water. Then he colored red.

Victor leaned forward and lifted his chin. Bloody hell, the boy had soft skin. Time hung suspended in air as for a moment the urges Victor tried to suppress must have shown. Leonard stared at him, fear and yearning both in his open young face. Oh, God, this was not happening.

Four years without a woman's welcome between her legs had not sent him chasing after boys. It did not, could not. Lord Byron might happily move back and forth between the two sexes, but Victor liked women. He'd always liked women. He might not have Keene's skill at seduction, but he just needed a woman who would not spurn him. One who would not find relations with him an unbearable burden.

Victor jerked away and stood. He wouldn't touch Lenny. Everything would be all right if they did not touch each other. "We need to rejoin my other guests."

Leonard looked miserable. "That would be wise."

Victor closed his eyes and leaned his palms on the table. "I don't offer anything more than friendship. Is that clear?"

Confusion creasing his forehead, Leonard stared at him. Was it possible he did recognize the animal magnetism of the moment? Was it possible he didn't know what he was, or didn't have a name for it?

Victor felt torn. At the same time that he would never consider participating in an act he considered unnatural and immoral, he hated that Leonard might have unwittingly made himself vulnerable and exposed inclinations he would rather have kept hidden.

For God's sake, just when Victor had made some peace with himself, he had to acknowledge that his father's wicked, depraved, hedonistic blood had tainted him in unnameable ways. "I don't care what you are, Lenny."

Leonard backed away until he ran into the wall. "I don't know what you mean."

"You need protection in more ways than one." Lord, there were men who would kill him if they had any idea what he was. What was he? It was more like he wasn't quite man enough to be male, but not female either. The boy's body didn't look like a woman's. He was too tall, too straight through the waist, his voice lower than most women's, yet his face was feminine, his hands were feminine. It was if nature had created a confusing creature between male and female.

"You are cruel and arrogant," whispered Lenny.

"Am I?" Victor straightened up and folded his arms across his chest. "If you mean to be rid of my patronage then you may return to America."

"You are a . . ."

"Bastard?" supplied Victor, when Leonard couldn't seem to form an appropriate insult. "Son of a bitch?"

Leonard's eyes widened.

"Don't be too free with your insults, or I shall have to call you out."

Leonard swallowed hard, and Victor again felt that horrible desire to comfort him.

"I didn't . . . you . . ." Leonard fumbled for words. "Oh, fiddlesticks!"

Fiddlesticks? The mild word reminded Victor how very young Leonard was. "At least allow me to write your father and assure him of your well-being."

"No!"

"You have no idea of the agonies of worry a parent feels."

Leonard blinked and stared. "Are you a parent?"

"I have a daughter." He shouldn't say that much, but he needed Leonard to know that he slept with women. Only with women. "Come along. We'll have Amelia play the piano while the rest of us play whist. Be civil, and I shall call the carriage round after a rubber, if you so wish."

Leonard looked miserable.

Victor sympathized. "We get along well enough over cards, do we not?"

Leonard nodded.

Victor reached for the door, since the servants at his direction always left him to his port alone. Leonard darted into him as they both tried to go through the doorway.

Victor closed his eyes and willed down the shudder of sensations. Bloody hell, if Sophie offered the same kind of comfort Amelia did, he would take her up on it, his loyalty to Keene be damned, he told himself. Although he knew the thought was a lie.

He put his hands on Lenny's shoulders to move him out of the way, but Victor was caught by a web of desire. When in Rome, one . . .

When in Hades, when in Sodom or Gomorrah . . . Why was it that the longer the evening had worn on and Victor had witnessed Leonard's shy awkwardness and now this side of him, the more his conviction that the boy needed his protection grew? Why was it that he felt bound to test the limits of his own sanity with another's folly? Why did he care so much about people who rejected him? His wife—hell, Keene had shot him—and now Leonard had made it clear he didn't want to be around him and resented his half-hearted rejection.

But as much as Leonard didn't want to be around him, there was an odd compatibility too. There was a sense of familiarity and comfort that occurred when people were destined to be great friends.

Whether this was his test of sanity or Leonard's, Victor knew he would not be able to let the boy out of his sight. His heart pounded and his blood heated and he desperately wanted to pull Lenny against him . . . .

CHAPTER 4

Lydia trailed after Victor. A footman opened the drawing room door, and she waited until Victor entered. Their bumping into each other while exiting the dining room had made her freeze. Had he felt the bolster that hid her waist? Or sensed the strange charge of energy that sprang from the contact?

The moment stretched out until a footman with a tea tray rattled past.

Lord, she thought she'd been found out, that her infatuation showed and he'd . . . they'd . . . well, a spark or connection or desire had flowed through the air. She'd feared he'd realize she was a woman.

In any case, he had scowled at her. What a time to finally feel a budding attraction, now that she was trapped into a disguise of being a man. She had definitely bloomed too late.

"Come and have a spot of tea, Mr. Hall," said Sophie as she poured him a cup and held it out. "We do not stand on formalities much among us. Do you mind if I call you Leonard?"

Amelia looked oddly at Sophie but quickly dropped her gaze to her lap and seconded the invitation. "Yes, do come tell us about your home,

Leonard. I have heard that you could fit all the states of Europe into the land held by your country."

"Yes, but most of it is wilderness. I suppose we shall spread across it all one day."

For a few minutes, the two women gently quizzed Lydia about her home and upbringing. She could feel Victor scrutinizing her as she answered their questions. She started to cross her ankles and remembered men didn't sit like that, so she pointed her knees out, rather than locking them together.

Victor asked Amelia to play for them, and walked her over to a spinet in the corner of the room. With his arm around her waist, he helped her choose sheet music.

The sight of Victor's head so close to the other woman's made Lydia swallow hard against a lump in her throat. They looked as if they belonged together, with their matching dark hair, his with rich waves, and hers in loose swirls. Amelia's head only came up to his shoulder, so he leaned down toward her. She tilted her head back, emphasizing the graceful length of her swanlike neck.

She even walked with a floating grace as if her feet never touched the floor. Lydia with her unnatural height could never have managed either the feminine head tilt or the gliding walk. Her strides had always been too long, kicking her skirts out in front of her. To take shorter steps made her look like a mincing fool. Although she didn't stand quite eye-to-eye with Victor, there would never be any need for him to bend over her.

"Would you like a biscuit?" asked Sophie, startling Lydia away from her observation of the low conversation between Victor and his other guest. "You didn't eat much for a growing lad."

She'd eaten a lot, but she never could have matched the amount her older brothers could consume at a single sitting. Was there an insinuation in Sophie's words? Her blue eyes were inquiring and sincere, guileless. "Thank you, no. I'm not as young as I look," said Lydia.

Sophie smiled and then said playfully, "I'm not as young as I act. So how do you find London? Have you been to a balloon ascension?"

Her husband, who had remained silent up until this point, snorted.

Lydia shook her head. She preferred to limit her exposure during the daytime hours. She wasn't that confident in her masquerade. Candle and lamplight could mask a multitude of deficiencies.

"I admit I have a fascination with balloon ascensions. I am quite determined to ride in one."

"No, you will not," said Keene.

His wife ignored him and went on. "I understand one might purchase a ticket. Keene thinks they are too dangerous. I quite have a fascination with heights. I should imagine one might be able to have the experience of a bird."

"Only a featherhead should wish to be a bird." Keene stood and crossed over to his wife. In spite of his words, or perhaps because of them, he leaned over and pressed a kiss on his wife's cheek.

"A balloon ascension sounds like a great adventure," Lydia said, because she was sure that was what a young man would think. But as she thought about it, why couldn't a woman enjoy it too?

"Pray, don't encourage her," said Keene. "She is far too careless with her health as it is."

"You know, you have never lost anyone dear to you to an accident," said Victor.

"I should like to keep it that way," answered Keene. "I have come near enough to it by my own hand that I should not like it."

Lydia looked between the two men. They were similar in height and build and even their features were alike, although Victor looked a shade leaner, with more of an edge. But Victor had said his family name was Bartlett. Perhaps they were cousins. That would no doubt explain it.

Yet as she looked between them, she realized an uncomfortable undercurrent hung in the air. Sophie's animation had drained out of her, and Keene squeezed his wife's shoulder as if offering comfort.

Victor rubbed the red discoloration on his forehead. Lydia wondered at it. Was it a scar? It didn't detract from his looks, but made him appear human, vulnerable, when she thought him arrogant and controlling. She wanted to touch it, to press her lips there, because it seemed to bother him.

She jumped to her feet and paced. A fluttering in her stomach, not entirely fear, made her restless. "Are we to play whist then?"

The question was unforgivably rude. Oh, good, now she managed rudeness, when everyone was around. However, insulting Victor, when he supplied cruder terms than she ever would have thought of, wasn't working well, and Sophie reacted with an indulgent smile. Could these people not be insulted?

"Ah, Lenny is no doubt anxious to show his

prowess at cards." Victor tossed her an amused glance. "Be warned, cub, you shall not find any easy marks here."

Sophie sprang to her feet and moved over to a round table and picked up a chair to pull it to the table. "Shall we play here?"

"Darling, let us arrange the furniture," said her husband, but he crossed to the far side of the room to take a chair, as if the only way to stop his wife from pulling all the chairs to the table was to beat her to them.

Lydia belatedly took another chair. "I'll get them."

As she neared the table, Sophie leaned into Victor's arm. "Do not forget I have a favor to ask of you," she whispered. Then she said louder, "Are the cards in the dining room sideboard? Shall I go for them?"

"I'll get them," said Keene, casting a stern glance in his wife's direction.

"I'll send a servant." Victor stepped toward the bellpull.

"Oh, Ludcakes, it shall be faster if Keene fetches them. He knows how very eager I am to practice before the season is in full swing. I may be sick of the card table before it is over, but I want to be sharp for when it is no longer seemly for me to dance. Leonard, you must promise to ask me to dance often. I quite exhaust Victor and Keene."

Lydia ducked and mumbled something. Good gracious, she didn't intend to dance with other women. She went to the far side of the room and grabbed the final chair needed. She lifted the sturdy piece of furniture and held her breath straining to carry the chair. Her brothers would have made the task look effortless.

Lydia glanced at Amelia as she played the spinet, gracefully, with more feeling than Lydia would have expected from her reserve. Did her womanly charms never end?

As Lydia neared Victor and Sophie, she could not help but overhear their low conversation. If the chair were not so heavy, she could move faster.

"If the favor you intend to ask for is for me to help you ride in a balloon basket, I must decline."

"Oh, pish, that is just diversion. I mean, I should like to ride in a balloon, but what I really wanted to ask you is . . ." she hesitated, looking at Lydia.

Lydia tried to look as if she couldn't hear and the chair weighed no more than a feather. Victor looked nervous, as if he didn't really want to handle Sophie's request. Lydia wished she could intercede for him, but she was at a loss.

Sophie continued. "You see, Keene is excessively concerned about my safety and it is rather wearing. I thought my father was horrid." She leaned close and batted her blue eyes at Victor with a mixture of charm and innocence. "Now that I am in a delicate condition, he is too worried that harm might come to me, if I . . . exert myself and he won't . . ."

Victor really looked uncomfortable.

"I thought that you might be willing. It is my greatest desire to . . ." She bit her lip with the most effective of pauses.

Lydia was fascinated by their conversation, although she tried not to watch directly. Was Sophie a natural flirt or were her pauses and hesitations rehearsed?

"For God's sake, just say it, so I might say no," blurted Victor.

Sophie blinked. "It's just a hunter."

Lydia tripped, the heavy chair crashing to the floor and her about to join it. Victor caught her across the chest and a thousand rocket bursts could not have startled her more. Her breath caught and her bound breasts tingled and ached. Her momentum brought them close, his long lean body rubbed against hers. Time hung suspended and he stared at her, an expression close to horror on his face.

He did not know she was a woman. Could he sense her excitement? Oh, fiddlesticks! She pushed away. "I told you I was clumsy."

Victor shook his head and raked his hand through his hair. With one hand, he righted the dumped chair.

"Victor?" said Sophie as if she was concerned by the dazed look that had crossed his face. "You did not hurt yourself, did you? Are you all right, Leonard?"

Victor looked at Sophie. "I thought you meant to offer me comfort as Ame—"

Amelia played a wrong note on the spinet.

Victor turned and Lydia backed away to the far side of the table.

Sophie cast a knowing glance in Amelia's direction. "No wonder you look so green about the gills. The only time I have ever—"

Victor glared at her.

"—was when I mistook you for Keene. No, silly, I want you to buy a horse for me. A hunter, well, if it has half the spirit of its sire, shall be a grand horse. I mean, I shall keep Daisy for town use, but Squire Ponsby is offering the two-year-old he bred from Sala- manca—remember the horse that threw me, the one I kept calling Grace?—he is offering the horse at Tat- tersall's and I want it. He won't sell to me directly, but if it is auctioned at Tatt's—as my agent, you could purchase him for me."

"You want me to buy you a horse?" asked Victor.

"Yes, oh, he is a sweet goer. I saw him when visit- ing my parents and I offered for him then, but Mr. Ponsby was there when Grace, I mean Salamanca, threw me and he refused to sell me the colt. I should imagine this horse could take a seven-foot wall, he has such beautiful lines. If you won't pur- chase him for me, I shall have to steal your clothes again and sneak into Tatt's and buy him myself."

Lydia sucked in air. Was Sophie on to her?

"Sophie, my dearest, even in my clothes, you never passed for a man." Victor glared in Lydia's direction.

He scanned down her body, and she resisted the urge to shrivel. In fact, as his gaze seemed to rest on her special appendage sewn in her drawers, Lydia held back the urge to check and make sure it was properly positioned, not that she had been that aware of that portion of a man's body and how it should be positioned until she'd attempted to cor- rectly wear a crude imitation.

She kept her eyes down as she needlessly shoved a chair further under the table. Well, and then she couldn't help but look at that area of Victor's body, and she shouldn't have, because heat coursed madly through her blood. She plunked down in one of the chairs.

"Leonard!"

What? Oh, heavens. Sophie still stood. "Sorry." She slid out of the seat, hoping that her embarrassment over her social gaffe accounted for the rise in her color, and she surreptitiously checked that her fake parts were still in position. A prickle of curiosity for what a man's private parts really felt like made her shift. What did Victor's look like, feel like?

Victor scowled ferociously in her direction. Maybe she hadn't been inconspicuous enough. Heavens, when she was rude in a way that bothered him and might cause him to reject her, she couldn't stand to continue. Lydia stared at the chair. Did she dare sit back down?

"Oh, sit, do. Do not stand on ceremony with me," Sophie said. "Please, Victor, say you will do this little favor for me, before Keene returns and I have to do something drastic."

"Sophie, I—"

"You would do it for me, would you not, Leonard? If you had a sister and she was a very good horse-woman, you would help her to buy a horse worthy of her?"

"I don't know anything about buying horse-flesh," muttered Lydia. Not to mention that horses scared her.

"Have Keene buy the horse for you."

"He won't because *I'm breeding.* I'll promise not to ride him until after the baby is born. Quick, promise me you will purchase him for me, before he returns."

Amelia turned from the spinet. "How can you afford a top-of-the-trees hunter, Sophie?"

Sophie let out an infectious laugh. "I know it

quite astounds everyone, but I am quite good with accounts. I have enough set aside for him."

Lydia looked up to realize that Victor was staring at her. "What do you mean you don't know anything about buying horseflesh, Lenny?"

She didn't even know how to ride. She was a city dweller year round in Boston. She could sail a small sloop, but there was never any moving back and forth between country and city, so she never had a need to ride a horse. She rode in a carriage to any destination that was outside of walking distance. Lydia swallowed a sick feeling. Another shortcoming in her man tricks. "I have never had a reason to buy a horse."

The door opened and Keene walked in, holding two decks of cards. "For God's sake, Sophie, you are not talking about that dratted horse again."

"I thought Victor might be interested in him," Sophie said, her chin jutting out.

"Without a habitable country estate, I doubt I shall be doing much hunting. However, since Leonard needs lessons in horseflesh, I believe we shall visit Tattersall's on Thursday."

Sophie bounced up and gave Victor a peck on the cheek. Once again Lydia felt a surge of jealousy. And damn, she seemed to be embroiling herself deeper and deeper.

"What is Tattersall's?" asked Lydia.

"The premier auction house for horses. It is also the place to go to settle or collect on racing bets," Keene answered as he set the decks of cards down on the table. He turned and crossed the room to stare out the window.

Lydia felt caught in a situation beyond her understanding. These people were obviously old friends of Victor's, but there were moments when tension thickened like overcooked porridge.

"Shall we play?" Sophie's gaze followed Lydia as she sat down. She offered Lydia a conspiratorial smile.

If Sophie was on to Lydia, was she keeping her peace?

Once again, Victor leaned over Amelia at the spinet. He was whispering to her, and Lydia was surprised at the anger she felt. Sophie she liked; Amelia made her feel gauche.

And Victor, no matter her clothes and studied mannerisms, made her feel like a woman, but she would bet he had that same effect on Amelia, too.

Victor stared out the window as his carriage moved down the street with his valet escorting Leonard. Was the man who had dressed and bathed him for the past half dozen years enamored of the boy? Victor rubbed his forehead.

Victor and Keene had stepped into the library for a nightcap.

Keene handed him a glass of brandy. "I meant to surprise Sophie with that horse, you know."

"Didn't know," said Victor, taking a drink. "Shall I tell her I lost it to another bidder?"

Keene smiled enigmatically. "Perhaps that would serve best. She grows too used to getting her way. And I shall rather miss the fights over who rides Brutus."

Victor dropped the drapery he'd been holding

back. His carriage had long ago passed into the darkness. "I won't miss the matrimonial discord."

He wouldn't miss it at all. Although he suspected Keene and Sophie's disagreements had a rather enjoyable conclusion, his and Mary Frances's fights had never led to anything so pleasant. Nothing in their marriage had ever led to anything so pleasant.

"Mr. Hall is an odd project for you."

"I'm not sure I understand it either," said Victor. "But my valet assures me it is better for me to rejoin the living by my interest in him, than to sit in darkened rooms, drinking myself to a stupor." He lifted his glass in a mock toast.

"There is something off about him," said Keene. "But Sophie appears fond of him."

"She's not always the best judge of character."

"No, and she is more maternal right now. My biggest fear is that she'll feel an overwhelming need to crawl out on a roof to rescue a kitten or some such. Do tell your Mr. Hall to stay off roofs, if you please."

"I'm not sure if he needs rescue or a thrashing. You do agree that he is not of age, don't you?"

Keene tilted his head to the side. "I'm not certain. There is a maturity to him I would not expect in a youth."

"He doesn't shave yet. I would give him no more than fourteen summers. Gave me a tarradiddle about Indian blood and Indians not growing whiskers."

"Ask Sheridan. If he doesn't know about Indians, he will know someone who does."

"Mmm, there's an idea. Does he still offer discreet investigations?"

"Very discreet. But I was thinking of his military days. He is bound to know an officer or two who has served in North America."

"Does he still have our pistols?"

"They're his now. He bought them. I never wanted them after I knew how inaccurate they are." Keene shook his head. "Tried to shoot you in the leg and damn near killed you. He found some Spanish writing under the lining of the box, and he's been trying to decipher the curse."

Victor waved off thoughts of the cursed dueling pistols. "I'm half tempted to put Leonard on a ship and send him home."

"But?"

"He might have had a valid reason for fleeing."

"Mmmm," said Keene. "As a parent, I'm not sure I would agree with his complaint." Keene stared into his glass. "Whatever it is."

"You would send him home?" asked Victor.

"Most likely. Unless he offered up evidence of abuse or mistreatment."

"He resents my interference."

"Do you want his friendship or his best interests?"

"Both, but too many times the two are mutually exclusive." Victor felt a wave of sadness wash through him. When had he ever been good for anyone? "I shall see if I can convince him it is in his best interests to return home."

"Oh, thank the Lord, a fire." Trevor Hamilton stuck his hands out toward the flames roaring in the common room of the inn. He had been chilled to the bone so deeply the last three months that he thought he'd never be warm again. "Remind me never to sail from Boston to England during the winter again."

Oscar Sullivan gave him a despairing look.

"Never fear, we'll find her. At least we know she made it here." But they'd known she booked passage to Plymouth before they left. Finding out how she'd left Boston had been fairly easy. All ships kept detailed logs of passengers and cargo on land, in case a vessel went down.

They caught the next passenger ship to England, but winter storms delayed their arrival. They had put into port at Dover and had to travel the breadth of England to get to Plymouth where Lydia's ship had docked.

But then the trail went cold.

"We need supper," said Oscar.

"James is talking to the innkeeper about lodgings. We might have found which way Lydia went and been on her trail tonight."

Trevor decided he'd warm his hands first, before moving to see if there was food to be had. He knew Oscar was impatient with the whole process of finding his runaway bride, but he didn't need to despair yet.

They'd searched high and low, visiting all the inns in Plymouth, and then all the coaching houses, anywhere a girl might hire transportation. At first they thought they'd found her; one innkeeper remembered leasing a room to an American woman and her maid, but no one remembered seeing the tall blond American girl leave town. Yet, she wasn't here.

Trevor had spent the better part of the day checking ship manifests to see if she had booked passage on another ship. A storm had been blowing in from the sea, making his trek from one shipping office to the next fraught with the sting of sea spray and a biting wind.

"Where could she be?" moaned Oscar.

"I'd bet money she headed for London."

Oscar's near desperation had kept them searching long after they should have quit for the day. Trevor was fairly sure that no stone in Plymouth remained unturned. The question was if they should turn the same stones again tomorrow, or just move on to where they suspected and Trevor hoped Lydia had gone.

Oscar sank down on a bench and covered his chiseled features with his hands.

Damn, the man was melodramatic. Then again, so was Lydia at times. Perhaps it really was love. "She had Jenny with her. If anything was terribly wrong, Jenny would have sent word. She's got a sensible head on her shoulders, even if Lydia doesn't."

Trevor probably shouldn't have said anything so disparaging about his sister to the man who wanted to marry her. That the man was willing to travel across the ocean in a freezing and damp cabin spoke of his earnestness. For the love of Peter, what did Oscar see in Lydia? Trevor didn't know that he'd go to such bother for a woman if she weren't his sister.

A certain English beauty he'd met five years ago during his Grand Tour sprang to mind—but when the time came to go home, he'd gone.

Although the memory of Lady Helena haunted his dreams, he never would have made the journey back to England if Lydia didn't need retrieving. He simply didn't believe in grand passions. When it came to a wife, an American girl was likely to be much less bother.

When he met Helena, she was eighteen, beautiful and perfectly prepared to marry a prince or royal dignitary. Her bloodlines were exemplary, her loveliness beyond compare, her manners and sense of propriety perfect. Not to mention there was always someone watching over her, just in case her decorum slipped.

He'd wanted to let down her fiery hair, and wrap his hands in the strands of shimmery copper laced with molten gold. The luster of pearls tinted her skin, and her eyes glowed emerald green. All in all, she was priceless, too precious for a common man like him, but that never stopped him from wanting her.

He'd been tolerated in London society because as an upstart American, they didn't know what else to do with men of his ilk. While tolerated, he was never allowed to forget that the stink of the merchant class followed him.

In England, the gentry made their living by owning and managing land, and they excluded those who made their living in trade of any sort. At least many of them tried to keep out those who had labored for their money. The lines tended to blur around the edges of society. That acres and acres of good land were free for the taking in America struck Trevor as ironic.

"But how could Lydia just disappear?" Oscar asked. He dropped his hands and looked around the common room as if she might be hiding in a corner. "How could she be all right with no man to protect her?"

"If you haven't realized, Lydia can be headstrong. She got it into her head that she should move to New York after Mother died. Had her bags packed and everything."

Seeing how far the six-year-old would drag her carpet bag down the lane had amused all five of her older brothers. She trudged a mile, the bag bumping awkwardly against her leg and making her list heavily to one side. She would have gone farther, but James had tossed her over his shoulder and carried her like a sack of potatoes. Even though she was clearly exhausted, she'd fought them the whole way home.

"I can't imagine why she ran away. I was so careful with her. I always showed her the greatest respect," Oscar said.

"Maybe too much respect," offered Trevor.

Oscar shook his head. "No, I had it from Benjamin Lee that she cried off after he stole a kiss in the apple orchard."

Well, perhaps that explained his sister's sudden reversal on her decision to marry Benjamin. Perhaps she didn't know that kissing could be a pleasant experience, and she needn't worry. If she found a gentleman too forward, one yell would have all five of her brothers at her side ready to defend her honor, with force if necessary. Besides, she always seemed like a girl who could handle any situation.

Years of defending herself against the rambunctious antics of five older brothers showed in her manner. Her forthright and bossy manners had scared more than one suitor away.

James entered the common room, his towering

blond head nearly touching the ceiling beams. He glowered as he crossed the room and patrons and waitresses alike sidestepped, even if they weren't in his path. Trevor had the same imposing height, but he tried to temper it with easy smiles.

A smaller man, wearing a bold scarlet coat with blue lapels and a brass horn hanging from his belt, followed James.

"Listen to what he's got to say," ordered James.

Trevor signaled a waitress with four fingers and pointed to a tankard on a nearby table.

He slid onto the bench seat beside Oscar as James and the stranger took the opposite side of the scarred wooden table.

The waitress set down four pewter mugs filled with a dark liquid. James drank with an absentminded scowl. Oscar curled his nose, but Trevor and the older man drank heartily and enjoyed the beer.

"As to your inquiries, we did have American passengers 'round about three months past. A young man and a girl."

James and Trevor exchanged glances.

"What did this young man look like?" Trevor asked.

"A bit like the two of you. Same yellow hair. Younger, though, not got the height of you two. He a brother of yours?"

"We think he's our cousin," said Trevor.

James frowned at the lie. Trevor rarely troubled himself to shade the truth, but he had his reasons.

"Where did this young man go?" James asked.

"Booked passage to London, he did. Set him off at the Swan with Two Necks."

"At the what?" asked Oscar. "How could a swan

have two necks? I don't see what this has to do with Ly—"

Trevor stood and knocked the bench to a tilt that made Oscar clutch the table to keep from spilling out of his seat. Size had its advantages.

"You big oaf," snarled Oscar.

Trevor clapped him on the shoulder. "Sorry, friend, thought I'd see about getting us supper." He just might see, while he was inquiring, if they could burn Oscar's portion.

"The Swan is a post inn in London," said James, frowning down into his pewter mug.

The dapper little man gulped down his dark brew and pulled out his watch. "Well, best be going, sirs. Can't be late. Mail coach is always on time."

James stood and thanked the man with a handshake. Trevor shook his head as the coachman stared blankly at his empty hand. Clapping an arm around his shoulder, Trevor steered the little man toward the door, and dug a couple of silver coins from his pockets.

"You've been most helpful," said Trevor, pressing the coins into the man's hand.

"This boy in trouble?"

"Not trouble, but he's too young to be traipsing around a foreign country all on his own."

"Run off wit' a maid, did he? Poor lad, fancied himself in love, I'll bet."

"Foolish notions youngsters can get," Trevor said noncommittally.

Lydia had gone to London as he'd hoped, as he wished. He wanted to hug his sister for bringing him back here, after she was properly chastised, of course. In London he might chance upon Lady Helena again, and that, as much or more than for Lydia, was why he had braved the bitter winter seas. But would Helena want to see him? Would she remember? Would she be married now?

It had been five years since Trevor had been to London. Five long years and there was no way she, his English beauty, had been waiting for him. Especially since he'd never promised to return. And she'd never really been his.

CHAPTER 5

Lydia reluctantly slid into the carriage seat across from Victor. She glared at him. In truth she was sweating like a stuck pig. She wanted to spend time with Victor, but a tailor would undoubtedly see through her disguise. "We should go to the Tothill Fields. There is a balloon ascension today." She held out a handbill she'd been passed in the street.

"Clothes first, Leonard. If you look like a country bumpkin, it reflects badly on me."

Lydia folded her arms across her chest. "Then you would do better to not be seen with me."

"Clothes, Lenny. They make the man."

Or they exposed the woman. Half of her feared her secret being revealed, half wondered if . . . but no. If Victor realized she was a woman, like all other men he would decide she couldn't make rational decisions about her future, couldn't exist without a man's support and protection, then he would send her home.

Or he could take advantage of her plight. She had been raised all her life to avoid being alone with a man not related to her. She had been warned that a situation like that could lead to too much temptation and too much intimacy. She shifted in her seat. "I'd really like to see the balloon ascension."

"Hoping to run into Sophie?" asked Victor with a saturnine lift of an eyebrow.

Lydia blinked. She was hoping to avoid being measured by a tailor. "I don't want new clothes." Just the idea of standing in front of Victor with nothing on but her shirt and breeches knotted tension in her stomach. "I cannot imagine a greater waste of time. I will not be able to stay in London forever, you know."

"No, I do not know. When will you return home, Lenny?"

"A few months, I suppose." Although she missed her brothers and father, she didn't want to go home. Here she stood on her own two feet and made her own living, albeit as a ne'er-do-well gambler. She didn't depend on any man's support. Her choices might be limited, but they were all her own. Where to live, what to eat, when to sleep, where to go. The freedom was heady.

A woman always had to live in the shadow of a man, her very identity tied to his talents. Pretending to be a boy gave her a glimpse of life where she was valued for herself.

Victor wore his habitual black, which both repelled and attracted her. His determination to take her to his tailor made her shudder. "I think when you are finished with me, I will look like an undertaker."

"Are you in mourning, cub?"

"No." Lydia stared at Victor. Was he?

"Then there is no need for you to dress in black as I do. Is that why you are kicking up such a fuss?"

"I don't need you to father me."

"I'm not old enough to be your father." Then he looked thoughtful. "On second thought, I might have managed it; how old are you?"

She didn't think she wanted to try and claim her real age again. She didn't look like a twenty-one-year-old man. Instead she searched her head for an insult. "You act older than Methuselah. I think you were never young."

Victor winced and Lydia wondered if she had hurt his feelings. She wanted to shrivel up and die.

"Don't be insulting, Lenny. If you get too carried away, I shall have to call you out."

Lydia blinked. Call her out? Now he was insulted? "I take it back. You have no maturity at all. Who settles disputes with fights?"

"Gentlemen do."

"Do you mean duels?" A chill of disquiet slid down her back. At times the male creature was as foreign to her as the hills of China.

"That or we could strip down at Gentleman Jackson boxing salon and go a few rounds, but that would hardly be sporting as I have several stone on you."

Not to mention that stripping down together in a boxing salon would be out of the question, although it might prevent a fight.

"No matter how elderly I may seem to you, I never was so young I didn't take an interest in being properly clothed. Now are you worried about the expense? I shall take care of it."

"No, I can afford new clothes." With the money she had won from him.

"Then what is the problem?"

Lydia couldn't tell him the real reason she didn't

want to visit a tailor. The carriage halted and her heart jumped into her throat. Anything to delay the inevitable exposure. "Who . . . who are you in mourning for?" she asked.

"My wife." He turned and studied her as he descended from the carriage.

"Oh God, I'm sorry," she blurted. She shouldn't have been so gushy and emotional. Boys, men, weren't known for emotions. Women were.

"Don't be. It was a release from a living nightmare worse than any hell."

Lydia stumbled down the carriage steps and looked through the window of a tailor's shop. Her heart thudded in her chest and her mouth grew painfully dry.

"Don't repeat that, cub."

"No, of course not." She willed back her panic by focusing on him. He had been married? He'd had such a complicated past. At once she wanted to know more, yet that he'd likened his marriage to a nightmare made her wary. "How long ago did she . . . pass?"

"Three months."

He rubbed the red mark on his forehead. In the daylight she could see it was a burn scar. The inch-long welt contained smooth reddened flesh at odds with the rest of his pale skin. How had he gotten it? He seemed to rub it when distressed. She wanted to ask more about his wife, but she could tell it bothered him.

He turned and walked quickly into the tailor's shop. The bell above the door knelled out a sprightly death toll for her.

The tailor in his waistcoat and shirt sleeves scurried forward. "How can we help you today, my lord?"

"Not me. My young friend here needs the help."

The tailor looked Lydia up and down, frowned, hemmed, then nodded. "Yes, I see."

Perhaps she could pretend to need the necessary and bolt out the back.

"Shall we start with six shirts, two with lace cuffs for evening wear—" Victor began.

"Four shirts, no lace," Lydia countermanded. "I won't wear lace." Not while in men's clothing.

"The lad is right. With his slenderness, lace would be too . . . effeminate." The tailor stared at her and frowned.

"He'll need a couple of evening coats, waistcoats, breeches, day wear, two or three pantaloons and informal jackets. Can you broaden the shoulders, until he fills out?"

Lydia wanted to crawl under the nearest rock, counter, pin cushion, anything to get away from the scrutiny of the tailor. In front of her hung a brocade velvet robe of long full-bodied paisley fabric. The drape of that gown would cloak any figure. Hers, if she was ever caught again without all her binding and pads in place. "What's that?"

"A dressing gown."

"I want one." She crossed over and removed it from the tailor's dummy and draped it around her shoulders. "Doesn't it look good on me?"

Victor paused in his litany of items he seemed to think were necessary for a man's wardrobe.

Wrong, wrong. A boy would never ask if a garment looked good on him. *Oh, fiddlesticks!*

"I'm glad to see you're taking an interest in your

new attire, cub." Victor turned toward the tailor. "He doesn't want anything in black."

"Uh, er, given his youth, black might be too mature." The tailor frowned again. He pulled his tape measure out of his vest pocket. "Although I might suggest black breeches for evening, with a light blue coat. The contrast of color will give the illusion of more breadth on the upper portion."

Lydia looked around madly for an escape. Her heart jumped in an irregular pattern. The back corners were draped. Hooks on the wall and a low bench with cushions showed through the curtain opening. Changing rooms.

"If you would remove your waistcoat and jacket, sir, I might get your measurements."

She swung the dressing gown off, and handed it to Victor. She half wished she could have thrown it over his head. She strode back to a draped corner and shrugged out of her jacket. "In the fitting room?"

She hung her jacket on the hook and stepped behind the curtain as she unbuttoned her waistcoat.

The tailor had trailed behind her. "Sir, there is more light out—"

"Please," she whispered. She reached into her pocket and pulled out a five-pound note.

He stared at the bill in her hand. His gaze rose to the opening of the waistcoat. Not that there was the best place to judge her female. But even bound tight, she still had small curves there. She hunched her shoulders and locked her elbows in front of the opening.

"Please," she whispered again. She wiggled the money.

He backed away as if fearful. "I . . . I . . . I need to get paper." He reached behind his ear and grabbed his pencil, then held it in front of him like a weapon to fend her off.

He swiveled and rushed back to the main part of the room. She heard the low murmur of voices. She turned around. Cornered.

How ironic. She leaned head-first against the wall and squeezed her eyes shut. The five-pound note remained clutched in her hand. She didn't know if the tailor would come back to measure her, or if Victor would return. How could she think five pounds would overcome the loyalty of a tailor for his regular and rich client?

Would Victor be angry? Would he hate her? Would he force her to leave London?

"Uh . . . er, miss, if you could remove your waistcoat. I'll get these measurements," said the tailor.

Lydia turned. "You didn't tell him, did you?" she hissed.

"No, miss."

"Shhh then, don't call me miss." She held out the banknote again.

He eyed it reluctantly a moment, then took it and shoved it in his pocket. "I have my assistant choosing fabric with Lord Wedmont. He doesn't know?"

Lydia shook her head as the tailor measured around her waist.

He tentatively tested the padding around her waist by pinching it. "Interesting."

They both blushed as the tailor had her raise her arms and measured around her flattened chest. He turned her away from him and measured the length of her back and across her shoulders. Lydia closed her eyes as if that could distance her from the sensation of her dimensions being recorded by a man.

He finished after a few awkward moments over her inseam—she finally held the tape at the top. Relieved to get back into the concealing waistcoat and jacket, she buttoned while the tailor wrote the last numbers on his tablet of paper. He looked up and squinted at her. "You pass quite well for a boy. I would have never known, if I had not seen you without your waistcoat."

"Thank you," whispered Lydia. What else could she say?

The tailor pulled back the curtain, and she emerged. Victor leaned against the counter, his long legs stretched out. Her gaze moved up from his long black boots, to the perfect fit of his black unmentionables, up to shoulders that would never need any padding.

A wave of longing hit her, so strong it shook her knees.

He turned and looked at her and smiled. "Never knew you'd prove so modest, cub. What do you think of this shade of blue?"

Lydia wanted to dissolve at his feet. "Everyone back home gets measured in the fitting room," she said and attempted to look puzzled that she'd done anything out of the ordinary. She turned and gestured toward the wall. "I thought that was what those hooks were for."

She moved closer as if drawn by an invisible force. He gathered the material from the counter and held it up against her chest. With every inch of resolve she possessed, she held her ground. Wave after wave of yearning spilled through her. His hand so casually pressing against her bound breast made sensations riot in her body. Then the urge to pull away melted into an urge to push closer. She stared into his dark eyes.

"Does bring out the color of his eyes, doesn't it?" said the assistant.

Victor shoved the material back on the counter and stared down at it. His voice sounded strained as he said, "Yes, the ladies will all be wanting him for a pet."

Lydia tried to catch her breath, which she had no earthly reason to have lost.

"We'll do quilted waistcoats. That'll add a bit of bulk on the top," said the tailor. "Not everyone has a fine manly figure like your lordship. Never have to work to disguise any flaws with you. And where shall I send the bills?"

"My direction," said Victor.

"No," corrected Lydia and she gave her address to the tailor, making sure he wrote it down.

"Have the clothes delivered there," said Victor. "Quickly, if you please."

"And the bills," said Lydia, but she suspected the tailor wouldn't listen to her, knowing there was a man in the room.

"Come, cub. We're on to the cobbler's for shoes and then we'll go to Gunther's for an ice."

The rest of the afternoon passed in easy camaraderie. They went to the cobbler where shoes for evening wear were ordered, and Victor didn't seem to pay much mind to the cobbler's complaint that her feet were smallish and her heels were too narrow. As long as Victor didn't remark upon those feminine traits, she was safe. Or was she?

The longer she spent with him, the more she wanted to spend time with him. The more she wanted him to learn she was female. She really should end this odd friendship. She should say something so cruel or insulting he would wash his hands of her. But the thought broke her heart.

Lady Helena Bosworth pulled back the last of the holland cloths covering the furniture in her family's London drawing room. Her marmalade-colored kitten sneezed with a vehemence that made his little legs wobble.

Helena scooped up the kitten. "Yes, I know, Sparks. As soon as Mama arrives with the maids we shall have quite a dust-up."

A stern lecture more than a fight, most likely. Her mother's censure had ridden on Helena for days. There had been months of discussion about whether or not they would even come to town for the season this year. Not that anyone had asked her opinion.

Helena rubbed her nose with the little tabby's. "All this uproar for me, and I should much rather have stayed away. Yes, I'm sure you think I'm silly. I should love the chance to dance and make merry."

The reason behind it all just blue-deviled her.

Helena heard a commotion down in the front entryway. She looked out a window over the street. Yes, her parents' crested carriage and the two baggage carts behind, trailed by the plainer coach that contained several of the staff, had arrived. Everyone piled out, and the street swarmed with servants removing band boxes and trunks. "I shall shut you in my room, so you are not stepped upon, all right, Sparks?"

The kitten mewed as if to protest. He had already been cooped up ignobly in a sack for over an hour as Helena rode ahead on horseback with several of the grooms to have the house open when the main entourage arrived. She wanted to be sure her father could sit and put up his gouty leg without delay.

The house was oddly quiet, all empty. In years past her twin sisters had been here too. But both of them were married now. Only Helena remained unattached.

Her father had been healthier too, and normally they all arrived together. But the carriage had to be driven at a snail's crawl to avoid jarring her father overmuch, and Helena had grown impatient with the torturous pace.

"Helena!" Her mother called.

Helena closed the door of her room on her mewing kitten and hurried down the stairs. Two footmen assisted her father up the stairs and into the drawing room.

"I have the covers all off. And there will be hot water for tea in just a spot, Papa," she said as she passed the doorway.

In spite of the lines of pain etched in his face, he smiled and said, "Ah, there's a treat. Whatever would I do without you, Helena?"

"Come into the morning room." Her mother pulled off her coat and gloves. Permanent worry lines made her mother's face appear harsh and haughty and much older than her forty-four years, although not as careworn as her father's at sixty-six. "We have to talk."

"Shouldn't we help the servants get everything situated?" Helena hoped to delay the lecture.

The Countess of Caine rolled her eyes and shook her head. "Everything is labeled. The servants should be able to manage under Meeks's supervision."

Her mother wasted no time in getting to the heart of the matter. "This is to be your last season. You must find yourself a husband by the end of it. We cannot have any more of your dilly-dallying."

Helena nodded. "Well, I shall do my best, and I shall quite understand if we stay in the country next season."

"It won't be just next season, and since I never produced a son to inherit the estate, I'm afraid we must see you comfortably settled in an appropriate marriage. Your father is not well, Helena, and the social season is very dear."

"Yes, well, we could do without a box at the opera, could we not?" They surely could practice a few economies. While it was understood that the bulk of her father's estate was entailed and would pass to his cousin on his death, they didn't need to bury her father just yet.

Her mother shuddered. "We must keep up appearances. Your father is an earl, and we must comport ourselves in a manner worthy of his station."

Helena clasped her arms behind her back. That meant a box at the opera, a box at the theatre, a subscription to Almack's, hosting at least two balls, a dozen other assorted routs, breakfasts and get-togethers. Helena would have to go through myriad fittings for morning dresses, day dresses, riding habits, evening gowns, and a dozen new ball gowns. Although she had acquired enough ball gowns in the last five years to stuff a whole room. Frankly, Helena would be content reading a good book with Sparks on her lap.

"Your father has had to offer the Coventry estate for sale. We shall have to let out the townhouse next season to hope to recover some of the monies spent on launching you girls in the last few years."

But the Coventry estate was to be hers—either as her dowry or a place to live if she did not marry. She'd half-pictured herself growing old there with a cat or two for companionship. She sighed.

"Helena, you are a beautiful girl," her mother continued. Surely you can offer enough encouragement to a gentleman worthy of you to receive an offer."

Ah, there was the rub. She'd only ever offered encouragement to a gentleman not worthy of her. Some would have said he did not deserve the appellation *gentleman*, that he was only a man. He would have surely been shown the door if he bothered to ask for her hand in marriage. The only trouble was he hadn't bothered.

It was the nearest she'd ever come to experiencing passion, and, all in all, it was a very puny nearness. For the depth of feeling most certainly was all on her side.

"So you see it is time to stop waiting for love or whatever nonsense that has you dragging your feet. You must concentrate on offering encouragement and bring a gentleman up to scratch. Helena, are you listening to me?"

"Yes, Ma'am." She wanted to be a dutiful daughter, she really did. She was just so afraid she would

have to settle for a man more than twice her age
or worse. Was it too much to ask to fall in love?

"Well, there is Lord Algany. He needs a wife."

"Yes, well, I believe he has decided to look for a
rich wife."

Her mother bit her lip. "Lord Brumly might be
available still. He certainly doesn't need a rich wife,
although your children would have little hope of a
decent legacy."

"Is he still alive?"

"You could do worse," said her mother sternly.
"At least he has a respectable title."

"Perhaps I could consider a viscount or mayhap
a baron." All the others named held the rank of
earl. In years past, she'd been pointed at foreign
princes and royal dukes. Then she'd been aimed at
just plain dukes and marquises. As the oldest
daughter and supposedly the most attractive, she
was predestined to make the best match, above her
father's position if possible. "What if I were to look
among commoners?"

Her mother gave her a hard look. "The Earl of
Wedmont was just made widower."

"Yes, and there are already rumors that he murdered his wife."

Lady Caine closed her eyes and pressed her fingertips to her forehead. "As a Cit's daughter she
was beneath him, and it is a good thing there wasn't
any issue. He will need to remarry. You cannot say
he is too old or ugly."

"No, I cannot say that. I shall toss my handkerchief
in his direction then. Although I cannot say how he
will find it among all the others." Being thought a
murderer would likely only increase his attractive-

ness. Helena craved passion. But to her, loving a man who murdered his wife was unthinkable.

Then again, she might have been hoping for something that was beyond her. Passion and love and all those intense emotions were perhaps reserved for people who were a bit more excitable. In spite of her red hair and green eyes, Helena seemed to have a quite moderate nature.

As they stood in the yard at Tattersall's, Victor hadn't really decided what his best course of action would be. He only knew that Leonard didn't appear to like horses.

The boy wore new chocolate-brown pantaloons with a fawn jacket. His jackets still fit too loosely to please Victor, but perhaps his tailor was worried the boy's shoulders might broaden. Last night Victor had rewarded Leonard's improved appearance— he wore a light-blue superfine jacket with black breeches and shoes, rather than boots—with a trip to his gentlemen's club. There the boy had won enough to purchase a decent horse for town use, if he wanted one. Watching the cub gamble and win filled Victor with pride.

Keene had joined them today and looked around for Mr. Ponsby, the owner of the horse Sophie wanted. Leonard had developed a distressing habit of sidling into Victor every time they came near to one of the horses to be auctioned this afternoon.

"Do you see a horse you like?" asked Victor.

Leonard looked around, his gaze darting from one horse to the next. "That one." He pointed to a swaybacked nag that would never manage more than an amble.

"Lenny, that horse looks ready for the glue-rendering plant."

Leonard turned his big blue eyes on him as if astonished that horses came to such an ignoble end. What did he think happened to them? One never saw them drop dead in the street. Well, almost never.

Nevertheless, Victor walked him over to the horse and showed him how long the teeth were.

Leonard shoved his hands in his pockets and nodded.

Victor pulled him away, so as not to talk disparagingly in front of the owner. "Not much bottom in this horse."

"I guess not."

"Wedmont, how are you?" said an acquaintance of Victor's.

Victor nodded and introduced his young American friend, Mr. Hall, as he'd done several times before. After a few minutes where Leonard said little to nothing, they went on.

Victor looked around the yard. One horse attracted a lot of attention. Keene stood to the side looking at the crowd with his mouth twisted wryly to the side. Hard to say how many of the lookers would actually bid on the horse, until the auction began.

Victor crossed the yard. "Can't say that Sophie doesn't know how to pick her horses."

Keene nodded. "The next thing is she'll want a smart pair and a fast curricle to race around the countryside."

"See, cub, look at the chest on that horse."

The crowd around the horse thinned, and they

stepped forward to get a closer look. Keene ran a hand over the flank. "Nice lines, Ponsby."

The large beefy man holding the bridle of the horse took one look at Keene and said, "I don't want Sophie on Waterloo."

Waterloo? But then his sire was Salamanca, so Victor supposed the name made sense. "I'm interested in the horse for my young friend here," Victor said and stepped forward.

Leonard looked at him as if he'd gone mad. The horse took exception and sidestepped, nickered and tossed his head.

"Come on, cub. Look at his teeth."

"Careful, he's spirited," warned Mr. Ponsby.

Leonard stepped forward, reluctantly. The horse flattened his ears. As Leonard reached up, the horse nipped at him.

Leonard squealed and grabbed Victor's arm, ducking behind him.

Lenny brushed against him. A rush of sensation drained the blood from Victor's head. "Bloody hell, Lenny, quit acting like a lily-livered pudding heart."

"I don't want a horse," mumbled Leonard as he backed away with his eyes on his feet. Unfortunately, he backed into a man leading another horse across the yard. Leonard swiveled around and stared as if horrified at the horse.

Victor couldn't tell which one was more startled, the horse or Leonard. Victor grabbed his arm and pulled him back to his side. "It isn't for you, it's for Sophie," he hissed. "For God's sake, play along."

When Victor pulled him back, Leonard leaned into him again. Heat fired his blood. Bloody hell, no. Then he watched Leonard's big blue eyes fill with tears. He shoved him away. "Quit . . ." Words to describe what was happening escaped him. "Don't you dare cry like a baby."

Frustration and horror overwhelmed Victor. He wanted to comfort Leonard, he hated that he wanted to comfort him, he despised himself for the extremely odd feelings that raged through him. And everything was happening with half the gentlemen of the *ton* surrounding them.

Leonard jutted his chin out. "If you would quit yanking me around."

Leonard had to go. There was no other answer for it. "Bloody hell, then act like a man. If you want to run away from home and pretend to be fully grown, you shouldn't behave like a scared little boy."

Leonard's face drained of color. "What are you going to do?"

"I'm tempted to throttle you!" Victor could feel his hands clenching in rage. "Or throw you in the Thames!"

"Toss me into a fire and kill me that way too?" Leonard taunted him.

Victor saw red.

CHAPTER 6

Lydia stared. What had just happened? All the men stared at them. Even the horses in the yard at Tattersall's seemed to have turned inquiring brown eyes in their direction. Victor had slapped her with his glove. As a slap went it hadn't hurt, but deep down inside she was bleeding.

"Tell him what to do," Victor growled.

"He couldn't have known," objected Keene, who warily looked back and forth between them.

"I told him just the other day. So tell him what to do," repeated Victor.

"You need to demand satisfaction," said Keene to her.

"I say, he's too young for that," said the giant of a man they called Ponsby. "Just let the lad apologize and be done with it. He won't refuse, will you, boy?"

Lydia looked at him and wanted to run over to him; his height and breadth reminded her of her older brothers. But she had no brothers here. She'd shunned their protection. She had to muddle out of this situation alone. "I'm sorry."

Victor shook his head. "He's not too young, he claims to be twenty-one. Are you a man or a boy, Leonard?"

Lydia straightened her shoulders. How could he turn so on her? He was angry, his scar bright red against his white-faced fury. She looked helplessly between Keene and Ponsby. She couldn't look at Victor. His anger would make her dissolve into tears, and she knew that would disgust him. Somehow in this moment when her world was crashing in, his respect mattered to her.

"Demand satisfaction, Mr. Hall. It will be all right," Keene put a hand on his sleeve and his voice was soothing.

"He apologized, Lord Wedmont, surely you can too?" said Ponsby. "And we can avoid this nonsense."

"I will not. His implication offends my honor, not to mention my wife's memory."

"You said your marriage was hell," she spit the words at Victor.

Ponsby ducked his head down, no longer her ally.

She had the sense that she had crossed a line that was very visible to the three men surrounding her, but invisible to women. But they all thought that she could see it too. "I don't understand."

"By the code of honor, one cannot accept an apology for being slapped," said Victor. "You have to demand satisfaction, and then we'll name seconds and they shall enter negotiations to avert the conflict."

She was puzzled by his patient explanation. He sounded weary, resigned. Her heart was splitting in two.

"Are you a man or a child?"

Neither, she wanted to call out. "I demand satisfaction," she whispered. She swallowed hard against the lump in her throat. *I cannot cry.* I will not *cry.*

"Very good, sir. Keene will stand your second. I will call upon Sheridan and name my conditions." Victor wheeled about and said, "Ponsby, if you will sell me that horse now, I shall write out a bank draft for five thousand pounds."

"Ho, wait," said Keene.

But Ponsby had already roared out, "Done, my lord."

Lydia couldn't take any more. She turned and walked rapidly toward the gate. She couldn't let the tears blurring her vision spill.

Only as she reached the sidewalk outside did she make the connection between what she'd said and his anger. She turned to go back and explain, but found Keene behind her. "Did his wife die in a fire?"

Keene nodded. "He tried to pull her out, but a beam fell on his forehead. His servants barely pulled him out alive."

Lydia drew in a shuddery breath. "I didn't know. All he said was that she died three months ago. I didn't mean . . . anything by it." But now that she understood the situation, she could see how what she said could have been deemed an insult or worse, an accusation of murder.

"Don't know how I shall pay five thousand pounds for that damn horse," muttered Keene. "I only meant to go to three. Where do you live?"

"Not far. I can walk."

"Fine. We shall walk."

"I—you—"

"I am your second in this affair. Victor suggested I explain the procedure to you. He said he would name conditions, so as your representative, I will offer to him the only condition he needs to meet is to offer apology for striking you."

"I don't care if he apologizes. I don't want to fight." Lydia caught Keene's expression of consternation. "Him. I don't want to fight him. He has been very k-kind to me."

"Yes, well, do not fret about it. All shall turn out well, you'll see."

Lydia didn't see how. In either case her friendship with Victor was destroyed.

Victor paced back and forth in the Sheridans' drawing room. The room had once been green with crocodile-legged furniture, but had been redecorated in ivory and gold with a touch of burgundy here and there. Something horrible had once happened in this room, but for all his questions, Tony would never reveal the exact details. Actually, that whole night had been rather eventful.

Sophie had been on the roof rescuing the Sheridans' son while a certain Lord Algany fell and broke his leg. During all the commotion, the man who ended up marrying Victor's half-sister Margaret had been shot.

One of these days Victor would get the whole story. Tony entered the room, his limp held to a minimum. They exchanged greetings and condolences and caught up on the past few months since they had last seen each other.

"Felicity is sending out invitations. She always feels she is obligated to start off the season with a small gathering. Let me get her, I'm sure she'd want to see you."

"Oh, no, don't bother her. I know she is probably elbow deep in ledgers."

Felicity ran the business left to her by her first husband. To fill his time, Tony had started conducting discreet investigations for the upper Ten Thousand while his wife made money hand over fist. "Are you doing any investigations?"

"Nothing I could speak about." Tony smiled. Lines crinkled around Tony's unearthly pale eyes.

Victor would swear Tony could look straight through a man and see parts of his soul. Now that he was here, Victor was reluctant to ask for Tony to second him, as if the whole episode with Leonard would disappear if he did not think of it.

Tony gave him an enigmatic look and said, "Do you need something looked into?"

How had he known? "I would like you to learn why my mother-in-law is in Newgate."

"There probably is a public record. Maybe newspaper accounts."

"Yes, well, I shouldn't like to be seen making the inquiries."

"I'll be discreet. What else do you need?"

"Very well, I need your services as a second."

Tony blinked and leaned back. "Of course, you may always count on me to stand by you. What about Keene, or do you mean to fight him again?"

"He is pledged to my opponent. And I'll need the use of the pistols; you do have them still, do you not?"

"Yes, got them back after they were stolen the last time. You don't really want to use them, do you? It's like opening a Pandora's box."

"I know they are inaccurate. That is what I want, just to stand there and aim at each other and miss.

I just want to scare a certain young gentleman who is too . . . above himself for his own good." Victor winced as he said that.

"The real danger is the curse. There is no telling who will win on that front."

"I'm not ever marrying again, and I don't know that I believe in the curse." Only God knew if he would feel anything for a woman ever again. Perhaps his first marriage had soured him so that only boys attracted him now. Not that he was winding down that twisted path. He'd send Leonard running back to Boston, long before that got out of control. "If you don't wish for me to use the pistols, then—"

"I'm happy to let you use them. Did Keene tell you I found writing under the lining? It's in Spanish and rather cryptic."

"The curse, I suppose?" Victor stood and followed his host down the stairs.

"Yes, pretty much as we've been told. The winner will get a happy marriage and the loser a marriage worse than hell. There is a verse about breaking the curse."

"Really?" All right, so he knew that he had lost the first duel he fought with the cursed pistols, but he really did not intend to marry again. There was no saying that his being the loser of the first duel wouldn't follow him forever. In fact, he rather suspected it would. Of course if all went as planned, Leonard would never actually fire one of the pistols.

Tony opened the door to the library and gestured Victor inside. "I haven't worked out all the verses. Spanish isn't my best language, and it does seem to be in an unusual dialect."

Tony pulled a walnut box out of a cupboard and

lifted the lid. He shifted the red velvet lining, revealing an etched copper plate.

Victor stared down at the ornate Spanish tooling and the mother-of-pearl grips on the pistol handles. They were beautiful weapons, and they made his stomach turn.

"I'll take my duties as second seriously," said Tony.

That meant Tony would do his best to see the disagreement settled without confrontation. "Yes, I should expect you to," said Victor.

A cold feeling skittered down his spine. Perhaps it was the memory of the day Keene shot him. Or that these cursed pistols had led to the horror of his marriage. Or perhaps some unease about the future, should he actually have to use them in a duel with Leonard.

The butler opened the door. "Mr. Davies, sir, my lord."

"What took you so long?" blurted Victor.

Keene gave him an odd look and brushed off his sleeve. "Whatever possessed you to offer Ponsby a king's ransom for that horse? I cannot afford so much."

"How is Leonard?" Victor didn't want to talk about the horse.

"He is upset. How do you expect him to be? He doesn't wish to fight with you, because he said you've been very kind to him. I expect he'll meet whatever conditions you set."

Victor threw himself onto a sofa.

Apparently ready for the moment, Tony handed him a glass of brandy. "Is this fight justified?"

"Of course it is," said Victor. "He implied I murdered my wife. I know there are rumors."

"Bound to be rumors after her last appearance in London," said Keene. "She provided a lot of grist for the mill."

Victor shuddered. "I didn't kill her."

"We know that. Not even Leonard suspected that or meant to imply it. Perhaps you inferred it?" said Keene.

"For God's sake, whose side are you on? You were there." Was his own half-brother turning against him?

"I'm *his* second. Remember? You appointed me. And he only said what he said after you threatened to kill him."

"I didn't threaten to kill him. I just threatened him with bodily harm or a nasty dunking." Victor leaned forward and rubbed his forehead. He didn't want to hurt Leonard, he just wanted to kill his unnatural urges toward the boy. "He needs to go home."

"Please, Victor, I have a bad feeling about this," Keene said. "Let me go back to Mr. Hall and tell him you have accepted his apology."

"No. He is not getting out of this so easily." Victor rubbed his face, hiding the wash of emotions.

"Then if you would name your conditions for satisfaction, we will see if Mr. Hall is willing to meet them," said Tony.

"I will be satisfied if he makes arrangements to return home to America immediately."

Victor raised his head from his hands, the others were silent so long.

"And if he does not agree to that condition?" Tony asked.

"Then he must give me the reasons he ran away from home in the first place. If there is merit in his need for refuge here in England, then I shall cede my request that he return home and offer my apologies for the blow with the glove."

Victor tossed back his drink. The brandy soothed and burned all the way down. He hoped it would reach inside his heart and warm it, if only for a moment.

He allowed that he might have killed his wife. Not so much by outright deed, but by his expectations and needs.

God forbid he should ever ruin another person's life with his desires. Getting Leonard out of harm's way was the best thing for both of them.

When Keene gave Lydia the condition of returning home to America to avert the duel, she refused.

He wouldn't force her to go home; she'd go when she was ready.

As for the alternative condition—to tell Victor why she ran away—she couldn't very well tell him she ran away from her own wedding. What *man* would ever need to flee a country to escape matrimony? That she now suspected her fiancé, the man she once thought she loved, would use her to take over control of her father's business was neither here nor there.

She could probably avert the whole duel by confessing her sex, but she was hurt and angry. And if Victor knew she was a woman, he would probably force her to return home anyway.

Drat. She had gotten along well enough before he interfered in her life.

Keene knocked on her door, early in the morning before the sun awoke. And Jenny—who up until then had followed orders to stay out of sight—tried to stop Lydia from leaving, by yanking on her arm and crying out, "Tell him the truth."

Lydia clapped a hand over Jenny's mouth and dragged her back into the bedroom.

"Stop it, Jenny. I have to go. I have to do this." Lydia untangled her legs from her servant's skirts. A man could have pulled the girl along, but Lydia had needed to wrap her arms securely around her servant and use the whole force of her superior height and weight to force Jenny into the back.

"You'll be killed," wailed Jenny, when her mouth was uncovered.

A sickening sense of dread slid down Lydia's spine. She would have to tell Victor. Although her mind refused to believe this would go forward. Surely it would stop before it went too far. Were men this uncivilized about a misunderstanding? Certainly, they couldn't be this barbaric in these days.

It all had to be a sort of male ritual, like two peacocks squawking and making feints at each other as if about to tear each other from beak to talon, but then after a ruffled display of feather and puffed chest they would swagger away as if they were both champion of a fight that never happened. She'd watched just such a display the day before between two of the extravagantly plumed birds on the grounds of the White Tower.

"Leonard, we need to leave. I can help you settle

your affairs in the carriage," called Keene from the other room.

Jenny followed her as far as the bedroom doorway and stood with her fist stuffed in her mouth and tears streaming down her face.

Keene held open the door for her. "Come, Leonard, we do not wish to keep the others waiting."

Lydia went down the stairs and found a lamp-lit carriage waiting for her. Keene studied her as she climbed up the steps and then he followed her in and shut the door.

"It would be customary to write out your last will and testament now, if you haven't already done so." Keene gave her an assessing look. He handed her a portable writing desk, complete with recessed inkpot. "In case anything should happen."

Fear made her hand shake as she lifted the pen.

"All you have to do is tell Victor why you are here. If it is because of your relationship with your maid . . ." Keene let the words dangle.

So that was what he thought. That Leonard had run away to have an affair with a maid. "It isn't because of Jenny."

Keene kept his silence as they traveled from the city to the countryside, the steady drone of the wheels and horses' hooves against cobblestone, fading to the crunch of gravel then to the muffled thrum of dirt roads.

She descended in the dawn air in a place that might once have been a drive to a grand house. Two rows of trees stood sentinel on either side of the grass corridor that led to nothing. Bare branches reached overhead like bony fingers ready to snatch her soul away.

Surely it was a reminder that her choice, to live freely as a man would live, led to nothing and she would have to go back to her future as Lydia Hamilton, daughter of a wealthy American shipping mogul and intended wife of Oscar Sullivan.

While she wouldn't mind returning to her life as a woman, if she could manage some means of income, she did not want to leave Victor. He may hate her and despise her, but as mixed-up and crazy as everything was, the world felt right when she was around him. Whether he was berating her clothing choices or giving her a quiet aside about the proper behavior of a gentleman, she liked being near him.

She'd even stifled her fear of horses to be with him that fateful day at Tattersall's. Or perhaps she hadn't been as in control of her emotions as she should have been.

The two carriages and a black hack were parked well away from the combat area. All the men were solemn as wisps of fog swirled around like ghostly witnesses.

A tall, tawny-haired man with unearthly pale eyes limped toward her and Keene. He held open a dark wood box.

Pistols with barrels twelve inches long rested inside the red velvet-lined box.

"Pick whichever one you would like to use," said Keene.

Oh, God, this felt too real. She pointed to the lower one in the box. One was just as bad as the other. She looked over and saw Victor standing by his carriage. His dark hair lifted in the breeze and his habitual black made him seem ominous. A harbinger of death, or at least no stranger to it.

Something inside her shattered, leaving her numb. Keene lifted the gun she'd chosen from the box. "Have you ever fired a pistol before, Leonard?"

As if she were a long way away, she answered, "No."

"Bloody hell."

The cool metal was thrust into her hand and Keene showed her how to pull the trigger. "Practice aiming it, Leonard. Sight through this." Keene pointed out a metal groove on top of the gun. "Hold your arm out and present your side to your opponent to give him less of a target." Keene grabbed her shoulders and turned her, then raised her arm directly to her right, aiming toward a tree. Her opponent wouldn't be a tree.

The pistol was incredibly heavy, much heavier than she would have expected. Her arm shook from the exertion of holding it out.

"Hold it steady, Leonard, and for God's sake, aim straight for his heart."

"No." She dropped her arm.

"Yes, don't fret. You are more likely to miss than not. The pistols are not that accurate, and you have no expertise."

"I cannot do this."

"I shall get Victor."

She tried again to aim the pistol, closing one eye.

"Do you have something to tell me, cub?" asked Victor. He'd removed his jacket and waistcoat. The breeze flattened the white silk of his shirt against his chest.

Lydia felt her gaze drawn to the firm, lean, muscled expanse. "I don't want to go through with this."

Keene took the pistol from her hand. "I need to load it."

"Then are you willing to return to the colonies?" Victor asked.

Lydia shook her head. A wave of despair wafted through her miasma of fascination. She just couldn't go home, now. Not with the way things stood between them. She couldn't bear to leave things like this.

Victor folded his arms across his chest, breaking her mesmerized stare. "Then tell me why you ran away."

"I can't. I did not think about your wife when I said . . . what I said. I didn't know you were there when she . . . at the time. I would never sland—"

"Keene told me. Did you leave home because your father would object to your setting up house with your Jenny?"

Why did he sound so angry? Lydia felt helpless. She shook her head. "I don't want to fight."

"If you want to be a man, then be a man."

"But," she started. She would have to tell him she wasn't a man at all. "I'm . . ."

Except at that moment, the light-eyed man approached with a pistol, while Keene brushed against her shoulder, the other pistol held in his hand. "They're primed and loaded."

"Don't disgust me, Lenny. Show me that you have the mettle of a gentleman."

"But—" she looked at the two men standing to their sides. She could tell Victor, but she didn't know how he would react and telling him in front of his friends might humiliate him. That she had fooled him more than anyone else would insult his male pride.

"Why won't you just tell me? We can end this now," said Victor in a low voice that radiated with exasperation. "Or at least tell me your real age that we may quit."

She straightened her shoulders. "I am one and twenty."

Victor shook his head as if frustrated with her.

"If I do this, will you stop being angry with me?"

"I cannot say. I am sure I should be proud of you." With those cryptic words he turned toward the field.

"Might I hold your jacket, sir?" Keene asked.

She shook her head and followed Victor out into the soggy grass. When they stood back to back in the middle of the field she would whisper her secret to him. She had to, but as she backed against him she savored the feel of his shoulders against hers. He was just enough taller than she to make her want to lean against him.

Then Keene or the other man was calling from the sideline to take their ten paces.

"Take long strides, cub. It'll be over in a trice," whispered Victor.

How could he still be offering her advice on the proper comportment of a gentlemen when they were about to point pistols at one another?

Their ten paces passed in seconds of nothing, over too fast for belief. She faced him and raised her pistol. He stood his body squared toward hers, where she was sideways as Keene had told her. His gun pointed straight at her heart. Fear thrust through her resolve. She couldn't do it. She couldn't shoot him. She couldn't even point the pistol at him.

Keene yelled deliver. She squealed and ducked to run.

She heard a click.

She took one step.

"No!" Victor shouted.

Two steps.

She heard the blast of a shot just before a force slammed into her left shoulder, spinning her around. Through the fog of surprise she heard the click of her own pistol. Oh, Christ, she had squeezed the trigger after all.

A deafening roar spit out of her pistol with a dragon's breath burst of flame. Then the kick of the gun lost what was left of her balance as pain seared through her shoulder.

Out of the corner of her eye, she saw another fall as she hit the ground. Where had her shot gone?

"Hell and damnation!" yelled Sheridan from the sidelines.

Victor's veins filled with ice. When Leonard dove to the side, the shot that should have missed hit the boy. Leonard's pistol had fired wildly, hitting Sheridan. Victor had already pulled the trigger when he saw the boy balk.

Victor's knees went weak as he stumbled across the field toward Leonard.

Although his focus was on Leonard, out of his peripheral vision, Victor saw the blossoming red stain on Tony's thigh.

Leonard moved. Oh, thank God.

Finally Victor reached Lenny and dropped to his knees. The surgeon knelt beside Tony. Of course

he would go to him first, he was nearer to him.
Damn, they should have brought two surgeons.

"Where are you hit, cub?"

Leonard moaned and gripped his left shoulder.

"How bad is he?" yelled Keene.

"He's conscious." Please let him be conscious.

Victor shoved at the coat, popping buttons in his
haste to get at the wound.

Leonard struggled against him, holding his arms
across his chest.

"I have to see the wound, cub. The surgeon will
be here in a minute as soon as he stops Tony's
bleeding. Don't fight me, you could make it worse."
Victor strived to keep his voice calm.

Leonard's struggles were too puny to be effective,
as Victor yanked open the jacket and waistcoat and
loosened the boy's neck cloth. He grabbed the shirt
at the hole made by the bullet and ripped it open.
Did the weakness of the youth's struggles indicate
serious injury?

Victor's heart beat frantically in his throat. "I wish
you hadn't moved. The bullet would have missed
elsewise."

Leonard gave a squeak of alarm. Victor had an
uneasy feeling that more than a bullet hole was the
matter with Leonard.

In fact, an odd bandage was pinned about his
chest, as if he'd cracked a rib.

A neat hole penetrated the fleshy portion between the boy's too-delicate collar bone and his
slender neck. An inch to the left and the bullet
could have ripped through his throat, killing him
instantly. An inch or two lower and he would have
been lung shot. Yet, blood pooled and oozed, and

Victor pressed Leonard's cravat against the wound and yanked at the binding to use it to tie the pad down. A bullet wound was more urgent than cracked ribs.

Leonard covered his face with his hands and moaned.

Was it to cover tears?

"Don't worry, cub. It's not bad. You shall be— bloody hell!"

Victor blinked and stared at one perfect rosy-tipped breast. Leonard was a girl.

Oh, hell, he'd shot a woman.

CHAPTER 7

At Victor's exclamation, Keene ran toward them. Victor grabbed Leonard's jacket and pulled it over the bared flesh of his—no, her—breast. Comprehending that Leonard was a girl confused Victor. How could he not have realized? All the signs were there.

"Is he bad?" Keene's hands were stained with blood.

The surgeon grabbed his satchel and started toward them. Victor waved them off and told not-Leonard to hold the wad of material against his shoulder. Keene kept approaching and Victor fought off the urge to throw himself across the girl's body to protect her—from what? He was the one who had shot her.

Victor scooped not-Leonard up and headed for Keene's carriage. He couldn't allow her to be examined in front of all these gentlemen and their coachmen too. "Not bad."

"Did my shot hit . . . ?" not-Leonard asked.

Keene appeared relieved to hear her speak.

"Hit Sheridan," said Victor. "You could have at least hit me."

"Oh, no," wailed the girl.

Keene turned his inquiring gaze to Victor as if looking for an explanation for his startled reaction when he pulled back the boy's shirt.

Victor shook his head as if to tell his brother to give him a bit of privacy. But he too needed to know how bad Sheridan was hit. "How is he?"

"Nicked a vein, but he says it is just a flesh wound, and he's survived worse." said Keene. "If you don't need me, I shall go hold pressure on his bleeding."

"Do. Seems to me Sheridan suffered the worst wound." If he could keep them focused on Tony, mayhap they wouldn't look too closely at not-Leonard.

Although Tony sat talking to the surgeon, Victor swallowed hard at the sight of blood staining the buff-colored unmentionables. "I'm taking . . . the cub to your carriage, have the surgeon come examine—do an examination there, once he has Sheridan's wound bound." Victor was having a damnable time, phrasing things so that he didn't reveal the girl's secret.

"I'm so sorry," she said, straining to look back at Sheridan.

"Me too, pet," whispered Victor. "Me too."

He set her on the seat of Keene's carriage and began easing the jacket and waistcoat off her shoulders.

"Will he be all right?" she asked. "I didn't intend to shoot at all, but when I fell . . ."

"If he says it is survivable, I'm sure it is. He's seen enough wounds to know."

She blinked.

"He fought at Waterloo. Who the hell are you?"

She recoiled and he left off learning her identity

and concentrated on her wound. Once he had her
free of the jacket, he gave her the carriage blanket.

"I have to take off your shirt, *Lenny*. Use the blanket to cover yourself."

She lowered her eyes and held the blanket in
front of her chest, while he pulled the ruined shirt
and undershirt over her head and right arm, then
gently eased them both down her left arm.

A larger gash on her upper back showed that the
bullet had passed through. That no pieces remained inside her shoulder to make the wound
fester was a blessing. He stripped off his own cravat,
folded it, then pressed it against her back.

He helped her drape the blanket over her right
shoulder and gathered the folds so she could hold
it closed with the right hand. What did she have on,
pillows around her waist? He tried to look at anything other than the expanse of her bared skin.
Such a beautiful, kissable back.

His fingers along her collarbone found no im-
perfections. She watched him out of those big blue
eyes, without a single moan or tear of protest.

"You will tell him, Mr. Sheridan, I am very sorry."
Her voice crested up on the Mr. Sheridan.

"I'll tell him."

Then the surgeon climbed in to examine her. Victor waited outside, giving the man room to work.

Half bewildered, he drifted over to the other two
men. With his arm draped over Keene's shoulders,
Tony stood on his good leg. A slowly reddening
bandage bound his thigh.

"Felicity is going to kill me," Tony said. "She hates
those pistols."

"Then I suggest you offer her my neck instead. It

was all my fault," said Victor. "My friend sends . . .
an apology." Thinking before he spoke had to be
the hardest thing for him. "I never expected this
turn of events."

"No, you expected everyone to miss," Keene said.
"You never listen to me when I express doubts
about your safety."

"You have doubts all the time," countered Victor.

"Not about you," Keene said.

Tony interrupted their spat. Well and good, because Keene had confounded Victor with that odd
cross between a reassurance that he cared about
him and that he respected his abilities—most of
the time.

"The outcome from yonder guns is never certain." Tony limped forward between them. He
seemed in remarkably good spirits for someone
who had been shot. "How is Mr. Hall?"

"Not too bad." Was it Miss Hall? Or Mrs. Hall? Or
was that part of her name a fabrication too? "Very
worried about you."

"You look battle-dazed," commented Sheridan. "I
need my leg elevated."

"By all means." Victor took Tony's other arm
across the shoulder.

"This leg always bears the brunt of any assault. My
punishment for insisting the surgeon not remove it
the first time I was shot, I presume."

The three of them lurched toward Sheridan's
carriage.

"My deepest apologies, sir," said Victor. Everything he had a hand in went from bad to worse.

"Think nothing of it. I needed a good bloodlet-
ting," said Tony. "I blame the pistols. What I want to

know is, why haven't you been injured, Keene? Everyone else who has dueled with them has also been shot by them."

"I do not know," said Keene. "Perhaps because I refused to keep them."

The surgeon descended from Keene's carriage, his mouth pursed in disapproval. "Lord Wedmont, if I might have a word with you."

Victor winced, but he made sure to shake his head to the surgeon. "Yes, sir."

Keene glanced at him oddly. Tony used concentration to climb the steps to his carriage.

"I shall call on you later this day, sir," said the surgeon to Tony.

"How is Leonard?" asked Keene.

"That person will be fine. I have administered sedation."

Keene frowned as the surgeon stepped away and waited for Victor to join him. "Person? Does he disapprove of Americans?"

Victor shrugged. "Will you see Sheridan home? I do not believe he should be alone."

"Of course I shall."

Victor reluctantly made his way over to the surgeon. "Before you start, none of us knew. If she had said, I would have called the whole thing off."

"What do you mean to do?"

"Take her home and see that she heals. What more can I do?"

The surgeon pursed his lips.

Victor ran a shaky hand through his hair. "My word of honor as a gentleman, I shall see that no further harm befalls her."

The surgeon opened his mouth to object.

"No harm of any kind. When I find her family, I shall see her safely restored to their care, her virtue intact."

The surgeon nodded. "I'll call later today to change her dressings."

"Very good, sir." It went without saying that the surgeon would be paid triple his normal fee. The man might be willing to patch up hotheaded young men, but he'd had a problem when one of them turned out to be a young woman.

Victor stared at the carriage. She was a woman, wasn't she? Of course she was. That was why she had a maidservant. Leonard having a maid had reassured Victor that the boy was normal and also angered him inexplicably.

Just one little thing niggled him. He moved to the carriage and climbed in. Not-Leonard lay on her right side, her long legs folded and tucked up to fit on the seat. Her eyes were closed and eyelashes appeared damp as if she'd saved her tears for the doctor. She had her torn shirt, jacket and waistcoat back on, but she suddenly no longer looked a boy at all. There was just that one thing.

Victor brushed her shoulder, but she didn't stir. He leaned down and her breathing was regular and deep. Sedated.

He had to know that she was not an it. Not an accident of nature that had no clear gender. He had glimpsed the outline of a very male piece of anatomy that had convinced him Leonard was a boy more than anything else. Victor reached down and cupped her crotch. Trying to guess what he was feeling seemed like a mad parlor game gone awry. One thing was sure, her penis felt nothing like his own. No, hers was too soft, and he could squeeze, twist and bend it in a way that would be painful for any man, yet she didn't stir.

Why would she have gone to such lengths to pretend to be a man? And what in the hell would he do with her?

Not sleep with her. He'd just given his word of honor he would protect her virtue. If God loved him, she'd have no virtue for him to preserve, but he knew that wouldn't be the case.

Drawing on green gloves dyed to match her riding habit, Lady Helena headed for the front door. A footman opened it for her, and she stepped outside where two grooms waited. One held the head of her horse and the other was mounted on one of the older animals from their stable.

Once the season got into full swing, and she was dancing until dawn, she wouldn't be able to enjoy these early morning rides.

A prickle of awareness stopped her in her steps.

The overnight fog had yet to burn off. Nothing appeared out of place in the nearly empty street, and the grooms did not act as if anything was amiss. As she neared her mount, the fog parted and a giant of a man stood there, like an apparition. She shook her head, wondering if he was a figment of her imagination or a hopeful memory. His blond hair glistened with diamond drops of dampness from the air. Not real, he couldn't be real.

"Lady Helena, that is you," the ghost spoke.

"Yes," she answered. Then she looked at the

grooms to be sure they had heard it too. "What are you doing here?"

Hope that he might have come back for her, that he might have been unable to stay away made her heart sing.

"I've come to fetch my sister home."

Her dashed hopes were childish. He would never have come for her. He hadn't stayed for her either. He wasted no time in returning to America with the ship he'd come to England to regain. He'd had to sue, but once his lawsuit concluded, he was gone. "I suppose that would be of more urgency than a boat."

"Ship," he corrected.

She retrieved the reins from the groom and reached for the sidesaddle pommel. The groom laced his fingers together and lowered down to give her a lift up.

He, Trevor Hamilton, moved beside her. "Allow me." He clasped her around the waist and lifted her onto her saddle, as if she had no more consequence than a feather.

For a moment she couldn't breathe.

"Perhaps you would allow me to take your groom's place as escort."

"It wouldn't be seemly."

He laid his hand on the neck of her horse, dangerously close to her thigh. "Who's to know besides us?"

"My grooms. Therefore, my parents."

He sauntered over and took the reins of the second horse. "You might tell them I am applying for a position in their stables."

"I do not find your comment amusing," she said.

She didn't understand his willingness to mix with
the lower orders. Not that she refused to speak
with the servants, or treated them with anything
less than kindness. But he always treated everyone as if they might be the best of friends.

"As I do not find any man's honest labor demeaning."

The groom dismounted. "More 'an we'd earn in
a month of Sundays, guv."

"You bribed my grooms?"

Lydia was in trouble. She felt as if she were floating. She half-realized she was being carried and
that felt nice, so she drifted in and out as she
floated up and up. The doctor had given her laudanum, which made her forget the ache in her
shoulder, forget that she had problems too big to
solve and forget to stay awake.

Then there were voices.

"Should I have a room prepared, my lord?"

"Prepare my wife's chamber," grunted Victor.

My wife's chamber. How nice. Except she wasn't
his wife. She struggled to raise her eyelids, but
failed.

She heard breathing, quickening breathing.
Then another voice she recognized, Millars's. "Do
you intend to put the young lady in your bedroom,
my lord?"

There was an air of disapproval and hushed secrecy. It was the manservant who had escorted her
home several times.

"You knew she was female and didn't tell me?"
Victor whispered. He was the one who carried her.

"You would have had the footmen carry a

wounded young man," said the servant with great affront.

"Right," said Victor with as much skepticism as Lydia felt. Fiddlesticks, she knew the servant had known.

"Are you sure this is best? I am forced with great reluctance to object to the arrangement, my lord."

"Bloody hell, man. The other room is not ready. She is injured, and you know I am capable of practicing great restraint," said Victor in a low undertone.

An odd thing for Victor to say, she thought.

"Yes, well—"

"It is only until she heals or . . . I can locate her family."

Was his hesitation because he thought she might not survive?

"Help me—she weighs a ton."

Oooh, that was not a pleasant thing to hear about oneself, even if it was true. She heard the snick of a door opening.

"You shouldn't have carried her up two flights all by yourself, my lord," said the valet as the door clicked shut.

"I didn't want anyone else realizing she's female. I do not have a chaperone for her. I do not know what I shall do with her. Turn down the bed, will you?"

She was deposited on a soft surface. Then her boots were tugged off.

"Perhaps an older female relative."

"I don't have any. Hand me one of my nightshirts, if you please." Victor breathed a little hard.

She was propped upright and pain shot through her shoulder. Her mental fog lifted a bit.

"Should I not fetch the housekeeper to remove her clothing?"

"No, after all my trouble, I deserve some reward."

Reward? What did he mean by reward?

"Very good, sir," said Millars as if it were anything but good.

"Why don't you make yourself useful and fetch her maid. However, I don't want this known to the other servants. You will refer to her as Mr. Hall outside of this room."

"My lord?"

"It's the best I can do to preserve her reputation at the moment. Although I daresay it shan't matter."

Why wouldn't it matter? Her jacket was pulled down, right arm first. She leaned limply into Victor's shoulder, breathing in the scent of him while she waited for the room to stop spinning. His hands were infinitely gentle.

"Go on, so I might settle her in bed."

There was the sound of the door and Victor eased her jacket and waistcoat down her left arm. She tried to thank him for using such care near her injury, but what came out was less than speech, more of a mumbled moan.

"Yes, I know, pet. I am being as careful as I can."

Then she didn't remember more than sensations of cold, then warm, until she was embroiled in a dream or memory of Victor pointing the gun at her and pulling the trigger.

She woke with a jerk.

Devoid of his jacket and waistcoat, he stood with his back to her, looking out a window.

"You shot me."

He turned slowly. "Yes, I did."

She looked around the spacious bedchamber. The room was filled with heavy, dark wood furniture, the walls a hunter green with dark wine hangings around the bed and matching drapes. A masculine room. Her inspection stopped when her eyes landed on a bowl of bloodied water on a night table beside the bed and a pile of stained bandages. "Where am I?" She struggled to sit.

"My bed." He moved quickly to her side and helped her, moving pillows so she had a backrest. She couldn't help but notice his sinewy forearms where his shirt sleeves had been rolled back. The open collar of his shirt exposed a masculine neck. Why had he undressed? Or had he never put his coat and waistcoat back on after the duel?

All at once she became aware that she didn't have a stitch of clothing on underneath the nightshirt she wore. Not even her smallclothes had been left on her.

He hadn't needed to remove all her undergarments, had he? Her muddy memory of being cold suggested he had stripped her naked, before pulling the nightshirt over her head and covering her with the sheets and blanket.

There was worse, she realized, as the left shoulder of the gown had been slit open. As she sat up, the front flopped open. Victor simply watched with interest as she grabbed at it and pain wrenched her injured shoulder.

He sat on the bed beside her, the weight of the mattress shifting to make her feel as if she should slide into him. Part of her wanted to, but his dark eyes held a predatory look that she had never seen before.

She stared at him, but then a frown furrowed his brow. "Oh, hell, you should not be moving around so much. You are bleeding again. I was watching for the surgeon. I would that he'd hurry."

Had she taken a turn for the worse in the interval between when she'd been shot and now? Her brain felt slow and muzzy. How much time had passed? How much blood had she lost? "Am I going to die?"

"Eventually."

Her squeak of alarm must have amused him, because he gave her a half smile.

She had two thoughts: one, that she wasn't ready to die, and two, that she didn't want to die untouched. That was followed quickly by the idea that she was a little uncertain about how everything would work, and Victor scared her at times, especially when he aimed a pistol at her. Oh, Lord, if she was confused about her feelings before, they were now even more complicated.

He put his hand in the neck of his shirt and pulled it out, exposing his right shoulder.

She suppressed her second squeak and slid down, staring up at him. Did he mean to remove his shirt? Her eyes were drawn to the discolored and puckered flesh of a scar.

"I lived through this. I should imagine you shall live through yours."

"Will I have a scar that bad?" she asked and then wished she could recall the words.

"I should not expect it. The bullet in my shoulder hit bone and had to be dug out. Then the wound had to be lanced and drained several times." His voice was matter-of-fact, but there were hints at the deepness of the damage in his wince. "Yours is just a flesh wound, and I know much more about how to care for such now. There are leeches I would not let within a league of you."

She tentatively reached out to touch his scar when he let go of his shirt, allowing it to slide back into place. Her fingers met silk. How peculiar, her shirts for Leonard had been made in linen. Yet, the slide of the material left her feeling bereft of what she wanted.

His fingers closed around hers. "Don't."

"Does it still hurt?" She looked at his dark eyes and saw not pain or a wish to avoid pain, but a hunger that burned through her.

"No. It healed long ago."

Then why didn't he want her to touch him there?

She let go of her nightshirt, hoping it wouldn't fall down since she was in a reclining position. Tentatively she reached for the neck of his shirt and pushed it back to see the scar. What she saw was the strong expanse of muscle and bone covered by smooth male skin and just the hint of dark chest hairs below where she held open the shirt.

His hold on her hand loosened, and she touched the marred and darkened skin. How many scars did he have? The one on his forehead, this one, were there more? If she were to look, would she find more battle wounds, as if he were a knight of old? He turned his head slightly away as if bearing her interest and examination was difficult.

That he had likely looked long enough to satisfy his curiosity when he stripped her of her clothing emboldened her. The flesh had healed, but the wound had been more than that. She didn't know how she knew that, but she knew with a conviction deep inside her.

She leaned up and pressed her lips to the mark. His taste was heady, slightly salty, all male. Her stomach fluttered and what she'd meant as comfort and an apology for her reaction of horror turned into much more.

Yet, his palpable tension made her unsure. Had she erred in treating him to such gross familiarity? Did he find her attention distasteful? Was her kiss an imposition? She reached to be sure the night-shirt was still covering her, while ducking her head down. "Do you have many scars?"

"With such treatment, would that I could claim more."

That brought her head up, and his face was so close to hers, his breath brushed across her lips.

He ran his fingertips across her bared shoulder. "Does that mean I am forgiven for shooting you?"

"I'm not sure." She wasn't sure at all what it meant.

He slid her slit sleeve down over her elbow. A welter of anticipation and fear and a deeper un-nameable expectation curled down her spine. His dark eyes held hers. He reached and eased her other sleeve down, while she clutched desperately at the front of the nightshirt. She clenched her eyes shut, knowing she should protest, wanting to delay her objection, but startled into silence by his casual removal of her gown.

"I daresay it is time you told me your name."

CHAPTER 8

Helena's horse sidled nervously. She smoothed a gloved hand down his neck, knowing the animal picked up her tension. The very idea of bribing her grooms astounded her.

"Yes, well, I always look for the easiest way about things, and it seemed expedient," said Trevor.

"But . . ." Her two grooms were neglecting their duty to be sure no harm befell her. He must have paid them a great deal if they were willing to risk their positions.

"You need have no fear that I will attack you," he said.

Her skin heated. He was so blunt. "I do not fear that you will behave with any impropriety." She feared that he never would feel an immoral urge toward her.

He gave her a sidelong look from his startling blue eyes. "If you are absolutely disinclined to go alone with me, then you might ask one of your groomsmen to fetch another horse. We can wait. But I should expect Rotten Row is deserted this time of the morning."

She nudged her horse. It was not proper, but what could happen while she was on horseback?

And a hope that he had actually sought her out because he wanted to be with her threaded a shining strand of optimism through her.

He asked after her parents and sisters, while she glanced at windows of houses they passed to be sure that none of her neighbors marked her progress with a foreign gentleman riding beside her. Or perhaps she hoped someone would see her.

She blushed when she told him her sisters were both married.

"And you are not?"

"No, although I have been told I cannot shilly-shally anymore. I shall have to choose a suitor this season." Heat crept up her neck. Why had she confessed that horrible, awful thing to him?

"So many men, such a hard thing to choose just one."

Helena stared at her gloves. Not so hard. And she was not like that. Yes, she had received odes written to her shell-shaped ears—weren't everyone's ears shell-shaped—and to her emerald eyes—more a mossy green than jewel-toned—and her lily-white complexion—that actually had a tendency to freckle and required countless treatments of lemon juice alternated with oil of talc. Even now, a swoop of netting from her hat protected her skin, but she truly did not set out to make any man admire her. And their admiration was rarely of a personal nature.

After all, beauty was only skin deep, but few men ever looked past that.

They quickly reached Hyde Park, and as he had said, it was nearly deserted. "I should like to give my horse its head," she said.

"By all means. I'll watch."

She smacked the flank of her horse with her riding crop and the horse smoothly cantered. She would have liked to indulge in a run, but that wasn't the thing. Not in the park. So she cantered around the paths, feeling self-conscious that Mr. Hamilton watched her.

But for the moment she had his full attention. Had he sought her out, or just happened upon her as she was leaving for her morning ride?

After giving herself and her horse a judicious amount of exercise, she trotted back to his side. He had dismounted from his horse at some point, making her wonder if he had bothered watching her at all.

"If you dismount, we'll walk your horse so that he might cool down."

She stared down at him, for once in a superior position to his imposing height.

"You don't want to stable him like that."

Of course not. She would hand him off to a groom who would walk him if that was needed. She hesitated, because it was totally improper. "You are taking your duties as groomsman too seriously."

"Please, walk with me. I must ask you something." He held up his arms.

Helena leaned into his grip, and he lowered her down with great care. When her body brushed against his on the way down, he gave no indication if the contact was intentional. He stepped back quickly and gathered the reins to lead his horse along the path.

She picked up the train of her riding habit and pulled the reins of her horse over his head. With her riding quirt, her train and the reins held in her gloved hands, she was disappointed that she would not be able to slip her hand into the crook of Trevor's elbow.

They had gone several steps and he said nothing.

"You wished to inquire about . . . ?" She bit her lip. In her fantasy, he would ask her for her hand or at least permission to pay his addresses to her, but half an hour of being in his company after a five-year absence was hardly a precursor to that.

"I know I may count on your discretion." He paused.

"Of course."

"And you know everyone in London."

That might be an overstatement, but she was brought up to know everyone who mattered in the hierarchy of the Upper Ten Thousand. She inclined her head rather than dispute his statement.

"My sister is missing."

A thousand horrible thoughts ran through Helena's head. Was she abducted, suffering a fate worse than death, or was she hurt in an accident or . . . murdered? "Oh, my! Oh, how horrible."

"She ran away from home."

Helena stared at the ground, her alarm winding down a few notches, and feeling dim-witted that she reacted so strongly. "I see."

Trevor—Mr. Hamilton, that is—allowed the corner of his mouth to lift. "It seems she had a hard time choosing a husband, too."

Helena stole a glance at her companion. Was he teasing her?

"She was to be married last month, but before the wedding took place she fled Boston."

"Perhaps she takes issue with the man chosen to be her husband."

"She picked him. No one was going to force her to marry anyone." Trevor shrugged his broad shoulders. "He thought all was well between them, and he doesn't know why she left him at the altar. He's an all-right fellow, he's thought handsome, comes from a good family."

"Good family, hmmm?"

"No one would have cared if she picked the green-grocer as long as he was responsible and considerate of her."

"I see."

"Do you? Because in America class distinctions don't matter as much."

"Yes, you have said so before." And they had argued about it before. While she regretted that she wasn't as free to choose a husband as his sister, Helena was what she was.

He stopped walking. "I apologize. Here I am asking for your help and we digress into this."

"Ever it is so."

He turned to face her. "We believe she may be masquerading as a young man."

"Oh!" Helena dropped her train and raised her hand to her throat, nearly slapping herself with the quirt. She was shocked, horrified. If his sister was such a disgrace, his suit would never be acceptable to her parents. Any chance that he could ever . . . Helena had gone from horror over the fate of this girl to horror over her actions. "How could she?"

"She's rather tall for a female," said Trevor, taking her question literally.

Helena was rather tall for a female. She swallowed hard against her distaste. If she was to have any hope at all, she must help him recover his sister before she created a huge scandal. "As tall as I am?"

"Taller. And less curvy. You could never pass for a man."

For a second, both of them focused on her fulsome figure. Her curves were rather lush. A fierce heat fired Helena's face. "I cannot imagine any circumstance in which I might try."

He turned and looked over the park, and she felt bereft of his gaze, but then she had probably imagined that his comparison of their figures was anything more than an explanation of his sister's form.

"So you see, discretion in locating her is of paramount importance."

"I agree."

"We have considered whether we should consult a Bow Street runner, or just make inquiries on our own." He clasped his hands behind his back. "Either way, I believe we risk drawing too much notice to her situation."

"Oh, then you will want Major Sheridan."

"A military man?" Trevor looked skeptical.

"He sold his commission, so he is just Mr. Sheridan now. His older brother holds the title. But that is neither here nor there to you. Mr. Sheridan does investigations for the *ton*. He recovered Lady—well, a certain lady's jewels after her house had been robbed. I believe the runners told her they would just concentrate on catching the felon and the recovery of her heirlooms was unlikely."

"Lydia is not missing jewels."

"I don't know the whole of it, but he is reputed to

have stopped at least one murderer. I know he cleared the name of one of his officers who was thought to have died by his own hand. He also uncovered another attempted murder plot. It was all a seven-day wonder with cursed pistols and a duel, but we never learned all the truth of it. He is thought to be quite extraordinary at solving mysteries."

"And discreet?"

"Quite so. He has a sterling reputation, and he *never* speaks of his investigations. The only things that are known come from those who have enlisted his services."

Helena stepped forward. Trevor leaned over and picked up the train of her habit. His blue eyes intent, his face hovered mere inches from hers. Her heart quickened.

"I like your hair like that."

Her hair was interwoven into a half-dozen coiled braids instead of elaborately arranged with the liberal application of curling tongs. While not a single braid, the style was hardly designed to draw flattery. When the season was in full swing, she would not be outside the house without a more elaborate preparation of her hair. "It is hardly fashioned."

"Yes, I know. It makes you look human."

His words stung. He thought her so cold, then? "Am I to suppose I look like an inanimate lump of coal otherwise?" She was relieved her voice sounded light, even mildly amused.

"Human, fallible, not perfect," Trevor said.

She had a sudden horror that one of the braids might have unraveled. She reached up. "Has my hair come undone?"

He caught her hand near her face. "Perhaps what I meant was approachable."

Time hung suspended in the morning air as his grip on her hand gentled and he stroked his thumb over the base of her fingers. She wished to strip off her glove and feel the light caress on her bare skin, but then he dropped her hand.

"We should go back now, before I have any thoughts of behaving with impropriety."

He lifted her onto her horse and she felt opportunity slipping away. Would he disappear for another five long years?

As his hands slid from her waist, she leaned over, planting her hands on his shoulders. Her move felt bold, although she could claim she slipped and only used him to steady herself. He looked up at her, the corners of his wicked lips turning up just slightly as if laughing at her.

"Do you ever have thoughts of behaving with impropriety?" she asked.

"I am a man," he answered, as if that explained everything.

"With me?" she whispered.

"What man wouldn't?"

She sat up straight and reached for the reins. Was he just being polite? When a lady fished for a compliment, a gentleman was supposed to comply. "I was not asking about any man."

His hand landed on her leg just above her knee, and she froze. "All the time, Lady Helena, but then I am reminded how very much trouble you would be."

"W-what?"

He nodded toward a lone horseman in the

distance. "Your groom followed after all." He squeezed her leg. "We come from different worlds. And yours is closed to me." He mounted his horse.

Helena sighed. But was his world closed to her?

Trevor didn't exactly get the welcome he'd hoped for. *What are you doing here?* She'd said it as if he had no business being in London. Then again, Lady Helena had always been haughty. But her parting held promise.

Had she thought of him in his absence?

In any case, he had what he was looking for—a name and address of a man who could help them find Lydia.

Divine providence. His early morning urge to go by Lady Helena's parents' home must have been inspired by an angel—and never mind that his desire to see her had a more earthly ring.

Truly, he was surprised that she had remained unmarried.

Now he just needed to convince James and Oscar that they should enlist the aid of this gentleman. He opened the door of their hotel room. Oscar slumbered on, but James was mostly dressed.

"I have learned of just the man to find Lydia," said Trevor.

James gave him a baleful eye and Oscar moaned and flopped over on the sofa where he slept.

"We can make inquiries on our own; we'll start at the Swan with Two Necks." James reached for his boots.

Trevor shoved Oscar's feet to the side and sat down on the end of the sofa. "Here's the thing.

This man is known to be discreet and a good investigator, and we don't want a scandal."

Oscar blinked sleepily at him.

"What difference does it make if there is a scandal? As soon as we find her, we'll just take her home. It can hardly matter what people in London think of her." The bed groaned as James pulled on a boot.

"The world is smaller than that. If word of her antics gets back home, she could very well be ostracized by Boston society. Oscar will need to be assured that her reputation is still spotless if she is to be a proper hostess."

Oscar eased up to a sitting position.

"Besides, we should open up a shipping office in England. A disgrace attached to our name would be an impediment to success."

"We don't need a shipping office in England," said James. "You just don't want to be put to any trouble to find her."

Trevor was used to his older brothers discounting his opinions, so he continued with gentle persuasion. "No, we don't need an office in England, but now that the war is over, it makes sense. With all of us brothers coming into the company, we should be thinking of ways to expand our operations and increase profits."

"Who would be in charge of a London branch?" asked Oscar.

Trevor started. He would want it, of course. He stared out the window. It wouldn't matter. He could be rich as Croesus and he still wouldn't be considered good enough for Lady Helena.

"Get dressed, Oscar," ordered James. "We need to start making inquiries."

"Wait. It wouldn't hurt to talk to this man, would it? While I should like to get Lydia back as soon as possible, I don't want her reputation destroyed." Oscar rubbed his face. "We don't want to ruin opportunities here."

"I'd rather avoid a scandal," said Trevor.

"I would hate for anyone to know that my bride went about pretending to be a man for three months."

Did Oscar care more about retrieving their sister or controlling the damage she might do to the Hamilton shipping business?

"Lydia might be in trouble," said James.

"All the more reason to use a professional to locate her." Trevor rubbed his jacket and wondered if he should find a good tailor. He doubted that Lydia was in trouble, but he wasn't above using the fear as persuasion. And damned if he could figure out what Oscar wanted in this.

One thing Trevor knew was, he couldn't allow any breath of gossip about his sister to reach Helena's parents, the Earl and Countess of Caine, or he'd never have even the ghost of a chance.

Why he still wanted Helena, he wasn't sure. What little time he spent with her, between her flitting between one appropriate suitor to the next, they ended up arguing. What he'd really wanted was to slide his hand under her skirt instead of resting it on top of it. Just to see if she could lose that haughty reserve of hers.

* * *

"You are still drugged, you know," said Victor as his
guest stared back at him with wide, shocked blue
eyes. Which may be why she had taken on the new
role of innocent temptress. She played it to perfection, clasping the nightshirt to her chest as he
lowered the sleeves and pulled her arms out of them.

"Now that you are awake, I shall change your bandages. With luck, we shall get them on securely,
now that you are sitting."

"Oh," she said on an expelled breath that wafted
sweetly across his face.

Hell, he wanted to kiss her. She seemed willing,
willing to let him do more than kiss her, although
her fear was evident too. But more than that she
was drugged and injured, she was under his protection, and he wasn't sure he would be able to stop
at kisses. Even now, he was in a state that her fake
male member could never have achieved.

He'd been that way off and on since he'd removed
her clothes and artificial padding earlier. He'd
known a gentleman or two to pad their shoulders
and calves, but Lenny had put a whole different twist
on the thing. On one hand, Victor had been busi-
nesslike about removing her clothes; she was, after
all, unconscious.

But the vision of her endless legs kept intrud-
ing into his thoughts. Her body was of a perfection
that he'd rarely seen. Her waist curved in as it
should, her breasts were high and pert. She was
slender, but not as devoid of curves as he would
have guessed from her pretense of being a boy.
Seeing her naked had convinced him beyond a
doubt that she was all female.

He shouldn't have looked, he should have been

immune to the sight of a naked woman, but her woman's mound was dusted with light brown curls and that had drawn his gaze more than was reasonable. Her secrets were laid bare in front of him, her physical secrets anyway, and he'd looked his fill. If that made him a cad and a bounder, well, he needed a woman. He wanted her—desperately. He didn't even know her name.

He couldn't allow himself to think of what her lips pressed to his shoulder did to him, or he would go mad.

He peeled back the cotton and linen pads and pressed new ones in their place. Working slowly to give her the illusion of preserving her modesty, he wrapped a length of cloth over her shoulder and down under her arm, so he might put pressure on the wound. Once he had her securely bandaged, he eased her arms back into the sleeves, even holding up the front of the nightshirt while she wiggled back into the gown. He took one last lingering glance at her bare, lovely back.

Would that he could draw his mouth and hands up and down her delectable spine. But she was not for him. And there were things she needed to know.

"My valet has gone to fetch your maid. I imagine they must be packing all your things to be taking this long."

"I don't have much."

He reached behind her to arrange the pillows and jolted as his body brushed against hers. "Lie down."

"I would rather sit up. Perhaps I should go back to my lodgings."

"Not until you heal," Victor stood. He wanted to

enfold her in his arms so badly he couldn't stand it. He walked away from the bed. "I cannot offer you proper chaperoning, so outside of this room you will be known as Leonard Hall. That seems the best way to preserve your reputation. Only my personal servant and your maid shall be allowed in here."

She made a sound of protest.

He held up his hand. "I know you are compromised living under my roof, but I will not violate your virtue. And I will not marry ever again, so do not think to turn this situation to your advantage."

"I didn't, I never thought—"

"Yes, well, I have no particular reason to trust you. You have lied to me about who you are from the beginning. Be warned, I have deflowered virgins and not offered them the shelter of my name."

"Oh, but I need have no fear of that," she said sarcastically. "You are not likely to . . . to . . . seduce someone like me."

She had every reason to fear he would seduce her. He wasn't even sure that he could keep his hands off of her for the duration of her healing. Really, he'd had only one virgin—one willing, encouraging virgin—and he'd been deep in his cups.

"Not while you're injured, cub, and not while I don't know your name."

"If I tell you my name, you'll just send for my family to come and take me home."

He had no answer for that. Were they so awful? "I cannot keep calling you Leonard."

There was a sound behind him that was suspiciously like a sniff. He turned to find the bedcovers tossed back, and her out of bed.

"What did you do with my clothes?" she demanded.

"You are not leaving."

"Where are my clothes?" she repeated as she yanked out a dresser drawer.

He moved behind her to push the drawer shut before she started pulling out his things. "For the most part, they're ruined, cub. Your maid will likely bring your things."

He put his hand on the blond curls covering her head. "Your unmentionables might be salvageable if the blood may be got out, but you should be in bed."

Not-Leonard put her hand in front of her face.

Her hair was feather soft and the curls twined around his fingers as he touched it. For such a tough woman, able to meet the demands of a male world without flinching, and bearing her wound better than a soldier, she was incredibly soft. "What is it, pet? What would convince you to stay?"

She dropped her hand and looked searchingly at him out of those big blue eyes of hers. That look from her when he thought her a boy had driven him mad; now, it caused a heady current of desire to thrum through his blood.

"You don't want me here. You have made that abundantly clear. You want me to go back to America," she said.

"That was when I thought you a boy." He trailed his hand down her neck. He really should stop touching her.

She turned to face him, frowning slightly. Her right hand was on her left shoulder, holding his nightshirt together. He was reminded how very little barrier there was between him and her skin. Her gaze dropped to his lips and sanity fled his grasp.

It was a simple matter, really, to move his hand to

cup her head and bring her forward. With her height, there was an easy fit, and no long delay to the meeting of their mouths.

She kissed with innocence that shifted to eagerness and her essence swirled on his tongue. Her willing participation was like ambrosia to a starving man. Need throbbed through him as he pulled her closer and deepened his kiss. He urged with a persuasive touch to loosen her hold on the slit nightshirt. She complied, wrapping her arms around him.

He wanted to touch every inch of her skin, to trace the lines of her every curve, to taste her flesh. The material slipped from her shoulder and offered him a tantalizing glimpse of heaven.

Only the glimmer of an awareness that she was both innocent and injured kept his pace slow and gentle, yet he had her tight against him. She ran her hands down his back and he was lost to sensation. He knew he should be caring for her, but all he could think and feel was how her touch fired his blood, flaming his loins and fevering his heart, and she kept stroking his back as if she wanted him.

In one smooth move, he lifted her onto the dresser, then yanked the bottom of his shirt free of his waistband. He would pull his shirt over his head as soon as he could stand to free his mouth from hers for long enough. Yet, she seemed to have the idea as her palms slid against the bare skin of his stomach.

His breathing rasped in and out, with half his intoxication coming from capturing her breaths in his mouth. Her touch made him quiver and throb and ache. Controlling his gentle easing down of her gown and caressing the soft curve of her breast with his fingers made his feelings soften and swell and become a thing of their own power.

Her kissing his scar and the memory of her naked flesh swirled in his mind. Would that he had a thousand hours for her seduction. Yet an unstoppable urge made him push forward and think seconds would be too long. Her knees opened at his pressure and he ground against her, hiding nothing of his thick, swollen desire.

Let her pull back and fight now, if she didn't want that part of him too. She made a sound deep in her throat, that could have been protest, could have been shock, and he tried to ease back.

Instead, she wrapped her long, long legs around his hips, cradling his hardness against her soft woman's core. His bed was just behind him, and he lifted her and took a step toward it when the rattle of the doorknob stopped him cold.

"Victor, are you in here?" asked Keene.

CHAPTER 9

Victor didn't know if he had ever moved so fast in his life. He dumped not-Leonard on the bed and ran to hold the door from opening all the way.

Keene stared at him, his dark eyes narrowing as he took in Victor's heaving chest and general disarray. "What are you about?" he asked, his voice low and riddled with shock and fury.

"It's not what you think," said Victor.

Keene crossed his arms and glared at him.

"Give me a moment." Victor shut the door, then turned the lock.

He leaned back against the door as he glanced at his guest. He had staked his honor upon offering shelter without assaulting her virtue. A gentleman who wasn't worth his word was not worth anything.

The door jumped behind his back as Keene pounded on it. "Get out here, now!"

"Are you all right, pet?" Victor whispered.

She was curled up on her knees, looking frightened and bemused and oh, so damn tempting. She turned those liquid blue eyes toward him and nodded. He wanted to comfort her, but he didn't dare touch her, not with the state he was in.

"Leonard, are you in there?" yelled Keene. "Are you all right?"

Victor released the lock, then planted his hand squarely in Keene's chest and pushed him backward. "You may be my elder brother, but you have no business barging into my bedroom."

"Devil take it. You have barged in on Sophie and me before," Keene paced down the passageway and pivoted.

"I have stood guard more often." Victor leaned over and put his hands on his thighs, trying to slow his breathing and get control of his wayward body. Obviously his half-brother could guess what was going on in the bedroom. "Thank God you are here."

Keene stopped and stared.

"It's not what you are thinking."

"Yes, you said that before. Perhaps you'd care to explain why you look as if you are engaged in an . . . an . . . amorous encounter."

"Not to put too fine a point on it," replied Victor, amused by Keene's delicacy of language. He headed down the stairs to the library and hoped a brilliant shim-sham story arrived in his brain box before he made it all the way there. He didn't know why he bothered. The truth would blurt out in spite of any tale he thought to spin.

"Do you mean to explain?" Keene trailed behind him and eyed him as if he were a monster of the most depraved sort.

"Not here."

Keene might not be wrong on the depraved part.

What had he been thinking? All right, he hadn't been thinking, he'd been feeling. Feeling urges he'd suppressed for years, feeling softer feelings of wanting to hold and comfort a woman. *Yes, that was so obvious,* he told himself sarcastically. Feeling like he wanted to *know her* in the biblical sense was hardly a desire to comfort and protect her.

Bloody hell, she was injured, drugged and probably a little desperate. And he was very desperate, but he knew better.

They reached the library and Keene pushed the door shut. "Do you mean to tell me what is happening?"

"I would rather not," said Victor as he walked toward the brandy decanter. He glanced up as if he could see through the floors to her. Was she still huddled on the bed like a frightened rabbit?

Remorse and guilt poured through him. When had he ever been good for anyone? He'd very nearly stolen her virtue because he needed a woman's touch.

He picked up the decanter and stared at the amber liquid.

"For the well-being of Mr. Hall, I must ask . . ." Keene hesitated. "I must ask if you are misusing him?"

Victor swirled the alcohol. He didn't want a drink. He didn't want to numb his feelings anymore and he didn't trust his control if under the influence. Hell, he couldn't trust his control when he was sober. "Misusing, yes, but he is not a him."

All right, he had only to look at his brandy and he started talking as if he were three sheets to the wind.

"What?" whispered Keene.

"She's a girl. Leonard is a woman."

"Oh," said Keene, and he sat down hard on one

of the leather chairs flanking the fireplace. "Pour me a drink, then."

Victor complied.

"How long have you known?"

"Since I ripped open her shirt after shooting her."

Keene winced.

"My sentiments exactly," said Victor. "Although I have to say it was a relief."

"A relief?" Keene echoed weakly.

"My feelings toward him were rather untoward. I thought I had lost my mind."

Keene looked at him. "I see. You, perhaps, desired him when you thought he was a boy, hence your fanatical need to see him leave England?"

"Exactly so. Although I could not quite decipher how the mechanics should work if I took a boy as a lover. I daresay I got carried away when I realized there was no such problem."

Keene gave a sound between a snort and a cough. He was probably amused, although it was no laughing matter. "I thought you were behaving oddly. Although my first concern was that you had mortally wounded the boy and weren't willing for us to see."

Victor felt shaky all the sudden. He could have killed her. "Her wound is not terribly bad."

"So the surgeon said. Sheridan seemed mightily interested in details of his, er, her injury."

Oh, God, had Sheridan figured out that Lenny was a female? He had an uncanny knack for ferreting out the truth. It was bad enough that Victor had to tell Keene, and he would have to call on Sheridan and offer his apologies to his wife, Felicity. But right now, he needed to protect not-Leonard from himself. "You had best stay until her maid arrives, and she is safe from my attentions."

Keene smiled slowly. "On the contrary, I should perhaps leave. Bottoms up." He tilted the glass up and downed the brandy.

"Bloody hell, no! Don't you dare. I cannot destroy her. The surgeon gave her laudanum. She is not likely to be clear of head, and I never meant to lay a hand on her . . . I just . . ." Any excuse would sound weak and pathetic. "I lost control. You interrupted in the nick of time."

"I hardly think you shall destroy her," Keene objected. "And I heard no protest from her. She had only to call out when she knew I was at the door."

Victor ran a shaky hand through his hair. "I dare not destroy her innocence." He destroyed nearly everyone he came in contact with.

"And is she innocent?"

"I would say so." Victor paced across the floor, too edgy to sit. She was enthusiastic in her approach, but her moves held an awkward bashfulness that could hardly have been faked. It was as if she had made up her mind to accept each move he made and contribute.

Keene leaned forward. "Then I would suggest you make it not so."

"I cannot believe you would counsel me so. You were not so encouraging with Mary Frances." His wife had never been so enthusiastic either.

Keene gave him an exasperated look. "We both know that Mary Frances was a curse, though her father's money was a blessing to you. No, I remember that I had Sophie flat on a bed within ten minutes of first seeing her and I was too gentlemanly to see it through. I had much more concern about her innocence than she ever did." Keene said the words *gentlemanly* and *innocence* as if they were offensive. "I would have saved us both much anguish if I had taken her then."

"But you . . . but you . . . you were there to propose to her."

"And I was not the least bit happy about it. My father had forced my hand. The last time I had seen her she was sitting in a cherry tree spitting pits. I mean, we were all enamored of Amelia back then, and Sophie was the converse of ladylike. How was I to know that she was everything I ever wanted?"

Victor didn't see what bearing Keene's short courtship had on his problem with his houseguest. Why had not-Leonard decided to welcome his seduction? An innocent rarely was driven by the pleasure that could be had.

Keene lowered his voice. "I only knew that she made me angry and I wanted to bed her."

"Yes, but Lenny is under my protection and I cannot ruin her." Victor threw up his hands. "I do not even know her name."

"To be precise, her staying here with you is compromise enough to ruin her."

"Not if no one knows her real identity."

"Do you not think others will find it strange, you shooting a boy and then bringing him home with you?"

"No stranger than our friendship, or that Sheridan and Bedford both lived under the same roof after their duel."

Keene pulled on his lower lip. "You could have her stay with Sophie and me."

"No!" The denial was out before Victor had time to think it through. He didn't want not-Leonard out of his sight.

Keene smiled. "Then finish your seduction."

"You are horrid. I cannot do that to her. I cannot be so lacking in honor. She is under my protection." Surely, Keene could understand the difference. Sophie was under her father's protection, not Keene's, when he nearly had his way with her. A good scream would have brought servants running in Sophie's case. Not-Leonard would have no such assurance of rescue.

"Not so. You never listen to my best advice anyway. You will have to marry her, you know."

Horror killed what was left of his ardor. He wouldn't do that to himself. He wouldn't do it to her. "That is what I mean to avoid at all costs. I shall not marry again. I cannot bear the thought of it." Victor gripped the back of a chair so hard his knuckles turned white.

Keene held out his glass for a refill. "Her bloodline must be at least as good as Mary Frances's."

"It's not that." Victor grabbed Keene's glass and headed back to the sideboard. "I have never seen anything but misery come of marriage. I'm not willing to put myself or any woman through that again."

"My marriage is hardly a misery," objected Keene.

"I have seen you in the agonies of despair when Sophie is crawling about on a roof. You cannot tell me all is pleasant."

"No, but the aftermath is heady. It is worth it."

"Would you say so if she fell to her death?" asked Victor, handing the glass of brandy to Keene.

"Probably not." Keene took a sip and looked

away. "It is as much or more my own fear of losing everyone I love that causes our discord."

"I don't fear losing loved ones, but I can make a royal mess of their lives. What madness did not destroy in Mary Frances, I finished off. I did my best to destroy you and my effect on George and Amelia's marriage is hardly to my credit."

"That does not mean you can discount marriage by comparing it to what you had with Mary Frances."

"You cannot name many happy marriages to those that are unpleasant. From Prinny on down, I know few that are worth the hell of it."

"Tony and Felicity."

"Her first marriage was not so happy, and she barely has time for Tony now. Were it not for their son, I do not know that they should hold together. What about George and Amelia, our half-sister and Bedford, or our father and my mother? Bloody hell, I watched my father break my mother's heart and put her in an early grave, as I in my own manner did to Mary Frances. No, I should not care to put so much effort into a thing that by its very nature is more likely to fail than succeed."

"You are still grieving," Keene said, as if surprised.

Victor's first inclination was to deny it, but this was Keene, who knew him better than anyone. "It has only been three months."

"Yes, but I thought Mary Frances was dead to you long before she actually died. You could hardly be responsible for the fire or that she ran back inside after you rescued her once. That was just her madness."

Victor faced the fireplace. It was his fault. He had pushed for concessions that Mary Frances could never have given. "She was never dead to me. I was still trying to salvage something and I wanted . . . I thought I wanted a son or at least a child I could raise. God knows, that was the final straw for her."

Keene put a hand on his shoulder, startling Victor. "That young woman up there could give you sons."

"No, I will never allow my desires to destroy another human being again. I have done enough damage. I want nothing. I need nothing. I have taken enough, and I have nothing left to give. No, I will not marry ever again."

Lydia shoved her feet between the sheets and pulled them up to her chin. What had just happened?

Victor had kissed her—and he had done a lot more than kiss her. He had touched her in places that shocked her and thrilled her. Her breasts still tingled where he had caressed, stroked and cupped his long fingers around her flesh.

She had touched him in ways that surprised her, as if she could only be satisfied to feel his warm skin against hers. It had all felt natural and intoxicating. She flopped to her side. Pain shot through her shoulder, ricocheting right down to her teeth.

Yet everything she'd been taught ran counter to what had just happened. Well-bred women weren't supposed to be so base. She was embarrassed by her lack of control, by her wantonness, by her ability to find pleasure in such an animalistic act. She knew men were supposed to enjoy such things, but a woman's liking was only supposed to extend through the opening salvos and the rest just tolerated. Conjugal joining was a gift to be given for a husband's enjoyment. Wasn't it?

She eased onto her back, but found that position no more comfortable. Her wound throbbed with an increasing ache that made the back of her throat dry. She shifted to sit, alleviating the pressure against her bandages. Moving like cold molasses, she rearranged the pillows.

The door opened just as she eased back and pulled the covers to her chin. Victor rolled down his sleeves as he walked across the floor, then opened the wardrobe. "The surgeon is here. I shall send him up to you."

He pulled on a waistcoat and jacket as he spoke, and he failed to look once in her direction. "Apparently, your maid refuses to leave your lodgings without the order coming directly from you. Would you care to pen her a note? Does she read? Would she recognize your hand?"

Oh, Lord, what was Jenny planning? And why wouldn't Victor look at her? She wanted to throw the covers over her head and hide. "Did your man tell her you shot me?"

Victor turned in her direction. He looked down at his waistcoat as he buttoned it. "I do not know. You need your maid here."

He seemed impatient . . . angry. Judging by his manner, he was just as mortified by her behavior as she was.

He moved back across the room and opened a drawer. He pulled out a neck cloth and wound it around under his shirt points.

Lydia put her head on her knees. Her head swam with confusion and hurt. Why would a man she had deceived from the moment they met, want anything to do with her? "Are you angry with me or my maid?"

He slammed the drawer shut. "Myself, mostly."

She jerked her head up, surprised by his answer.

He moved to the foot of the bed and Lydia couldn't help but drink in the sight of his long legs and the way the material shifted over the smooth muscles of his thighs as he walked.

"I owe you an apology for earlier. I never should have kissed you."

His apology hit her like a rock thrown at her chest. She hadn't expected it. What about the rest of what he had done?

"Or anything more. You are drugged and not yourself."

Lydia put her face against her knees and clenched her eyes shut. It hadn't been all him. Clearly he thought her behavior unladylike.

"I give you my word that I shall never . . . I will not touch you. I shall shelter you and see to your care. I do not expect anything in return. Do you understand?"

She shook her head against her knees.

His voice softened. "If you thought it necessary to repay my hospitality with your body, it is not."

"No." She hadn't thought that at all. But it was probably the only thing he could think in regards to her enthusiasm.

"In spite of my lapse, I do mean to keep you safe until you are well again. I shan't hurt you. If, however, you feel it best, Keene has offered to house you. With Sophie there, you would be more or less properly chaperoned."

Victor wanted to be rid of her again, and that hurt deep in her chest. "I suppose you want that."

"It might be the best thing *for you,* cub."

She looked up and saw he was holding the bedpost with a tight grip. Did he want her to stay?

Victor raked a hand through his hair and wondered why he was standing in front of Amelia's house. He raised his hand to lift the knocker. He'd walked over, needing to burn off energy. Now it looked as if he was in for a soaking. Well, that was another way to kill his ardor.

Not-Leonard was asleep in his bed. He wanted nothing more than to crawl in with her and hold her until she woke again, but he knew he wouldn't stop there. He wanted to finish what they had begun earlier. He wanted to make love to her all through the rainy afternoon and long into the darkness of night. If she had made him crazed as a boy, her revelation as a woman broke his willpower.

His body thrummed with urges. His blood felt thick and he was aware of everything around him, the scent of rain in the air, the heavy gray clouds in the sky, the cool breeze lifting his hair from his scalp. He felt more alive and awake than he had in months, perhaps years.

After the surgeon left, with not-Leonard heavily dosed with laudanum again, Victor had gone to retrieve her maid. Mostly he'd hoped to learn his houseguest's real name, but the maid refused to yield any information. At least his knowledge of Leonard's sex had persuaded Jenny to bring clothes for her mistress.

Jenny would sleep on the cot in the anteroom off of Victor's bedroom. At least with her maid close at hand, not-Leonard would have some chaperoning. She needed it.

Victor slapped his top hat against his thigh as a footman opened the door. After being let inside, he was left cooling his heels in the entry hall as the footman ascertained if Amelia was "at home."

She would be, but the longer Victor waited, the more he doubted this would serve as solution. How was it he suffered the long years of his marriage without a physical union, but one week with a woman whose name he didn't even know and he was half-mad with desire?

He needed release, Amelia was available, making love to not-Leonard would shatter her life and complicate his. Amelia was not the one he wanted, but she was safe.

He was shown into the drawing room and Amelia rose from the sofa and moved forward to greet him. With each step she took toward him, he wanted to bolt.

"Hello, Victor. I am so glad to see you." She stretched up and pressed a cool kiss to his cheek.

"Amelia." Was she really that short? Not-Leonard's height made kissing her so easy. No need to stoop or bend.

"It is such a dreary afternoon, and I am quite bored with myself." Amelia stood in front of him. "I shall ring for tea."

He hadn't come for tea. "I should go."

"Oh, no, you must stay at least a quarter hour. It's only polite." She gestured to the window where water streamed down the panes. "You should stay until the weather lifts. I am not likely to have any other callers to interrupt us in this rain."

She reached out and gathered his hands in hers.

Victor felt a mix of alarm and consternation that Amelia did understand why he had come. Her hands were cold, and he belatedly realized she had removed her gloves. They lay draped over the arm of the sofa. Amelia would never be found without her gloves in her drawing room, except she'd removed them knowing he was on his way up. So would they move to her bedroom, or would they just make use of the sofa?

The sofa. She'd made love with him in a carriage before, and the idea of trespassing in the bed of his once-friend made Victor feel sordid.

Should he lock the door? He glanced toward it.

"Really, don't leave. What is wrong?" she asked.

"I shot Leonard." He hadn't meant to tell her that. Damn his mouth.

"Oh, Victor," she said and stepped back. "Is he badly hurt?"

She tugged her hands back, but he refused to let go.

"He . . . Leonard will be fine. I did not mean to wound . . . him." Victor squeezed his eyes shut and released Amelia.

"Well, what should you expect when you point a gun at him and fire it?" Amelia asked. "You forced him into a duel."

He didn't need a raking over the coals. He needed to be rid of his passion. He opened his eyes to find her with folded arms and trepidation in her midnight blue eyes. "I don't want to talk about it. I did not come here to talk about Leonard." He came here to get over Leonard.

He looked her over. Truly, Amelia was a beautiful woman, but he felt no urge to press her. "My apologies. I shall leave now."

"Victor, stay, please. I am a poor hostess." She stepped toward him and placed her bare hand on his shoulder. "I am just nervous. I am not used to doing anything like this."

Amelia brushed against him, and he tried to feel something beyond dismay that he felt nothing. No, he felt the hardness of her stomach that her high-waisted gown concealed. The mound jutted against his abdomen.

"You are with child."

She looked down at the small swell and placed her hand against the upper curve of her belly. "Yes, it shall be obvious to everyone in a fortnight or so."

How had he not noticed before? Why hadn't he noticed when he kissed her at his house?

"Sophie and I seem to manage to do this in tandem these days, although I believe I am in the lead this time." She looked back up at him, her eyes swimming with moisture. "Does it bother you?" she whispered.

It touched off a storm of emotions, but then everything lately seemed to affect him. His emotions toward Amelia and her pregnancy were along the line of regrets. He was fond of her, even if his desire for her had cooled with the passing years. He put his hand over the soft swell of her stomach, only to discover it did not feel soft at all, but firm. He had been excluded from her first pregnancy, the pregnancy he had created. "Not mine, this time."

"No. It is George's," she said.

"I want to be a godfather this time."

"George—"

"Will object, I know. But I want closer ties to your family." To his daughter.

She put her hands over his and gave him a weak smile. "My breeding bothers George."

"Why? He should be glad. I . . ." Victor didn't want to finish the thought, that Mary Frances had not given him any children. It seemed sacrilegious to think ill of the dead, and odd that he should have never experienced a woman's pregnancy this close and never would.

"I know." Amelia cupped his face.

He kissed her then, and she leaned into him. He felt but little passion for her, but he continued, sure that not-Leonard would be safer if he experienced a small measure of satisfaction. He hoped to comfort Amelia, to woo her with gentleness, to seduce himself with lies that her body was changing because of him, that he could love her again. Instead, he filled his mind with images of his houseguest so he could feel the thickening that would see him through this act.

He guided her down to the sofa, easing her shoulders against the cushions, and positioning a pillow behind her head.

"I shall not break," she whispered as he debated lying beside her or whether she could bear his weight in her condition.

He winced, not wanting her to talk. She didn't have the alluring, throaty voice not-Leonard had. But it did settle his debate. He covered her mouth with his, thinking of how different his houseguest had tasted, how much more urgent he had felt then. He shifted to lean over Amelia.

She circled her arms around his neck. "Am I hurting you?" he asked.

She shook her head. He continued then. As he closed his eyes and remembered his houseguest's attention to his scar, he found enough desire to go on, but damn, he wanted Leonard. He wished he were with her and felt awful for Amelia as if he were cheating on her in his mind.

"No! What are you doing to my mama?"

The patter of little feet running across the floor reminded Victor he should have locked the door.

"Oh, no," whispered Amelia as tiny fists pummeled Victor's back.

"Don't you hurt my mama." Thwack, thwack. "Don't you kill my mama."

He twisted around and grabbed the little fists intent on hurting him. "Reggie, stop. I'm not hurting your mother. I'd never hurt your mama, precious."

"Regina, stop misbehaving right this minute." Amelia sat up and pointed. "Go back to the nursery."

The little girl in front of him sobbed and his heart split in two. "No, wait. She doesn't understand."

"I shan't tolerate this behavior." Amelia's voice filled with fury. "She cannot hit people. I will not allow it."

"Amelia, she's just a baby."

His daughter stood before him quivering, but she looked up at him, her dark brown eyes so like his and filled with raging defiance. "You are hurting my mama. You are trying to kill her."

"No, sweetling, I would never hurt your mama.

You know why? Because I would never do anything that would hurt you."

"Victor," warned Amelia.

He held out a hand to stop her. "I would never, ever do anything that would hurt you, Reggie. I would rather die first. I am too fond of you."

As he looked into her perfect little face, he realized he could not do anything that would wound her. Even though he wanted her to know he was her father, the knowledge was more likely to damage her than to comfort her. He repeated, "I would never do anything that would hurt you."

As he said it, he realized it was true. She looked at him, her defiance melting into uncertainty. He smoothed her hair back from her face. He wanted to tell her he would always be there for her, for any need she might have, but that would only confuse her.

Why did his actions always lead to pain for the people he loved? What if Regina had walked in half an hour later?

CHAPTER 10

Lady Helena retrieved the morning post and sifted through it; a couple of invitations, and a note addressed to her. She put the note aside because she did not recognize the hand of the sender, but it was on stationery from Grillon's Hotel. It could be from any one of a dozen of her acquaintances. Then there was the expected invitation from the Sheridans, who always started the season with a dinner party followed by a small ball.

Helena sat down at the writing desk to pen an acceptance for her mother and herself. She would decline for her father, citing health concerns. She hesitated. Had Trevor managed to contact Major Sheridan? Should she ask that Felicity Sheridan consider Mr. Hamilton as substitute for her father?

Helena chewed on the end of the pen and wondered if that might be going too far. Putting anything on paper concerning Trevor Hamilton would be tantamount to announcing her interest. She could mention that she had sent him to Major Sheridan. She hurriedly added a postscript mentioning her acquaintance and that the major might be of assistance to Mr. Hamilton in a matter of some delicacy.

She reached for the note from the hotel, suddenly wondering if it was from Trevor.

She popped the wax seal and unfolded the single sheet.

One scrawled line.

Meet me in Rotten Row at five.

No signature. No flowery admiration. No avowals of undying emotion.

Yet Helena's heart beat faster. She turned the paper over. Yes, it was addressed to her. Thank goodness her mother had turned over many of the household duties such as answering correspondence. A year ago this note might never have made past her mother's screening.

The stark command had to have come from Trevor. Any London gentleman would have added flattery and coaxing and at least signed with a dash or an initial. But it was straightforward and to the point. An assignation.

Though it was in a public park that would be well attended at that hour, she would have to take either a groomsman or her maid with her. Or could she sneak out?

Her mother entered the morning room and Helena started.

"Are you unwell, dear? Your color is high." Lady Caine moved over to the chair beside the writing desk and picked up her embroidery.

Fie on her pale skin that colored so easily. "I'm fine, Mama. How is Papa today?"

"Eating his breakfast. He had a difficult night." Her mother looked as if she had had a difficult night too.

Helena wished she could ease her mother's burden. Unfortunately, she could only do little things like help the household run smoothly. "I have just written out an acceptance to Mrs. Sheridan's dinner for the two of us."

"Good. Wedmont will be there; he always is. You might take the opportunity to engage his attention."

"He will be in full mourning still." Helena slid the note under the invitation from the Sheridans.

Her mother set her embroidery down. "Yes, well, Helena, you may not have much time."

Was her father so ill? Helena had never really considered that he might not get better. "Is Papa worse today?"

Her mother's lips flattened and she shook her head. "He is much the same." She put her embroidery in her lap. "I have had several dreams lately and I am sure they are a portent of things to come."

Helena blinked. Her mother was usually a sensible sort, not putting stock in omens or superstitions. The dreams must have been disturbing if her mother was giving them any credence. "What kind of dreams?"

Her mother picked up the embroidery and pushed through a stitch. "Dreams about dying and death."

"About Papa?" Helena asked.

"No, not specifically. I just think it is wise to heed the message of urgency, Helena. You must be married soon, or you will be in danger of never being able to marry. And I do worry so for your future."

"Mama, what if I were to consider marriage to a commoner?"

"One who is an heir presumptive, presuming there is little chance of an heir apparent usurping his position, may be acceptable. Did you have a particular gentleman in mind?"

Helena shook her head. "I meant just a commoner in general."

"Absolutely not."

Helena fingered the note under the invitation. Would Trevor ever be acceptable to her parents? What would happen if they knew about his sister's antics? The truth was he would never be acceptable. Nor did her parents need the added burden of a disobedient daughter during this time. She would have to set her cap for the Earl of Wedmont and tell Trevor that . . . that their relationship was over. Only it had never really begun. She would have to tell him . . . that she could offer no encouragement.

She would meet him in the park and tell him. But for a few hours she would imagine that her purpose in meeting him was far, far different than spurning him.

Victor rubbed his face. Regina's nursemaid ushered the girl out of the room, leaving Amelia and him alone again.

"We could go to . . . the other room," said Amelia.

He supposed she meant her bedroom, where presumably they would suffer no further interruptions. "No. I had better leave."

"You do not want me because I am with child?" Amelia's voice quivered.

Victor dropped his hands and looked at his former lover. She stood in front of the window staring out at the sheets of water coming down outside. Her chin had dropped and her shoulders sagged. That wasn't like Amelia at all, but then neither was her tepid welcome.

He stood and crossed the room to her, wrapped his arms around her and put his hands against her swollen belly. "I cannot imagine you in a more beautiful state."

She pressed her hands over his, but she trembled. What she had said about her pregnancy bothering George niggled at Victor's brain.

"I cannot stay, Amelia. It is about Regina, not about you. She already thinks poorly of me, I cannot bear the thought of her opinion sinking any lower. Why does she think I would kill you?"

"Oh, it is what George said when he heard Mary Frances had died," Amelia said airily.

"And that was?"

"He did not mean it."

"What did he say?"

"He said you had probably done her in. Please do not mention it. It was a private statement, and he only said it to hurt me."

"I just fought a duel for a less slanderous statement than that." When his friends thought so little of him, how could he expect anyone to think otherwise? Yet to confront George would likely hurt Regina and he would not do that.

"It was just to me, and he did not mean it, and it was only unfortunate that Regina heard it."

Amelia shifted, turning in his arms and resting her head against his chest. "I am so alone."

He stroked his hand over her hair, holding her. "No, you're not alone. You may always count on me as a friend, but the time for us to be lovers has passed. I am tired of hurting people. I do not want to hurt you or Reggie or even George."

172   *Karen L. King*

"Keene will not even look at me. He is too in love with Sophie."

An old rage coursed through Victor's blood, but the intensity had paled over the years. "You know how to wound, Amelia."

"I did not mean . . . I only . . . You feel safe to me, and Keene I have known as long and I trust he would be as gentle as you. I did not . . . Oh, I am sorry." She clasped his lapels as if afraid to let go.

"What is wrong between you and George?"

"He . . . he . . . he will not make love to me while I am with child and we had a monstrous row about it. I did not know what else to do but to come up to town."

How could George just deny himself for months on end? Why would he deny Amelia, who Victor knew had a passionate streak? "What is wrong with him?"

"He thinks such acts are only for procreation and it should be a sin." Amelia pressed her face into his chest.

"Has he been associating with Sophie's father?" asked Victor, mildly amused.

Amelia hit him, which was so unlike her, it made him laugh.

He freed himself from her, holding her hands between them. "I shall take care of it."

"Oh, no. You cannot. How?"

"I'll take care of it. I know George."

She looked so relieved he was almost wounded. That was *if* he cared to sleep with her. "Ah, Amelia, I was never first with you. You always settled for me after George or Keene did not come up to the mark."

Her blue eyes clouded with tears. "That's not true," she whispered. "You were my first choice, but

you . . . but you said so many times that you could
not marry me."

"Oh, hell, Amelia." Back then he did not have the
means to support her as a wife, but she had never
sought his lovemaking after the one time, leaving him
to believe he'd failed miserably. He had not known
she'd carried his child until after Regina's birth.

His wife's money had restored his estate to him,
but being poor as church mice did not seem so horrible to him now. He and Amelia might have had a
future if he had known how she felt then. If she had
told him about the baby. But that was a time long
past and everything was different now. She had
married George and Victor was enamored of a girl
whose name he did not know.

"I do love George, he is everything I try so hard
to be."

"And I give you leave to be your worst." Victor
kissed her forehead. Perhaps he could mend the
damage he'd caused. Or at least he could try.
"What I did to you was unforgivable, and I am so
very sorry."

The rain streamed down in a torrent. Helena crept
down the servants' stairs and out through the rear
garden. A gate led to the mews and an alley behind
their house. Trevor probably wouldn't even be there,
but she couldn't miss the opportunity to see him. If
the day had been normal, her maid and a footman
would have attended her during a walk in the park,
but no one expected her to go out in this deluge.

Most of the afternoon Helena sat quietly with her
embroidery in the drawing room, while her father

slept on the chaise longue, and her mother sat at the escritoire making lists of tasks to be done in preparation for the season. Helena watched the clock slowly tick away the minutes, until she could stand it no longer.

She told her mother the rain gave her the megrims and she would be resting in her room with a cloth soaked in lavender water on her head. Helena asked not to be disturbed before time to dress for dinner. Her mother had nodded and shooed her out of the room, with an admonition to not take sick before the Sheridans' party.

Her mother fussed with the coverlet over her father's legs, which was a good thing, for it kept her mother from noticing much else.

Helena kept her head down so the rain would run off her bonnet as she hurried toward Hyde Park. If he failed to show, she was ruining her boots and muddying the hem of her dress for a wild goose chase. And she was the goose.

She had always prided herself on her common sense, but this had to be the most illogical thing she'd ever done. Try as she might, she could find no good explanation for her stubborn hope.

By the end of the alley her walk turned into a scurry and by the third block, a trot. Oh, this was insane. She had gone quite mad and that would likely make her a good wife for Wedmont.

How many years had it been since she ran? Not since childhood, but as her feet splashed through the puddles she wanted to laugh, which was hysteria, most likely. How long had it been since she'd been outside alone, without a maid or footman trailing her every step?

A lone carriage drove by, splashing dirty water over her pelisse. She knew she should turn back, but she could see the park just ahead. She crossed the street, and hurried toward Rotten Row. Normally the carriage, walking and bridle paths would be thronged with traffic, but the park was eerily empty. She scurried along the graveled pathway, grit clinging to the hem of her gown.

She would have to hide her ruined clothes or risk being found out. She knew she should return home, that being out in the rain alone unchaperoned was the height of folly. A rumble of thunder made her start. She stopped, telling herself to go back, but the broad tree-lined path of Rotten Row beckoned.

She lifted her head and looked. Just ahead she could see a figure under a tree. He stood with the heel of one boot propped against the bark and he leaned back against the trunk. The rain had turned his blond hair dark, yet he wore the sort of caped greatcoat that one should wear in the rain.

She took a step toward him, and another. The rain penetrated the loose straw weave of her bonnet and a rivulet of water ran down through her hair and under her collar. Another trickle ran down her face. She dashed it away and her steps quickened. He pushed his foot away from the tree and stood on both feet as she flew toward him.

He held his arms open and she stopped three steps in front of him, out of range of his embrace. She stared into his blue eyes and wondered what innate modesty had made her forgo flinging herself into his arms. She failed to think of any reason to not leap into the expression of passion she craved, except it wasn't seemly. It wasn't done, and she was here to give him his congé.

He lowered his arms slowly. "I didn't think you would come."

"I was sure you would stay away." She sounded out of breath. She hadn't thought she had run so far, nor so fast to be winded.

He smiled gently.

She could watch his face forever. The way his cerulean eyes crinkled in the corners, just an instant before his sculpted lips curled up. His cheekbones were high, almost exotically so, and his forehead broad. She had not noticed so much before, but with his wet hair pushed back, she could drink in his features.

"Where are your minders?"

Helena glanced over her shoulder as if waiting for her maid to catch up. Then she looked down at her muddy pelisse. "I left them at home."

He stepped toward her, closing the distance she foolishly left between them.

With his height and the caped coat making his broad shoulders look even wider, he appeared indomitable. Her heart skittered in her chest. A feeling close to fear whispered through her veins. She took a half-step back, but she did not want to run.

"Do you not have a hat?" she asked inanely.

"I only brought one with me. I did not care to ruin it."

"You only have the one?" That anyone could make do with less than a dozen, surprised her. And she was only delaying the inevitable with talk of hats.

"We do not plan to stay long in England."

Helena felt each dull aching thud of her heart, as

a drop of water trickled down her face. She dashed it away with her soggy glove. "Only long enough to retrieve your sister, I suppose."

He looked over her head across the empty park. Helena resisted the urge to swivel and see if she could follow his gaze. "Unless I should stay long enough to retrieve . . . another woman."

Did he mean her?

He looked down at her with tenderness in his eyes. "I volunteered to fetch Lydia home. You realize, I did not have to come back to London."

"Why did you?" Helena mopped at the water on her face.

He shrugged, distracting her momentarily as she stared at the broad expanse of his chest. She could have been held against that wall of masculinity if she would have taken three steps forward into his proffered embrace. She condemned her temperate nature that kept her from passionate gestures, but then her even disposition would be a blessing as she watched him leave England again.

"Why did you ask me to meet you here?" she asked, wanting more than hints, more than vague implications.

"To see if you would show. I have often thought that I could open a shipping office here, expand our family business."

Horror spilled through Helena. If he was ever to be accepted as even an acquaintance to her parents, her mother specifically, he would have to appear free of the taint of trade, rich enough to live on its proceeds, without ever actually conducting business. She knew her expression reflected her dismay, and she took another tiny step back.

"If there was ever reason for me to stay in England," he said.

A trickle of icy water slid down her back, making her shudder.

He looked her over and smiled ruefully. "I suppose not. Why did you come to the park in the pouring rain, Helena?"

She unexpectedly burst into tears.

He stared at her a moment before he curled his arm around her shoulders and led her under the boughs. "Stand here, the rain is partially blocked by the tree limbs."

"It should hardly matter as I am supplying my own watering pot." She hiccupped.

"Shhh," he soothed, brushing tears off her cheeks with his thumb. "Whatever is the matter?"

Helena tried to get control of herself, but only succeeded in slowing the flow of tears. "I have come to tell you that I cannot encourage you. You see, I really must settle this season. My father is ill, and he said he will have to sell the Coventry property, which was to be my dowry. These last few years have been too dear, and my parents have determined I shall have to set my cap for the Earl of Wedmont."

"And is the Earl of Wedmont old and ugly?" Trevor continued to rest his hand against her cheek. Actually, just his palm, because his fingers curled around the edge of her bonnet. With such great hands, he could be trusted to hold anything securely, from her kitten to a baby. His touch, so gentle and reassuring, calmed her.

She shook her head. "Actually, he's rather handsome, and a very young widower. He's mayhap seen thirty summers."

"But you don't want to marry him?"

"No. But I must." Another fat tear dribbled out of her eye and down her cheek. Oh, la, and she thought she had gotten control of her fit of the vapors. "I do not know why I tell you these things."

He caught her tear with his thumb. "Actually, I am surprised to find you still unwed."

"Yes, well . . ." When he had been here before, she had been held apart as if a proper bride for a prince. How silly those ambitions seemed now. Yet her parents still considered her worthy of a better bargain than to marry a commoner, let alone a man in trade. She could not imagine a circumstance that would make Trevor acceptable to them.

He brushed her lower lip with his thumb. She tasted the salt of her own tears. His expression turned intense. The intimacy of his gesture surprised her. It was less than a kiss, but much, much more.

He moved his thumb under her chin and her lips tingled where he had touched. He tilted her head back and leaned toward her. He hesitated only a moment, his intentions clear in his blue eyes, but giving her the last chance to protest or turn away. Turning away was the last thing she wanted to do.

Then his lips met hers for the gentlest of kisses. Her eyes fluttered shut as his firm lips encircled her lower lip. With the lightest of tugs, he made this kiss unlike anything she had ever experienced before. His thumb traced down the underside of her chin, across the ribbon of her bonnet and down her throat, stopping at the hollow just above the top fastener of her pelisse.

The urge to throw open her wrapper so that his touch would find no impediment surprised her.

Just as had the mad shivers that such a simple little kiss provoked. Instead, she found the end of her bonnet ribbon and pulled the bow loose.

He transferred his attention to her upper lip, giving her the opportunity to mimic what he had done to her, back to him. She nibbled ever so slightly and his low moan made her fear she had done something wrong, but he tugged her against him, eliminating the gap between their bodies. Then his tongue touched her lips.

Her lips rounded into an "oh" of surprise as much from this variation on a kiss as from the rush of sensation that made her breasts tingle, and, lower still, provoked a tightening between her legs.

She could feel Trevor's smile as he explored her mouth and coaxed her into responding.

He was laughing at her ineptitude, and just a slight sting of regret that she was not a passionate creature made her wince. His amusement was not so great that he stopped, and Helena wanted nothing more than for this moment to go on and on.

Yet he seemed intent on letting her grow comfortable and then pressing on to a next step. He ended the kiss and pressed his lips against her neck. She tilted her head back to enjoy his attentions and her bonnet tumbled down her back. Trevor grabbed it before it dropped to the ground.

Shudder after shudder rippled through her. He was so talented.

He pulled back, and she reached for him. He secured her bonnet to the tree, tying the ribbons around a branch.

"You are sopping wet, you know."

Yes, this fustian pelisse had been a poor choice,

and being splashed by the carriage had made it worse. "And muddy."

He opened his coat. "Let me share with you."

She hesitated while he waited, the sides of his coat held open. He looked warm and dry and oh-so-inviting. Unwilling to drench him, she stripped off her wringing wet gloves and stuffed them in her pocket. With near desperation she undid the catches and dropped her pelisse, while stepping forward.

He caught her coat and tossed it across a branch before enfolding her in his warm embrace.

"Helena," he whispered before once again covering her mouth with his.

The rain continued to pour down around them, but she felt safe and warm in the cocoon of his seal-skin coat. She was warm and alive in his arms. Alive and enthralled by the power of his kisses.

Only now his hands slid down her back, below her waist, cupping her curves and pulling her tight against him. A hard object prodded her stomach and interfered with their closeness. Helena tried to ignore it, but she thought it a part of his clothing that she could push aside. She reached and as her fingers curled around the hard length, she realized her mistake.

"Christ Almighty! Oh damn!" he swore.

It was not part of his clothing, it was under his clothing and it throbbed under her hand.

"What is that?" she whispered, shocked, confused. How could he conceal such a large part of his anatomy?

She tried to pull her hand away, but Trevor pinned her against the tree, so tight she couldn't move, nor could she pull her hand out from between them. Stars above, what had she gotten herself into?

CHAPTER 11

"Don't move," Trevor gritted out between clenched teeth. He was in danger of falling over the edge and losing control. Helena probably had no idea what she had done, grabbing him like that. Hell, undoing her bonnet, stripping off her gloves, tossing her coat and the way her damp white muslin gown clung to her breasts, revealing more than she could know, had driven him to the brink.

He knew he scared her, but knew she had to feel his penis pulsing against her hand. His problem should be clear to her. He could only think to pin her against the tree so she couldn't wiggle or rub or clench her fingers around him. Any move might spiral him into release.

"Just give me a minute," he whispered. In any case he had to stop. They needed to discuss how far she intended this tryst to go. She had gone out without a chaperone, but he doubted she meant to be seduced in a public park, against a tree, in the pouring rain. Any one of those factors should have rendered her safe from an excess of attention.

"I do not know what I am about," she said with a rising note of panic in her voice.

"Yes, but you have damn good instincts." He kissed her forehead. "Don't fret, we are stopping."

She blinked her green eyes at him and bit her swollen lower lip. "Is that what you want?"

Another wave of desire crashed through him. "That is the last thing I want."

He could hardly believe that she had been kissing him, with all the abandon he could have ever hoped for. He had been sensitive of her inexperience, but that was not enough to stop him in the moment he dreamed about for five years.

"I do not understand. Why . . . what . . . oh, I feel so strange."

"I could fix that."

She stared at him. "How?"

For the life of him, he did not know if she wanted him to explain or persuade. "I fear I will shock you, sweetheart."

She flinched at the endearment, or perhaps at his reminder that they had crossed boundaries they should not have ventured past. One bit of encouragement, even another question, and he would see to her education in the art of seduction.

She shook her head as if she could not believe what had happened. The haughty reserve dropped back over her face. A tense stiffness replaced the pliable softness in her body.

Finally, able to ease his hips back, he pulled her hand away, just in case she had any ideas of exploring further. She possessed an incredible amount of command over him.

She had run toward him, then drew up before he could embrace her. Her penchant for turning hot, then cold, with him reduced to a beggar. She had only to beckon and he would follow her to the ends of the earth. But he wanted more than stolen moments of passion.

"Helena, my intentions toward you are honorable even if my behavior is not."

She lowered her gaze. Not an auspicious beginning to a proposal.

And it was a lie. His intentions weren't honorable, especially since he knew his suit would be refused. The best possible solution he could hope for was to be her lover. She was not raised to be the wife of a working man, not even a well-heeled business owner. He was not an owner and years would pass before he had substantial wealth in his own right.

He twisted, pulling his coat off and draping it around her shoulders.

"You shall get wet." She pulled his coat tight. His overcoat swamped her, yet she still managed to look regal with water droplets glittering like jewels in her coronet of braids and clinging to her eyelashes. She was a woman made for court functions in palace ballrooms. Boston had no palaces.

"Helena, not a day has passed in the last five years that I have not thought of you."

She closed her eyes. Her white skin paled and her expression grew pinched.

"I do not know if that is love, but you cannot deny that there is something between us."

She held out her hand. "Do not. Oh, pray stop. I am sorry. I have misled you. I did not mean for things to go so far. I came to tell you I must not see you again."

He yanked the ribbons of her bonnet loose, pulled it off the branch, then brushed it out, making sure no pieces of bark clung to the inside. "Come, I will walk you home."

With such a reception for his declaration of feelings, what else could he do?

She nodded and busied herself with tying her bonnet. He carried her saturated coat as they left the park and walked toward her house. The torrents of rain hid the last gray light of the day. The darkness crashed around them, mirroring his mood.

He hardly looked at her as they walked with heads down. Another block and she would be home. He would not see her again. He would not put himself through this again. She hesitated before crossing the last street leading to the square where she lived.

He turned back to look at her.

She pressed her hand against her lip and trembled. With his winter coat, she could hardly be too cold. "What?"

"I left through the mews," she spoke to the ground and he could not make out her features under the brim of her bonnet. Ashamed to admit her sneaking or afraid to enter through the front door? In either case he cared little. He would not cast so much as a shadow upon her reputation, and he doubted she would be punished.

"It is dark, Lady Helena. I will see you to your front door and bid you a good life." He bowed like any good English gentleman would, although he did not have a hat to doff and his clothes were wet through, which was a good thing, because he needed the dousing in cold water.

A plain black carriage turned into her square.

"I do not wish for things to end so." Her voice quivered.

"I do not wish for us to end either, Lady Helena. But you give me no choice. I cannot be your toy to play with when the mood suits you."

"Trevor, I truly do not mean to toy with your affections. I just—my father is ill. I cannot do anything that would upset him. And my mama is very worried, she cannot tolerate any more burdens." Helena gingerly placed her hand on his arm.

He hated that his heart pounded at her slightest touch. And she actually spoke his given name. "You are of age now." She had not been when he was here before. "You do not need your parents' permission to marry."

"If that was a proposal, it was the worst in all time," she said lightly.

Damn her, and she was right. He dropped to a knee in a puddle of icy water. "Helena, would you—"

"Oh, no!" She clapped a gloved hand to her mouth. "That was the physician's carriage. Oh, heavens, he is entering my house." She skirted around him and darted toward her home.

Trevor stood and winced. Then he walked after her, the cold material of his trouser leg slapping his leg. So much for noble gestures. He should have told her to send him word after she married and was ready to take him on as her cicisbeo.

Marriage was a business affair to her, an alliance of bloodlines. The English upper classes often looked for love outside of marriage. He was the outsider, challenging their long-established protocols.

As he stood in the rain outside the open front

door of her house, a footman walked out, extending Trevor's coat.

Passing Helena's soggy coat to the servant while he took his own back, Trevor stared at the house. Light shone from the windows, but its welcome excluded him. The door clicked shut and he remained alone in the darkness of the street.

Lydia woke in the darkness and for a moment wondered where she was. Her shoulder throbbed and she remembered. Victor's bed. She had slept in long stretches most of the day and well into the evening. She did not know what time it was, but it was very still.

When her shoulder began to throb, she would climb out of her drug-induced fog long enough for Jenny or Victor's manservant to give her another dose of laudanum. Victor had been noticeably absent for most of the day, even after the surgeon had arrived.

At one point there had been food, but Lydia ate only a few bites, before falling asleep again. A gnawing emptiness in her midsection suggested she had not eaten enough.

Lydia vaguely remembered Victor standing in the doorway a time or two, but then again she might have just hoped for his presence.

A pale strip of light framed three quarters of the connecting doorway to the other room. His wife's room.

Was Victor in there? Did he have the door cracked so he might hear if she called out?

She pushed the covers down and swung her feet to the floor. A shawl lay across the foot of the bed and, miracles of all miracles she had undergarments on now. She still wore the nightshirt that belonged to Victor, but Jenny had whip-stitched ties on the shoulder so the slit would stay closed when the surgeon was not attending her. Lydia wrapped the shawl around her shoulders and tiptoed toward the connecting door.

She pushed it open. It glided silently on its hinges. The room revealed was clearly a mate to the one she slept in, although softer with more delicate furnishings, including a full-length cheval glass. The drapes were a matching wine, but the walls were papered with vistas of English gardens; the only green to match that of Victor's room was in the stems of flowers and piping about pink cushions.

Square in the middle of the room stood a bed with rumpled sheets and twisted pillows. The covers dragged on the floor to one side. The bed had been slept in, or at least thrashed around within. A nightshirt lay crumpled on the floor as if it had been flung down in haste.

Lydia stepped into the room.

Victor sat sideways to a desk on the far side of the room before the window. His legs, sprawled akimbo, were encased in habitual black, but his feet were bare, making her smile. His untucked white shirt was open at the neck and the sleeves rolled back, and as she studied him, her heart beat faster.

She could not tell if he was asleep or awake. His elbows rested on the arms of the chair, but his head had fallen forward into his hands, blocking his face from her view.

On the writing desk, near the burning lamp sat an open pot of ink and a paper with sand scattered across it. To whom was he writing? Had he learned her identity? Was he contacting her father? A bolt of alarm struck her chest.

She inched toward the desk, squinting to read the words through the blotting sand. It looked like one line, scrawled in an expansive angular script.

She leaned over to blow the sand away. Victor moved. She jumped.

"What are you about?" he asked.

Lydia pulled the shawl tight across her chest, trying to still her trembling. "Are you writing to my father?"

Victor glanced at the sheet of paper. He lifted it, dumped the blotting sand into its box, then folded the sheet. "This has nothing to do with you. Besides, I suspect a letter directed to Mr. Hall of Boston would be returned to me, forthwith."

He opened a slim drawer and pulled out a wax sealing stick and held it over the lamp. When the end was gooey, he applied it to the flap, and then turned his hand backward and pressed his pinkie ring into the red wax. "Do you need more laudanum?"

"No." She did not want to sleep any longer.

He glanced at her. "How is the pain?"

He quickly returned his attention to his letter as if he could not bear to look at her.

"Not so bad." Actually the pain made her jaw clench, but she tried to relax and not fight it. A dull ache, which she assumed was due to the repeated doses of laudanum, thrummed in her head.

"You should return to bed."

"I'm not tired. I have slept too much."

He turned the folded and sealed letter over and scrawled a name on it. George Keeting, Esquire.

Not her father, not anyone she knew, and an address in England.

Was she an afterthought? He steadily ignored her, a far cry from the pointed attention she had received earlier. She drifted over to the nightshirt on the floor and leaned over to pick it up.

"Leave that."

"I was just going to fold it and put it on the bed."

"I have servants to pick up after me." He stood. The lamplight behind him left him in silhouette to her. Just a menacing shadow, which made her step back.

"Yes, well, I am used to helping the servants. My brothers . . ." Her voice trailed off as she scooped the garment from the floor. Her brothers often left their clothes lying about and it became a daunting task for the maids to get them all picked up. In America, the mistress of the house who did not labor alongside her staff was thought lazy.

He snatched his nightshirt from her hands and tossed it across the room. "You should not be in here."

A pain not due to her wound or her headache scorched her heart. "I know. You do not want me here."

"On the contrary, pet. I want you here overmuch." He raked one hand through his dark hair. One curving strand sprang free and settled across his forehead.

She wanted to touch the stray lock, to push it back into place. She wanted to trail her fingers over the dark shadows that had grown on his cheeks and chin. She wanted a repeat of their earlier embrace.

"Bloody hell! Do not look at me like that."

She ducked her chin, staring at her toes peeping out under her hem. How was she looking at him? Could he read her unnatural desire in her expression? "I'm sorry," she mumbled.

"Hell, Lenny, have I not done enough damage already?"

She jerked her head up. What lure drew her even though he had shot her? But he had said right after that if she had not moved he would have missed. She put her hand to her shoulder. "You did not mean to shoot me, did you?"

"I never mean to cause damage, but I always do." He planted his hands on his lean hips.

The bed showed evidence of tossing and turning, rather than peaceful slumber. "I do not think you are my enemy."

"Not your enemy, but not good for you either."

She shrugged. "No worse for me than those who are supposed to be looking out for my best interests."

The moment teemed with energy, yet it was quiet and intimate in the soft lamplight, with a disordered bed so very near them. What would it be like to share a bed with him? But this was his wife's bedroom. Would he think of her?

Restless, Lydia pattered toward the window. Her instinct was to straighten the bedcovers, but Victor had reacted so strongly to picking up his sleeping clothes that she felt she trespassed upon his privacy.

She realized now why the quiet sounded so complete. The rain had stopped.

"Is it not time for you to tell me what you are running from?" he asked.

She pulled back the drape to look outside. No visible stars or moon, the darkness a cavern. Was there any point in keeping it secret? "My wedding."

"Mmm."

Silence settled over the room, like a comfortable blanket. She tensed, waiting for the next question, for the belittling of her reasons, which did not sound so important, even to her. But he did not ask.

Lydia let the drapery slide from her clasp. "Do you miss her?"

"Who?"

"Your wife. This was her room, was it not?"

He did not answer for a long time, and she suspected she had offended him. She turned around. He stared at the bed.

"At times I miss her, other times I don't. I hope she is at peace now."

That answer told her so little. Did sleeping in his wife's bed disturb his rest? Were those the times he missed? She leaned back against the window, feeling the coolness of the glass through the heavy curtains.

"Would you be more comfortable sleeping in your own bed? I could make use of another room, or this one." She gestured toward the rumpled bed. "It does not look as if you sleep well in here."

He turned and stared at her. "Possibly because I have never slept in here before."

He had never slept in his wife's bedchamber? Had she joined him in his bed, or did he just never stay to sleep? Heat rose in Lydia's face. Her curiosity about his marital relations was far too indelicate. "I only thought if you should be more comfortable in familiar surroundings. I have no memories to disturb my rest."

"And plenty of laudanum to ensure sleep. I have no memories of this room to haunt me. My wife was seldom here."

He had described his marriage as worse than hell. Was that why he did not question her decision to run away from her wedding? She could not stem her curiosity. "Was your marriage so horrid then?"

"I asked you not to speak of it, when I said so before."

"I did not realize it was important, your characterization was so offhand." Lydia bit her lip. A strong desire to ask him about her own situation welled up in her. She had not spoken to anyone about what Oscar said.

"I am like that. I speak my mind to those I trust to know when to repeat things or keep their own counsel."

"I am sorry to have failed you." She had not thought that he had taken a boy he was mentoring into his confidence. "I think I would have done better if I fully understood the situation."

He gave a quick snort and shook his head. "Even I do not fully understand and no one of my friends knows everything."

Lydia felt a lump in her throat; she was not likely to still be considered his friend. "I hardly thought that we had reached such a level of intimacy that you were telling me your secrets."

"Especially since you will not even tell me your name. And I was not aware that you were deceiving me." He pivoted and paced away from her. "I married my wife for her money. She married me for my title. Although I did my best to make my marriage work, it was inevitable that I would wound her."

Had he been cruel to his wife? Lydia could not see it. Had he been an adulterer? She could hear the pain in his voice. Whatever he had done, he had been hurt by it. She pushed away from the window, following him to the dark side of the room. "In what way did you wound her?"

He glanced over his shoulder and took a step away from her, until he reached the washstand. He leaned his palms down against the marble surface. "I made demands of her she could not fulfill. She was not well."

Fearing his reaction, but needing to touch him, Lydia reached out and put her hand on his shoulder. She wanted to soothe him, to calm the stormy waters she sensed in him. "She was ill?"

He winced, but did not pull away from her touch. "Not physically unsound, but she had demons. She could not be a real wife to me, yet I pressed her again and again."

Lydia flattened her palm, relishing the firm flesh and bone under the silk of his shirt. She wanted to reassure him, that no matter his guilt, she did not think him an ogre. "She could not be a real wife in what way?"

He spun, catching her wrist and pulling it away from him. "I have not fully made love to a woman for many years. You are playing with fire. I am fair near starved for a good bob."

His expression intense, his dark eyes bored into her. His chest rose and fell with a heavy cadence. Had he picked a crass term to shock and repel her? Instead, she was drawn to the flame.

Her thoughts spun around what he had said. As a husband, he had every right to force his wife to his bed, yet he had not. Nor, if he told the truth, had he sought solace outside his marriage. She suspected he always told the truth, even when it was not the best course of action for him.

She glanced at the disordered bed. "If it would give you comfort, I would . . ."

She hesitated at his scowl, and her courage deserted her, but she stumbled on. "I would . . ." *be willing to make love with you, would gladly become your lover.* Her mind supplied fitting phrases, but she could not get them out. "I would do, wouldn't I?"

His expression flickered, softened. "You would more than do. I daresay knowing you are so near is why I cannot sleep. As much as I should wish it, I cannot bear the thought of hurting you any more." He folded his arms across his chest.

Pain washed through her. As desperate as he claimed to be, he still did not want her. She turned to flee the room, to run from the sense that she would never be woman enough to tempt a man. Every childhood jab about her unusual height, her lack of female form did not hurt so much as his refusal.

Before she could round the bed, he grabbed her around the waist and yanked her back. He slid one arm down across her hips and pulled her against his hardness. His male member jutted against her backside, nestling firmly in the crevice between her curves. She could feel his shudder as he touched his lips to her shoulder.

He spoke, his lips so near to her ear that his breath tickled. "Make no mistake. I want you more than I can stand, but I cannot take advantage of you under these circumstances."

In an odd way he offered physical proof that he did not find her repulsive, that his body craved hers. But she did not want him to think for her, to make decisions because he did not believe her capable of making a good choice. "What circumstances are an impediment?"

He breathed out hard. He flattened his hand against her stomach and slowly shifted it up to her lowest rib. "You are injured." Her next rib. "Your sensibilities are impaired by the laudanum you have been given this day." He reached just under her breast and paused. "You are under my protection and I have given my word that I will not assault your virtue."

His hand closed around her breast and sensual pleasure poured through her. She could feel his member throb against her as he pulled his hand up and circled her breast with his fingertips. She leaned her head back as he kissed her neck, just below her ear. His slow circles grew tighter and tighter until he gently rolled her beaded nipple between his thumb and forefinger.

Jolt after jolt of pleasure rippled through her and a gasp left her lips.

He pushed her away. "That is how I feel around you."

She blinked, feeling bemused. He expected her to take pleasure in this act? And if he felt that much intensity of pleasure, then why would he ever stop?

"But I would hate myself for ruining you."

She turned and studied him. His chest heaved and his dark eyes were glittering with desire. He would deny himself pleasure because of guilt? "Don't you think it is time you forgave yourself?"

"You do not understand."

"No, I don't."

He walked back to the writing desk. He picked

up a glass paperweight and looked into it. "There are rumors that I killed my wife."

Lydia folded her arms. "But you did not."

He looked up at her, his expression stark. "Not in deed, but by my demands, I forced her to choose death. She ran back inside the fire, after I had pulled her out once. That is the kind of influence I have over people. I destroy people, just as my father did before me. I do not wish to destroy you."

Helena stared out her bedroom window into the darkness. The clouds blocked any light. She saw only the globes upon the gas lamps, too faint to brighten the stormy night. Holding her kitten against her chest, she stroked Sparks's fur, while relishing his tiny heartbeat against her palm.

What had she done?

The evening had provided too many shocks, and she could not sleep. The physician had not come for her father, as she feared, but because her mother had fainted and could not be roused right away.

Helena had sat on the edge of her seat in the drawing room, waiting for the physician's diagnosis and hoping her father would not comment on her wet hair or muddy hem. Her stomach tightened with lingering tension from her encounter with Trevor. Instead, their butler brought her a shawl.

They waited still longer. Helena feared her mother had discovered her absence and that had triggered her mother's sudden illness. Although as Helena sat, it occurred to her that her mother had been overly tired lately.

She was such a horrid daughter. She had put her

mother's exhaustion down to the burden of caring for her father and never given it another thought. Other than minding the minimal tasks of correspondence and minor household emergencies, she had not eased her mother's burdens.

After a long spell, the physician was finally ushered into the drawing room. Helena jumped to her feet as he crossed to the chaise longue to speak with her father.

"Is she all right?" she had asked before the physician could utter a word.

"May I offer my congratulations, my lord. Your wife is with child."

Helena sat down hard. It had been nineteen years since her mother had last given birth. How could she be with child?

"Are you quite positive?" asked her father.

"I did do a thorough examination. With women of a certain age, we do not want to mistake her condition. I am quite sure. She should feel the quickening soon."

Her father nodded.

Helena was not sure what he meant by quickening. After this afternoon, she knew she was too ignorant of the functioning of the female body or the male body and exactly how procreation took place.

The physician continued to speak. "She is a bit hysterical. I could give her medicine to calm her down, but it would be better if she applied more natural methods, given her delicate condition. And it is essential that she eat properly."

Helena sprang out of her chair. "I shall take care of her."

When she entered her mother's bedroom, her

mother lay propped up in her bed while tears streamed down her face. Seeing her indomitable mother in tears tore at Helena. She rushed forward and took her mother's hands. "Do not cry, Mama, everything shall be all right."

"I cannot believe this. I am too *old* to have a baby."

"The physician seemed sure of it. He said he examined you."

"I thought my menses had stopped because of the change. Oh, I cannot believe this." Her mother's voice ended on a wail. "It was so very personal, his examination. I have never allowed any man to look at me or touch me so."

"Mama, you must calm down." Helena swallowed back her own panic at seeing her mother's anguish. "I am sure this cannot be good for you or the baby."

She smiled brightly at her mother and squeezed her hands.

Lady Caine shook her head. "Even if I can carry this child, it will be another girl, or a simpleton. I cannot believe . . . I thought it would raise your father's spirits to . . . with his health he could not get out to visit his mistress."

Her mother froze and stared at Helena. She blanched white, which was how Helena felt.

"Oh, my God, I cannot believe I spoke so to you. What is wrong with me?"

"Mama, you are just overset. Please do not fret. I am not an infant. You may trust me in your confidences. I hardly think it shall harm me to know of these things, since I shall be a married woman before too much longer." Helena suppressed her frown. Either that or she should be an old maid.

"We cannot allow this to interfere in your season.

You must marry soon. Oh, Lord, how shall we ever manage to dower another girl? We have almost nothing left for you."

"Yes, Mama, I will take care of everything. Do not worry about me. I am sure that if I set my mind to it, I can bring Wedmont up to scratch."

"Yes, yes, you must. Oh, I cannot believe this has happened. If I cannot escort you to events, what will we do?" Her mother seemed to be working into a panic again.

"Mama, you must trust me to see to my season. If you cannot chaperone me, I shall enlist the aid of one of my sisters." Helena winced, thinking of the embarrassment of answering to one of her younger siblings. "The important thing for you to do is take care of yourself. I shall do everything I can to help you deliver a healthy brother or sister."

"I should be helping you with a pregnancy. This is so wrong."

"Yes, well, I should have to marry first, and perhaps this was meant to be. Surely, God has planned it this way."

Her mother looked at her sharply. "Why are your clothes damp, Helena?"

"Ah, well, the physician seemed to take such a very long time, and I walked a little in the rain." The distortion of the truth rolled off her tongue with ease. But the last thing Helena could risk was upsetting her mother further. Her mother would be very distressed to know she had been out alone with Mr. Hamilton and indulging in sins of the flesh.

Helena had not allowed herself to think of what had happened between them. She could not allow it to happen again. "Now, do you feel well enough to come down for dinner, or shall I have cook prepare a tray?"

Other recollections of the strained evening rolled through her thoughts as she stared out into the silent night. Then there had been that moment when Trevor went down on one knee in the street. Her view of the physician's carriage and the knowledge that he was entering her home had nearly stopped her heart. Her one moment of passion, her first real proposal, shattered by fear for her father, who apparently kept a mistress.

Even at that, she nearly had to shame Trevor into declaring himself. Yet his kisses meant something, did they not? His near loss of control said she was not a total failure at provoking physical passion, at least.

Helena rubbed her cheek against Sparks's silky orange and amber fur. He blinked at her sleepily as if he did not understand why they were not long abed. "I did not even ask after his sister, Sparks. Am I not a selfish beast?"

Leading Trevor on with kisses and yearning to hear him declare himself, although she had known she could not accept his suit, was unforgivable.

She should apologize. She should not see him again. She should forget how he made her feel, liquid and tense, awake and aware as if she had woken from a long slumber. Only his lighthearted offer to fix the strange way she felt kept spinning in her head.

CHAPTER 12

Not-Leonard seemed unimpressed with Victor's warning that he would destroy her. Her head tilted to the side and she looked skeptical.

"I'm hungry," she announced, as if their conversation had little merit. As if he hadn't just told her his darkest secret and his deepest fears about himself. As if they weren't dealing with his barely restrained desire.

She amused him mightily. "Ah, pet, so am I, but then I presume you are talking of food."

She crinkled her nose and looked absolutely adorable. "I am a bit thirsty too."

He grinned. Her lack of concern about his ability to destroy people he cared about put him in his place. He crossed behind her into his room and tugged the bellpull.

"Must you summon a servant? Couldn't we just tiptoe down to the larder?" She sounded dismayed. "Surely, your staff are all still fast asleep."

"I do not want you out of these rooms. Your reputation would be besmirched forever."

"I did not expect you to wake one of your servants."

"Just my valet, and he is well paid, pet." Besides

that, the less time they spent together alone, the better.

She looked at him with calm assessment and he suddenly realized she had diverted their conversation, that his waking a servant was hardly the point, but a way of breaking their intimacy.

She crossed the ends of her shawl and folded her arms across her chest, and looked down at the floor.

A moment earlier, her consternation at his refusal of her offer to provide outlet for his desire had been clear in the crumpling of her expression. Showing her how much he wanted her was not difficult, although pulling away had been like wrenching his soul free from a demon's grasp.

Now, he was unsure what thoughts churned in her head. He felt locked out, held at arm's length, and he cursed himself for a fool. He could have had her, were it not the wrong thing to do. Yet, she did not trust him with her name.

Yearning burned under his breastbone. In her own way, she had been spurning him from the minute he rescued Leonard from a thrashing.

He had just told her more than Keene knew about him. Did he think that by sharing every skeleton in his cupboard, she might tell him who she was?

A light tapping prompted Victor to head for the door of the feminine bedroom. When he opened the door, his servant stood there impeccably dressed, as if he had slept standing in a corner, fully clothed, just in case he was summoned.

"Miss Hall would like a food tray." Victor swiveled. "What would you like to eat?"

Not-Leonard shrugged. "Whatever is easy."

Victor rolled his eyes and turned back to his valet. "Buttered eggs, scones and hot chocolate."

"Very good, milord," said his butler and Victor turned to face his houseguest.

He wanted to close the space between them and carry her to his bed, either bed. He wanted to break down any barriers between them. His body thrummed with energy, and he had to admit that more than her proximity made him want her. If his desire was based just on deprivation, then Amelia would have done.

How could he want her so much, when he knew so little about her? Was it because, like his father, he relished destroying innocence? Was Amelia's maturity and experience what left him cold? Did Lenny's many secrets hold Victor in thrall?

"Why did you run from your wedding? Is your betrothed a beast?"

She crossed the room to the window and edged back the curtain.

"A tyrant? Cruel to you?" He needed to know. He needed to understand. He needed to have a part of her to hold.

"No, not on purpose. For the most part he has been quite kind and considerate." Her answer was mild in tone, confusing him. "I thought myself quite in love."

Victor folded his arms, ignoring the knot below his ribcage. "In what way did he hurt you then?"

She shook her head slightly.

Her refusal to allow him a glimpse of her world, her real world, made his heart ache. "Come now, I have confessed my secrets."

"Yes, but candor comes easily to you."

"As well as the curse of speaking my mind."

She turned and gave him a half-smile. "Not so much a curse. I admire your ability to share your thoughts without a care to their reception."

He blinked. She had not been exposed enough if she thought his tendency to be brutally blunt was anything short of hurtful. "Perhaps my words have not wounded you yet. They will sooner or later."

"You have said things that have hurt me." She stared at him, her blue eyes guileless. "But I do not fear you say one thing to me and have a worse opinion that you share with others. I know how poorly you think of me."

Victor stared at her, feeling remorse at causing her pain, yet sure he had not given her a true glimpse of his view of her. Yet, he knew he could not offer encouragement.

"I hate that you will not share so much as your name with me," he said.

She turned her back to him, her head bowed. "I would share much with you."

He felt torn in two, because he wanted her touch. He wanted . . . her trust. He wanted her in totality, not just physically, not just in part.

He sat on the edge of the bed. In truth, he knew that the things he told her, the worst of his past, were in part to warn her. Now that she seemed to be heeding his counsel, he wanted to take it all back. Yet, none of this was any help to her.

He desperately wanted to hang on to her, to encourage the tenderness of her emotions, to bask in her concern and care, but he knew he could not offer anything in the balance. He no longer had anything of himself left to give, nothing beyond

pain and suffering he could share. He knew he
might take and take and take, and she deserved
better than that. She deserved a man who could
love her.

Even though the idea of her with another man
made Victor want to tear this man apart limb by
limb, perhaps he could help her find the happiness
she deserved. "So why have you run away from this
man? You are obviously not afraid of the physical aspects of marriage."

She gripped the drapery in one hand, holding it
as if it were a lifeline. "He wants to marry me only
for my birthright."

"No man wants to marry you only for your
birthright," blurted Victor. "No man with eyes in his
head."

"I heard him say as much. He wants his place in
my father's company." She let go of the curtain and
stepped away, pacing with her long-legged stride.
"He wants more than what would be mine if I had
been born a male. He wants to wrest control from
my brothers and take over the company when my
father passes."

"So he is ambitious," Victor said cautiously. The
business world was ambiguous to him. There would
have to be one person who must take control of the
company when her father was gone. Without a
clear primogeniture system, Victor assumed the
person best qualified would take control of a company. "That does not mean he does not care for
you, and would not be a good husband."

Her steps quickened as she paced back and forth.
He wanted to leap up and soothe her, yet he
wanted to know why she was here, why she had

turned up in his life, why she had protected the secret of her identity to the point of risking death.

She stopped and bit her lip. "Are you pushing me at him because you do not want me here?"

"I am not pushing you at him, I just have not heard that he or your family has done anything so dreadful to make you flee across an ocean and risk your entire future, let alone your life."

Her blue eyes were stormy. "I do not know that I ran from the man, so much as I ran from marriage."

Victor shook his head, surprised, shocked even to hear a sentiment so close to his own from an innocent such as her. Had he unduly influenced her with his own cynicism? "And why do *you* think marriage so bad, pet?"

She put her palms up. "I will lose who I am. I will be nothing more than property of my husband. If he causes dissension with my brothers, I will have no choice but to stand by him. I will have no identity, except as his wife. If I had been born a boy, my birthright would be mine. I could make all my own decisions."

He stared at her. Was that what her masquerade as Leonard was about? "So you wish you were a man?"

"Helena," said her father after he limped into the breakfast room and sat heavily.

She jumped to her feet to fill a plate for her father from the warming dishes on the sideboard. "What can I get for you, Papa? Would you like some kippers or poached eggs?"

"Sit, dearest, we need to talk."

Helena slid back into her seat. She repositioned

her napkin in her lap, although her appetite deserted her. Her father had always left talking to her mother, filtering his requests and commands through her.

He reached out a hand toward Helena, and she noticed how knotty and gnarled his knuckles were, the joints thick and his spotted fingers crooked. When had he gotten so old?

"I am worried about your mother."

Helena took her father's hand in hers. She was more worried about him.

"At your mother's age, carrying a child could be quite difficult."

"I will take good care of her."

He patted her hand. "I know you will, but I want to speak about you. I have found a buyer for the Coventry estate. I will set some of the proceeds by for you to have a dowry."

Helena nodded, although she felt a burn behind her eyes. Her property would be gone. It was never truly hers, so she should not feel its loss so keenly, but it had always stood as a solace to her. A place she could withdraw to if she never married, but that option was gone now.

"I do not want to frighten you, but if this pregnancy proves fatal for your mother, and I am an old man . . ."

Helena understood. She would have no place to go. No place to live. Her mother would be entitled to use of the dower house, but Helena would not. She had to marry now, or she risked becoming a poor relation with no welcome anywhere. Her younger sisters might allow her to spend time in their households, but the twins were close to each other, not to her. "I have told Mama that I will set my cap for Wedmont."

"I hope you understand the urgency, Helena. I had hopes that you might have married one of the royal dukes, but . . ." her father shook his head.

Helena wanted to protest that her youngest sibling might be a brother.

"Wedmont is not likely to object to your dowry. He is nearer your age and more likely to make you happy."

Except Helena suspected Trevor might be the only man who could make her happy.

"Now, there is a favor I would ask of you. The physician recommended that we seek the services of an accoucheur. I do not wish to trust this to a servant. I would ask you to take a maid and pay a call on William Knighton's offices, as he is reputed to be the best of these doctors."

"Of course, Papa."

Helena was relieved to have a task, even a task as little as finding a doctor who specialized in delivering babies.

Her father gave her hand one last squeeze. "Now, I will take kippers, poached eggs and a roll with clotted cream, if you would be so kind."

She stood again to dish up his plate, relieved to have the emotional conversation over.

"Helena," her father said.

She turned, thinking no more than he had an item he wished to add to his request.

"I do not know where you went yesterday in the rain, and I am sure I do not want to know, but I trust we will have no more of that."

Helena nearly dropped the plate. Instead, she

bit her tongue and busied herself with serving her father.

Her father sighed behind her. A tremble started at her toes and moved up her legs as if a cold draft had suddenly found its way under her skirts.

"I should not speak of such things—your mother would have my eyeteeth—but after you marry and then deliver an heir, you might seek your pleasure elsewhere. Do you understand what I mean?"

She did drop the plate then and stood staring dumbly at the yellow yolk splattered on her skirt. "I do not wish to speak of it," she whispered.

She heard her father trying to rise out of his seat.

"I need to change, please excuse me." She ran to the door and up the stairs to her room. Her chest hurt at the realization that there was no love in her parents' marriage, and she had no hope of anything better.

Lydia stared at Victor, wondering if it was ever her curse to be accused of being too masculine. Except he was not regarding her with the horror that she had heard in Oscar's voice.

In fact, Victor swallowed audibly and said with a rough edge to his voice, "You should not stand directly in front of the lamp, pet. Unless of course you are trying to make me insane."

Lydia twisted, looking at the lamp behind her. She caught a glimpse of herself in the cheval glass. With the light behind her, the outline of her body was clearly visible through the nightshirt. She stared at her reflection, noting the slim feminine form. Female, yes. Curvy and voluptuous, no. But not male. She did not know that she had ever paid attention to her body before dressing as a boy. Her height and the lack of female influence in her life had always made her feel out of place, as if she did not quite belong within the ranks of women.

Yet, it was clear she was not male. Pretending to be Leonard proved that much to her.

She tried to form the thoughts that seemed hazy and vague. "I do not wish to be a man. My brothers have all taken positions in the company, and although I am just as capable of understanding shipping, I would never be allowed to contribute to running the family business. I cannot earn my own way in the world, unless I masquerade as a man."

Victor stood and moved behind her. He put his hands on her hips. "So you became Leonard as a means of seeking your independence?"

"My freedom. My self-reliance. To prove that I did not need men to make my every decision for me. That I could stand on my own two feet and support myself. To hear them, when I became a woman, I became incapable of rational thought. My brothers and father discount my . . ." Lydia took a deep breath realizing how miserable their disregard for her opinions had made her feel. "They never listen to me."

Victor met her eyes in the looking glass. His fingers tightened on her hips. He waited patiently.

All of a sudden, Lydia felt stupid. What must he think of her? "I suppose because I lost my mother when I was so young, I do not have a proper appreciation of the benefits of being a woman. I just . . ."

"What would your father have done with his business, if he had no sons?"

Lydia shrugged. "Sell it all outright or try to find

a husband for me to marry who could run everything."

"Mmm."

What was he thinking? She wanted to run back in the other room and jump into the bed and pull the sheets over her head. He probably thought she was suffering from hysteria and when she was done he would pat her on the head and tell her she was a pea goose, or she should not worry about a thing. Her heart thudded painfully under her ribcage. "I have never been very feminine."

"I cannot believe I could ever mistake you for a boy." He rocked her hips lightly. "Your proportions were all wrong."

Lydia closed her eyes and dropped her chin. "It is my height. I know of no other woman so tall."

He was silent for a long time. Although she had her eyes closed, she could feel his gaze on her. Finally he said, "I should introduce you to Felicity."

He had lost her.

"Who is Felicity?"

"Sheridan's wife." He inched closer. She could feel the heat of his body behind her. A powerful wave of yearning swept through her.

"The man I shot?" Lydia winced. The woman would likely hate her on principle.

"Yes, but you see, she runs all the business left to her son by her first husband. There are manufactories and mines, a shipping company and even a sugar plantation in the West Indies. I do not know of anyone, man or woman, who manages so much with so much success, not even my father-in-law. Her advice as I was rebuilding my fortunes was invaluable."

He knew a woman with business success, and admired her for it? Excitement coursed through Lydia's veins. His long elegant fingers shifted on her hips and a different kind of thrill pulsed through her.

"But you have to admit, pet, that your choices have not always been sensible."

Disappointment curdled her blood, and she crossed her arms in front of her reflection. "I managed until you came along."

"You were about to be beaten senseless when I came along. And your actions have in part led you here, where you had better hope my valet brings that tray soon."

She twisted out of his grasp, disappointed that he had seemed to understand her, yet not. "I was here in London for almost three months. I supported myself by gaming, but I was getting by. I did not depend on any man."

"Is allowing a man to protect you so terrible?" he asked, stepping toward her. His eyes were dark and bottomless, his breathing too rapid and visible. A strong and rapid pulse thrummed in his throat. "I could have killed you, those brutes at the gaming hell could have killed you. If anyone had penetrated your disguise, you could have been raped or worse."

"I thought you understood. I do not want to be dependent on any man to think for me, to decide what I should and should not do, to, to . . . to—"

"Speak for you when you cannot form the words?" He lifted one eyebrow.

She wanted to smack him. "To override my decisions."

He folded his arms and glowered at her. "As

addlepated as your decisions have been, I have never countermanded them."

Lydia opened her mouth to speak, but instead she gaped like a fish out of water. He had forced her to follow his dictates. Or had he?

"I should, though. I should put you on a ship back to America or send you to stay with Keene and Sophie. You should not be here."

She clenched her hands together. He may not let her do as she pleased, but he gave her options and honored her choices. "I could go back to my apartments and take care of myself." Although she knew as she spoke that the burden of her care would be too much for Jenny alone until she was better.

"Bloody hell! If you want to earn a living so badly you turn your back on honest proposals and your family's protection, then name your price and I will take you as my mistress."

Lydia could not have been more shocked if he had thrown a bucket of water over her head. "I'm not a whore."

He stared at her, his chest still heaved. "No, but I would make you one."

Her heart pounded in her chest and heat rolled off of him, charging the air like a storm on the verge of breaking. Undercurrents hung heavy and ominous.

She wanted to explore the dangerous world of making love to him, but not as a transaction. Not as a business exchange. Not when he would take all the responsibility for what was done and hate himself for it.

She reached out and pressed her fingers against his chest. She could feel his thundering heartbeat, feel his gasp, feel the power of desire burning through his skin. She was tempted, oh, so tempted, but, "Not like this, and never for a price."

His expression went stark. "Oh, hell, pet, I am sorry."

"No, you are not sorry. You are relieved."

She turned and went back into his room, carefully shutting the door between the two rooms. He was relieved, and she was furious. Her hands shook as she dropped the shawl on the foot of the bed. Dawn crept through the cracks in the drapes, but never had she felt more bleak.

CHAPTER 13

Helena waited until her footman thumped the brass knocker of the house in a respectable middle-class neighborhood and the door opened. She stuffed her hands in her muff and descended the carriage steps.

As she approached the doorway, her footman stepped to the side. A middle-aged woman wearing a large white apron and utilitarian mobcap stood in the doorway.

"I need to speak with Doctor Knighton," Helena said. "Is he available?"

The woman cast a glance at the footman and Helena's maid, who stood behind her. "He's been all night delivering a baby and he's washing up now."

Helena waited, uncertain if that was an answer.

The woman threw open the door. "Come in, my lady, I'll tell him you're here. I'm Nurse Antton."

The footman would have announced Helena when the door opened, so she did not respond. She followed the woman into a small antechamber with straight chairs lining the unadorned walls. A young woman with a very large belly slumped listlessly in one of the chairs.

The nurse clopped across the bare hardwood

floor and entered a door on the far side of the room. After saying a few muffled words, she turned and announced, "My lady, the doctor will see you now."

The listless young woman looked up, flattened her lips, then shifted her gaze away.

"I shall not take long," whispered Helena as she passed her.

Helena entered a room with smells that reminded her of the tooth drawer's office. However, instead of a chair that leaned back, there was a high, narrow table in the center of the space, with odd stirrups fitted to the end. A wooden stool sat at the stirrup end, and Helena blanched thinking how the two might be used together.

Moveable white screens on iron rods ate up a lot of the floor space. Jars of all sizes and contents filled the shelves lining one wall. Lying on a cabinet top were odd metal instruments, including ones that looked like giant hinged spoons.

The doctor stood with his back to the room, splashing his hands in a washbowl. A few instruments dripped on a towel-covered table next to him. Had she stepped into a torture chamber?

He glanced over his shoulder at her and nodded toward the screens. "You can step behind the screen and have your maid help you get undressed."

His command was so unexpected, Helena froze.

He turned, his expression impatient and tired. "There are wrappers on hooks you might wear, but do hurry. I have other patients to see."

He had mistaken her for a patient. "I . . . I am not with child."

He seemed to slump. "Oh, that is why you did not

summon me to your home. Well, I do not deal in that. You may ask Nurse Antton for the name of one of the midwives who might give you advice."

"No, you don't understand," said Helena. She winced, thinking she could have phrased her correction more mildly. Gentleman do not like to be corrected. She started again to clarify, "I have been unclear—"

"You either want assistance with becoming pregnant or you want to prevent it. I do not deal with such matters. Now, if you please, I have had a difficult night, and I have patients who need me."

Helena blinked. "My mother." She looked down at her toes. Were there ways to indulge in sins of the flesh and prevent pregnancy? She had never even thought such a thing possible. Women had to stay pure until their marriage night for that very reason, while men were under no such restriction. "My mother is with child. Her physician recommended she consult with a specialist, with you, because of her age."

The doctor wiped his wet hands on a towel. "I apologize. I gravely mistook the matter."

Helena gave a tiny shake of her head. "I am sure I do not know of what you speak, but my father has requested I solicit your services, and I thought it best that you are warned that my mother is not . . . not likely to be a good patient, before you actually called upon her."

He met her eyes as if measuring her.

"My father and I are quite concerned about my mother, although she is in good health and did give birth to my sisters and me, but it has been a good many years."

"Give your direction to Nurse Antton and I will call on your mother this afternoon."

"Thank you, sir."

He looked like he wanted to say something, but was uncertain, and Helena hoped her embarrassing interest in preventing pregnancy was not apparent in her telltale skin.

He opened the door and Helena walked across the floor. Biting her lip, she wrote out her direction in a ledger book Nurse Antton opened for her. She sent her maid out to the carriage as she handed back the pen. She looked behind her and saw the room was filling with young women in various states of breeding, along with a baby or two.

Now or never.

Helena leaned across the table. "Mrs. Antton, the doctor mentioned that you could give me the direction of a certain midwife."

The nurse looked up and her cherubic face crinkled in a frown. "You do not have need—"

"For my mother," Helena spoke in a rushed whisper. "After she has the baby, she wants to be sure this does not happen again. With her years, she fears . . ."

Helena knew her face was flaming.

The nurse looked down and Helena feared everyone in the room stared at her, and Mrs. Antton could see right through her lie.

"I'll see whoever is next," said the doctor behind her and Helena nearly jumped out of her skin. He would be in her house, discussing everything with her parents . . . Oh my heavens, what had she done?

Victor had made sure his houseguest ate a decent

breakfast. Her winces and the gingerly way she moved convinced him her pain was greater than she would admit to. He insisted she take another dose of the laudanum. Her listless acceptance said it all. He told her the pain would lessen in a few days.

He sat beside her bed until she fell asleep. As the furrows between her light brown eyebrows smoothed out, he knew the pain medication was taking effect. He bent forward, resting his elbows on his knees. What was he to do with her?

What she had said about coming to England because she had no opportunity to live an independent life at home worried him. He could take her to one of the many bluestocking societies, give her the Wollstonecraft woman's book on the rights of women, introduce her to Felicity or try and to convince her she had better resign herself to her lot as a woman.

She could not live as a man forever, nor did he have the right to force her to be his mistress. Bloody hell, when he thought of the way she made him feel, he could not seem to remember that she was injured by his own hand.

He had thought he had learned a measure of self-control living with Mary Frances all those years, but his impulses toward Leonard were uncontrollable. Thank goodness she had possessed enough sense to reject his outrageous proposal to make her his mistress, although it was the time-honored fashion for an independent woman to make a living.

As soon as her maid woke and entered the room, Victor went out. He walked to Sheridan's house, knowing he owed Felicity an apology.

He found the Sheridans in the morning room, and he was surprised to find Felicity perched on the arm of the chair where Tony sat with his injured leg propped on a footstool.

Victor walked over in front of her and bowed. "My deepest apologies for your husband's wound, madam. I should not have embroiled Tony in my mess."

"I blame those awful pistols. I told Tony not to bring them home last time. Do sit down and tell us how your young friend is doing." Felicity's brown eyes held nothing but sincerity and welcome. "Tony explained the accident to me."

"Uh, er, Leonard is fine, fast asleep when I left. It was just a flesh wound." Did everyone know of his sponsorship of Leonard?

Victor sat down as instructed. Immediately he felt pinned by Tony's pale gaze.

Bloody hell, could the man see straight into one's soul? Victor shook off the feeling. If Tony could see how very dark Victor's soul was, Victor would not be allowed in the house.

"Are you ready for the season?" asked Felicity. "We have been speculating on how many handkerchiefs might be tossed in your direction this year."

Victor shuddered. He supposed in the marriage mart he might be considered a great catch, because now he had not only the title, but the wealth to go with it. Assuming that the lack of a standing house on his estate was only a minor drawback, all said. "I am in mourning."

"Oh, well, you must give me a wink if you find yourself swarmed too unmercifully," Felicity said with a little smile. "You are coming to our dinner, are you not?"

"I would not miss it," said Victor, wondering if he could cry off later.

"You should bring your young American gentleman, too."

"No!" Victor winced. "The wound . . . will not be healed by then."

Now, Tony really stared at him.

Felicity seemed in a mood that nothing fazed her. "At first, I thought to call it off, but Tony assured me he would be well enough by then. Besides, he will be glad of the excuse to avoid the dancing afterward."

She rubbed her hand across her husband's shoulder and the two exchanged a look so full of tender meaning, Victor felt like an intruder. He rarely saw Felicity and Tony together, although they had been married a couple of years now. Usually he ran into Tony at masculine haunts, while his wife spent most of her time with her ledgers.

"I am surprised you are not closeted with your work," Victor said, and then wished he could bite out his tongue.

She smiled. "Ah, I should be. I have much to do today, along with the plans for the party. I do seem to have a surfeit of women accepting my invitations this year."

"Really," said Tony, his eye on Victor.

"Are you sure you would not like to bring your friend? I thought inviting him would be a way I could show him that I bear him no ill will for shooting Tony."

Victor shook his head, not trusting himself to open his mouth for fear he would blurt out that *his friend* would make her too-many-women problem worse. And he was not taking not-Leonard out as a male ever again. Victor rubbed his forehead. He wished he had never taken him anywhere in the first place.

"Lady Helena mentioned a Mr. Trevor Hamilton that she sent to you for advice, dear." Felicity turned toward her husband. "Perhaps he might be invited. I am sure I have heard that name before, and if Lady Helena knows him, he must be acceptable."

"Yes, I am expecting him and two of his companions this afternoon," Tony said.

Felicity brushed a kiss on Tony's cheek and slid off the arm of the chair. "I cannot dally any longer. If you will excuse me, Victor. I'm sure you gentlemen have things to discuss."

Victor stood and bowed, while Felicity left the room. When he turned back to Tony, the man eyeballed him.

Victor paced away. "I thought she would be angrier."

"She was," said Tony.

Victor picked up a decorative marble ball and transferred it from hand to hand. "What eased her mind?"

"Ah," said Tony.

Victor turned and glared at him. "Do you never answer questions put to you?"

Tony grinned and stretched his arms overhead while looking incredibly smug. "She is reassured that my new injury does not interfere in my ability to perform my husbandly duties."

He shouldn't have asked, thought Victor. It reminded him he had a woman sleeping in his bed, a woman whom he should not touch, yet could not resist.

"What are you concealing about your little American friend?" asked Tony.

Victor turned away. "Nothing."

Tony waited.

His silence often made Victor feel he had to fill it in with the truth. Instead, he asked, "Have you learned anything of my mother-in-law?"

"Yes. Why don't you want to bring your friend to Felicity's party?"

Victor tossed the marble globe and caught it, feeling the heavy cold weight. "That, sir, is no concern of yours. What have you learned of why my wife's mother is in Newgate?"

"Sit and put that rock down. Are you sure you want to know?" Tony's expression turned stoic, then unreadable.

Dread crept up Victor's spine. If Tony thought he might not want the truth, then there was probably good reason for it.

Victor carefully placed the decorative ball down and returned to his chair. "I need to know."

"You might think better of it." Tony gave one last shot. "Why are you hiding your American friend?"

Victor popped up again. "Bloody hell, what do you know?"

"Nothing, just guessing."

Victor raked a hand through his hair. Had Tony used a he or she in reference to Leonard? Or had he avoided the subject the same way Victor did?

"My lips are sealed in any case. I have not even mentioned my suspicions to Felicity." Tony said. "Although the curse is beginning to make sense to me."

"What do you suspect?" demanded Victor. He did not know why he bothered; Tony always got at the bottom of every mystery.

"Sit. I'll tell you what I learned about your mother-in-law. I warn you that part of her sad tale concerns your late wife."

Victor suspected as much. He also suspected Tony would not tell until he knew beyond a doubt that Leonard was a woman. Hell's bells, how would he ever preserve her reputation if everyone knew his protégé was really his protégée?

Trevor stared at the engraved invitation in his hand. He'd meant to say no, but the major's wife had startled him when she said, "Lady Helena has already accepted. You do know Lady Helena Bosworth, do you not?"

"Other than the invitation to dine, that was a waste," said Oscar.

"Who is this Lady Helena?" asked James.

"I got the feeling he knows where Lydia is," Trevor said, choosing to reply to Oscar rather than answer his brother's question. "And it is dinner and dancing afterward."

"Trevor," said James sternly, pulling rank on him. He'd meant never to see Lady Helena again. "Perhaps we should hire a runner." Get the business of finding Lydia done and leave England and never return.

"I thought you just said you think Major Sheridan knows where Lydia is." James pushed a chair back in the inn where they had stopped for their evening meal. "He's very hard to read."

"I'm not sure he is a very good investigator. He did not ask much after learning how she looks," Oscar said.

Trevor laid the invitation down on the table top. He'd hoped this Major Sheridan would solve their problem quickly, and they could be on their way home to America. "That is why I believe he already knows where she is."

"Then why not have done with it and tell us?" Oscar rubbed his forehead. "What reason could he have to keep silent?"

"He does not know positively? Maybe he only has strong suspicions," offered James. "In any case, he only asked for two days before he will report his findings."

"Report if he has findings," corrected Trevor. How could it be that if Lydia was here in London, he had not run across her? He had spent the last few days walking every byway and lane where a young woman or woman pretending to be a young man might be found in this city.

He had not seen Lydia, but every woman bore a striking resemblance to Lady Helena until he got close enough to see they were not her.

Lydia shifted listlessly on the bed. She rotated her wounded shoulder and lifted and lowered her arm a few times. Victor had told her she needed to start moving her arm in spite of the pain, or the stiffness might become permanent. Other than that, he had hardly said boo to her in the last couple of days.

At first, he had been in such a dark mood that she thought it best to leave him be, but then as she realized he was avoiding her, exiting the room the minute she woke, locking the door between their two rooms at night, she tried to convince him to stay to talk to her.

Truth to tell, she was bored to tears, even though an eclectic selection of books had shown up in her room. From several marble-paper-jacketed books, which contained light fiction from Minerva Press, to Mary Wollstonecraft's treatise about the rights of women, as well as *Emma,* by Jane Austen.

She'd read them all, and she was tired of reading. She wanted to do something. Her shoulder was on the mend and she bore the pain without the laudanum. She should just return to her apartments and be done with this odd business of living with Victor.

A tap on her door made her heart leap. She ought not to be so ridiculously happy to see him. Besides, it was more likely to be Jenny or Victor's valet, the only two servants allowed in his bedroom.

"Come in," she called.

"Where is your maid?" Victor asked as he entered the room with several packages wrapped with brown paper and tied with twine in one arm and a hat box dangling from his other. He kicked the door shut with his heel.

"I am sure I don't know," said Lydia.

"I thought you might wish to go for a walk." He dumped the packages on the bed. "If you are feeling well enough."

As usual, he hardly glanced her way as he spoke.

"I would like nothing better." His distance made her eager anticipation drain away.

"Should you not open these?" He gestured toward the packages. Then he looked at her.

Her heart missed a beat as she drank in his dark gaze. But she was uncertain of his intent. She lowered her chin, before he could read her hungry expression. She wanted just one tiny spark of acknowledgement that those kisses and caresses were real, not a laudanum-induced hallucination.

She reached for the package on top and undid
the string. After pushing aside the paper, she unfolded a morning dress of pale blue silk with a
ruched bodice and embroidered green leaves
along the hemlines of the skirt and long sleeves.

She looked up at him.

"Should I duck?"

She shook her head, failing to understand. He had
bought her a dress, a beautiful dress. Did he really
see her as a woman? Want to see her as a woman? Yet
she could not accept such a gift without being fully
aware of the implications. Men bought their mis-
tresses dresses. She clasped the gown to her chest,
feeling tears sting at her eyelids. "Why?"

"I was not sure if you would want to throw something at me or would be pleased. I had my tailor
take your measurements to a dressmaker. If it fits
well, we should order more dresses for you. Jenny
says you only have the traveling dress you wore
when you left Boston." He paced away from the
bed. "There is a pelisse and muff in one of the
other bundles."

"I cannot accept such gifts from you."

"Think of it as compensation for the death of
Lenny."

"I'm not sure that I am ready—"

He turned and leaned his palms on the bed.
"Lenny has to go, Lydia Margaret Hamilton."

Dear God, when had he learned her name? Her
full name? She stared at him, too shocked to speak.

"You have two brothers and a fiancé in London
looking for you, and we need to talk about what you
should do." He pushed away from the bed. "What
you want to do. We have to walk, because I cannot

keep my mind on any subject beyond seducing you while we are in my bedroom."

He walked across the room and put his hand on the door.

Fear and doom crashed together in her heart, jolting her with the unpleasant wash of sea-cold dread. Was he taking her to them? And Oscar had come too?

A thud and shouts drifted up the stairs. Fiddlesticks, had her brothers learned where she was and come to rescue her?

"He's not here." She heard Millars call out.

"I'm going to kill him! I'm going to kill them both!" came the next shout.

Lydia stared at the door and Victor, not recognizing the voice. Was it Oscar? She had not heard him in months, yet the rage and anguish was clear.

Lydia could hear the futile protests of "Sir, please come away. Sir! Sir!" from the servants.

Victor had paled. He turned toward her. "Hide."

His one-word command jolted her into action. Lydia scrambled off the bed and yanked back the wardrobe door. She scrambled in among Victor's black jackets and waistcoats.

She heard the bedroom door open, and Victor sounded as calm as ever as he spoke. "Hello, George."

Who on God's green earth was George?

CHAPTER 14

George planted a hand in the middle of Victor's chest and shoved. With his other hand, George waved the letter Victor had sent him. His face mottled with anger. "What the bloody hell do you mean by this?"

"I thought it fairly straightforward." Victor glanced over his shoulder to make sure that Lydia was out of sight. "I meant what I wrote."

George followed his line of sight and must have seen the dress on the bed. "Is she here?" He dropped the letter and wrapped both his hands around Victor's neck.

"Your wife?" Victor managed to sputter out. Fearful that Lydia would take it into her head to rescue him, he clawed at the fingers around his neck. Had he cast himself into a coil too tangled to unwind?

"Where is she?"

Veins popped out on Victor's forehead and spots danced before his eyes. With all the equanimity he possessed, he folded his arms and pointed one finger at George's murderous grip.

A contingent of his servants burst into the room and pulled George free of him. Millars must have assembled reinforcement. Victor sucked in a lung-filling gasp. "I cannot very well . . . answer questions . . . while you are choking me," he managed to get out between rasping breaths.

He pointed to the door. "Everyone out."

His footmen looked unsure.

"Go ahead, release him."

Wide-eyed maids filled the doorway. All he needed now was for Lydia to pop out of the wardrobe and all his precautions to keep her identity secret would be for naught.

"I shall not tussle with you, George. I find it undignified these days. Perhaps we could go downstairs and discuss this like gentlemen over . . . tea." He wanted brandy, but George no longer drank, at least not that Victor knew.

George's chest heaved and he looked mad as a tortured bull in an arena.

"Or we could air all our dirty linen in front of the servants," Victor glared at his staff, "who cannot be trusted to keep gossip to themselves."

Several of the maids must have recalled their duties as they backed away from the door. The footmen released George and filed out of the room. He hoped none of them noticed the dress on the bed, or their speculation about his pet boy would really run rampant.

George stepped forward and shoved him anyway. "I ought to call you out."

Victor brushed at his sleeve. "I've had my quota of duels for the month, nor would I care to roll in the mud with you again. Is it not time we moved past this animosity?"

George stared at him as if he had grown horns. Since the man had hated him for half a decade,

Victor suspected the concept of being friends once again was beyond him.

"For Regina's sake, as well as my new godchild's," prompted Victor.

"Where is my wife?"

"I should imagine she is home, or if not, you might ascertain if she is with Sophie. They do spend a fair amount of time together."

"Why would you send me such a note?" asked George, the fight draining out of him. He sat heavily on a chair, leaned over and buried his face in his hands.

"Why would you refuse to make love to your wife?" Victor asked softly. He glanced toward the wardrobe. He did not want to have this conversation here. "Come, let us go downstairs."

George shook his head, paying him no mind. "It is not right. It is only for procreation and I take too much pleasure in our congress."

"That has to be the stupidest thing I have ever heard."

"What do you know? You have no religion or God," George lashed out.

Inexplicably, his words hurt, but Victor was determined to make his point. "We both know Amelia is too passionate a creature to be ignored. If you will not share her bed, she will take a lover, so all your morality shall be for naught." He had to get George out of his room, out of the earshot of Lydia. "Besides, the midwives say that regular intercourse helps ease the pains of childbirth. Would you deny her that?"

George dropped his hands and his eyes were red-rimmed. "Are you quite sure?"

Victor looked him straight in the eye and lied as

he never had lied before, and then calculated how much he would have to pay a midwife or an accoucheur to attest to his fabrication. Could one bribe a minister to tell George relations between man and wife were never a sin?

Then, just to be double-sure George understood him, Victor kicked his boot. "You should thank God every day that he gave you a wife who gives you much pleasure. God does not love me so."

George scowled at him.

Out of the corner of his eye, Victor saw the wardrobe door move. No!

Lady Helena walked as quickly as she could with her head down to the address given to her by Nurse Antton. She had left her carriage standing at the curb and her maid in a greengrocer's waiting on an order. Helena's heart pounded with fear. She would be found out. Her servants would report her absence to her parents. The midwife would take too long, refuse to give her the information she sought, or would not even be there.

But all those fears proved inconsequential. There had been a few moments of discomfort as Helena had to ask the midwife to explain how the device she was given was to be used, and Helena had made an awful excuse that she was to be married soon, but that she and her imaginary husband were planning a continental trip and they both felt it unwise to be encumbered by a pregnancy during their travels.

All the while, she was sweating each second that ticked by. Finally the transaction was complete, her silver handed over and the device wrapped in brown paper. The midwife gave her a final warning that the method was not foolproof, and not to be stingy with the lemon juice.

Her mission accomplished, Helena ducked out of the midwife's inner chamber only to find herself face to face with Amelia Keeting and Sophie Davies.

The two women stared at her as if just as shocked as she was to find her in such a place. But they were both married and had children; they probably had every need for the services of a midwife.

"Why, good day, Lady Helena," said Sophie. "How are you?"

Helena did not know how she did it, but she stumbled through a greeting and then excused herself as her maid was waiting. She could not help but hear Amelia ask, "Why do suppose she is here? You do not think . . . do you?"

Helena turned around. "I have been handling many of my mother's errands, while she . . . while she rests."

Fearing at her age miscarriage was more likely than a baby, Lady Caine had insisted there was no reason to bandy about the news of her pregnancy, and Helena was sworn to secrecy.

Amelia lowered her gaze.

"Send your mother our best wishes then." Sophie's gaze moved to the parcel in Helena's hand.

Helena stumbled out the door. Stars above, they did not believe her. And why should they? She was not here on any errand for her mother. Could she trust them not to gossip? Would her final season be clouded with rumors and speculation?

How could she land Wedmont if there was the slightest blot on her reputation? They were both friends to him. Even if they did not spread their knowledge of her errand throughout the *ton*, would their friendship obligate them to warn the earl? She looked down at the package in her hand and wondered if she had deliberately sown the seeds of her own destruction.

Lydia strained to hear what was said to this George. Victor lowered his voice. She leaned her ear against the cupboard door, and the unlatched door began to swing open.

She grabbed one of Victor's jackets to keep from tumbling out onto the floor.

"The dress is for whom?" George asked.

"A friend," answered Victor. "What are you about?"

"Where is she hiding?"

"No one is under the bed, George. I swear to you Amelia is not here."

Lydia froze, fearing the inevitable discovery. What would her brothers think? What would Oscar say? What would Victor do?

Nothing. He had already warned her that he would not offer marriage even if he seduced her, and he had offered a slip on the shoulder instead.

She could go home and marry Oscar, masquerade as a boy until she was found out again, or become Victor's mistress. Of all the choices, becoming Victor's mistress held the most appeal but the least sense of worth. Could she live with herself if she lived with him?

"I swear on Reggie's health that your wife is not here and has never been here in my room, or alone with me in any of my bedrooms," Victor said, just the other side of the wardrobe. Clearly, he did not want George to discover Lydia while looking for Amelia.

Apparently that avowal convinced George, because shortly afterward Lydia heard the bedroom door close.

She waited until she was sure the bedroom was empty, then she eased open the door.

Feeling slightly ridiculous, she tiptoed across the floor. As she neared the bed, she saw the letter on the floor.

She picked it up, looking at the address that she had seen Victor write out that night, the night when she had gone into his bedroom because she could not sleep. She turned it over, wondering what words had brought George Keeting storming in from the countryside and ready to throttle Victor.

If you will not make love to your wife, I will.
Wedmont

Lydia's head spun as she realized George was married to Amelia and clearly both men had intimate knowledge of her passion—was that how Victor had phrased it?

She rubbed her forehead, remembering her jealousy of Amelia at Victor's dinner. Had he gone to visit Amelia after Keene had interrupted their kisses that first time? He had written the letter that night. What other conclusion could she draw?

Lydia's hands began to shake. Did Victor make love to her by night and Amelia by afternoon?

And who was this Reggie? Regina? Another woman in Victor's life?

Pain twisted in Lydia's stomach. She sank to her

knees on the carpet. Was there anything special about the kisses they shared? Or was it just that she was convenient, sleeping in his bed and foolishly giving him every indication she would willingly indulge in pleasures of the flesh? He had warned her in so many ways that he would not treat her seduction as anything that might require redress. What was she doing here?

Every avenue in her life led nowhere and this one was no exception. She had been running from the reality of her life so fast that she had never really looked forward to see her destination. She had always thought if she ran fast enough and far enough, a magical solution to her problems would appear.

The door swung open and Jenny came in. "The master says I am to get you dressed for an outing. Whatever are you doing on the floor?"

Lydia stood slowly and folded the letter. "Nothing."

"Oh, miss, what a lovely dress!" Jenny scooped the pale blue silk off the bed.

"Yes, one should always wear a beautiful gown to one's own funeral."

Jenny turned around, puzzled.

"Two of my brothers and Oscar are here, and I am told Leonard must die." Lydia set the letter down on the dresser. "I suppose he is taking me to them."

As much as she hated the thought, Leonard had to go. Life had caught up to her, in spite of her running away. Now she had to decide what to do with her future.

With their enmity set aside for an uneasy accord, Victor was finally rid of George. Victor gave the signal to Millars, and then met Lydia at the garden gate near the stable entrance.

"Anyone see her?" he asked Millars and Jenny.

"No, milord," they answered in unison. Then Jenny giggled.

Lydia's face was hidden behind the drawn-down veil of her poke bonnet. He'd purchased it thinking that the wide brim would hide her face and the full crown would conceal her sun-bright hair. As he looked her over, the only thing she had in common with Lenny was her height. Few women were so tall.

Yet she was beautiful, willowy and slender. The ripples of silk caressed her gentle curves. Victor swallowed hard, thinking of her long, long legs, thinking of the nearly sheer undergarments she wore, thinking of the way she had kissed his scar.

He had worked to stay away from her, visiting Keene, visiting their half-sister Margaret. He'd found Margaret barefoot in the dirt, her chickens scrabbling around her feet. Although he'd talked with her briefly as she scattered corn for them, he'd spent more time with her husband, whose elegant shudder spoke volumes about his wife's interest in her chickens.

It did not matter how long Victor stayed away. Two seconds in Lydia's presence and he wanted to bed her, laugh with her, watch her concentrate over cards, but mostly he wanted to kiss her from now until eternity.

"I cannot conceive of why you would ever want to abandon dresses," Victor told Lydia.

She turned her head away.

He extended his arm. "Stay back several yards, Millars."

She slowly put her hand on his sleeve and he led

her down the alley, to the street. He thought if they walked through the neighborhoods they might have more of a chance at uninterrupted conversation. She needed to decide what she wanted to do. He already regretted buying a bonnet that hid her face so well.

Dressed as a woman, she seemed much more subdued than she had ever been as Leonard.

"That was meant to be a compliment, Lydia." He liked the way her name rolled off his tongue.

"Yes, thank you," she said.

"You must tell me if your shoulder is bothering you, or if you need to rest," he said, concerned that she was perhaps not up to walking. He slowed his pace, which he realized had been rather brisk.

"I'm fine."

"Then why so Friday-faced?" Was it because she knew she would have to leave his home? The thought made him pause too. He was not ready for her to leave, yet he knew that if she stayed he would make her his lover. Even now he wanted to stop and push up her veil and kiss her senseless, in spite of the passing traffic.

"Are you taking me to my brothers?"

Was there any significance in that she did not include her fiancé in her question? "Not this minute. Is that what you want? I could find out where they are staying and deliver you to them."

Her hand tightened on his arm.

He wanted to wrap his arm around her waist and pull her closer to him. "I do not presume that I could hide you forever."

She stopped walking. "No, I would guess not. Nor should you want to do so."

"On the contrary, pet, I should like to keep you to

myself forever." He could resist no longer and lifted the thick netting that obscured her face. Folding the mesh lace back over the brim, he searched her face.

Her blue eyes were wide and wary and her expression pinched. She lowered her gaze. He touched her cheek with his fingers, wanting to comfort her, yet not certain why she appeared so distraught.

Her skin was silky soft, calling him to make everything right for her. But how? Keene's admonition that he would have to marry her echoed in his head, but how could he? That would only transfer her care from one male to another, and he was the last person she should trust. He would destroy her and cause her immeasurable pain. That was what he did.

"What do you wish to do?"

She stepped back, away from his caress, and turned her head so he was left staring at the straw of her bonnet. "I do not know. Becoming Leonard was the only way I could be free."

He felt bereft, shut out and his heart slogged heavily in his chest. "Lydia, I do not pretend to understand your fierce need for independence, and I do not know that I can offer you any solution that would accomplish what you want, but I have thought much on what you said."

He folded his arms behind his back, rather than reach out and hold her. "I know there are a few women who make their own way in the world by writing, and I recalled that Lady Beauchamp has a successful enterprise of making fancy cards for St. Valentine's Day. She pens love poems on them."

Lydia turned to look at him. Relief flowed through him like a well-warmed brandy. How could just her willingness to look upon him make him intoxicated?

"I fear I have no talent for writing. I have thought much on my predicament too. There are a few women who make their own living by their art. Those who paint well can sell their paintings, and there are a few women writing books. I have no special talents in the arts. My artistic skills are passable at best."

"You give yourself too little credit," he said, but what did he know? He had never heard her sing or seen her draw or even compose a letter, let alone a poem or novel.

"A few women gain a measure of control over a business by inheritance." She shrugged. "Either from a husband or father who has no sons."

"And your father has many sons."

"And a business weakened by the years of war between France and England. Three of our ships were impressed into English service. Trevor recovered one of them through the courts, but . . . even if my father wanted to, he could not stake me in a business venture. As a woman, I cannot gain experience or footing by employment in a company."

"I could offer you venture capital."

She grimaced. "Then I might consider myself bought and sold. I have taken more from you than I should. I already feel half whore, wearing clothes you've bought for me." She gestured at the gown and then resumed walking.

Victor winced. His offer to make her his mistress was a raw wound. Bloody hell, he had watched her innocence die when he had made that statement, demand, whatever insanity it had been.

He had bought her a day dress that was suitable

for a married woman, not an innocent. His blood ran cold and the desire he felt for her seemed a seedy thing, a cruel and hateful need.

He should deliver her to her brothers and fiancé, but he could not bring himself to do so. He had to walk doubly fast to catch up with her rapid pace.

"Lydia, I can only offer my apologies again. I said unforgivable things, and I have no excuse. I have done many unforgivable things to you." Beyond shooting her, he had compromised her; only Keene's interruption had prevented him from taking her virtue. "I want you to stay in England. I would continue our friendship. But it is not about what I want. What do you want?"

She abruptly stopped again, and he brushed against her before he could stop himself. He had just the barest sense of her body, curved and oh-so feminine, nestling perfectly against his hip. A shudder passed through him. His blood heated as the primitive urge to just make her his fired through him.

He stepped to the side before he reached for her, before he said the hell with conventions and propriety, and carried her back to his bedroom, the consequences be damned.

"What I would have said I wanted when I woke this morning is different than what I would say now. I think it is clear that I must go back to Boston and marry Oscar."

Victor raked a shaking hand through his hair, feeling outraged and wounded and desperate to keep her here in England, near him in some way. "Do you want to marry him?"

She narrowed her eyes at him and gave the tiniest shake of her head. "No, but it is clear I cannot manage on my own. You were right, I have not always made sensible choices. I have been nearly beaten, shot, seduced, robbed—"

"When were you robbed?" interrupted Victor. What else did he not know about?

"Before I met you, so you cannot take blame for that."

Her dismissal did not entirely ease his mind, but she would hate him harping on it. "You were not entirely seduced, not if you are talking about me."

She stared into his eyes half a second and he felt his world tilt as if everything could right itself, then she made a dismissing gesture with her hand.

She turned to walk away. He grabbed her arm, spun her and pulled her up against his chest. "I could show you the difference."

She stepped back, and he was losing her. His soul wrenched. He should be used to loss by now.

"Ah, pet, stay for the season and we will find you a rich old man on death's door to marry and make you an independently wealthy widow."

She pushed him away.

"Lyddie, it was just a jest."

She turned and looked at him, pain filling her eyes. "My mother is the only one who ever called me that," she whispered.

Oh, God—he had wounded her again, by choosing a pet name that reminded her of the loss of her mother.

She dashed the heel of her hand against her cheeks. "I won't cry. I know you hate it."

"I hated it when you were Leonard."

She sniffed, and looked skeptically at him.

His heart thudded in his chest. "All right, I hate

it now, too, because I want to fix anything that is wrong for you, and I do not know how. Perhaps that is part of why I found it so disagreeable when you pretended to be a boy."

She gave him a small smile, and he felt as if the world had bloomed around him.

"I do not believe you have smiled for days."

Which apparently were just the right words to chase the sunshine from her face. Would he never learn to keep his mouth buttoned shut?

He rubbed his forehead. They had not made any progress on deciding her future. "What do you want to do, Lydia? Whatever you want, I will move heaven and earth to make it so. If you want to stay in London, I am sure that at my request Keene and Sophie will sponsor you for the season."

She studied him with that intensity that made him want to grab her up and make love to her from now until forever.

"Just when I am prepared to hate you, I find I cannot," she said.

Emotion twisted and knotted in his gut. Even as he knew he should just deliver her to her relatives, he wanted to keep her with him. "You would do better to hate me. Both of us would do better if you hated me," he said. With that he braved the lethal edges of her poke bonnet, leaned in and kissed her.

CHAPTER 15

Victor was shown into the drawing room at Keene and Sophie's. Laughter spilled down from the nursery on the top floor. A pang of regret that he would never know the joy of a full nursery in his own home hit his heart.

Keene greeted him and asked him to sit.

"I shan't be long," said Victor. "I have just come to see if you are still willing to house Lydia."

"Uncle Keene, Uncle Keene, come quick." Regina burst through the drawing room doors, her little black shoes pattering across the carpet.

Seeing Reggie so carefree warmed Victor's heart.

"Aunt Sophie is stuck on the roof."

Keene turned white as a ghost and then raced out of the room, not stopping to look at the little girl.

Regina looked at Victor shyly. She dug a toe into the carpet and twisted her hands together in front of her. She looked toward the door Keene had just raced out of, then said, "Would you help?"

"I should be greatly honored." He bowed and reached out his hand. "Now where is Aunt Sophie?"

Regina put her little hand in his and tugged him toward the door. "In the nursery."

"Oh, I thought you said on the roof. I have had to

help rescue your aunt from a roof before. She is very bad about climbing on roofs when she should not. I hope you never do such a thing." Victor said as they took the stairs up. Where had Keene gone?

Regina looked up at him, her dark eyes serious. "It is only the dollhouse roof."

When he got to the nursery, Victor saw the problem.

"I am ever in a predicament," said Sophie. "Richard threw his tin soldier up here and see."

The chair she had used to climb onto the four-foot-high doll-house had tipped over. She was not so high up she could not slide down, but her dress had caught on a miniature chimney.

"I shall either rip the dress or destroy the chimney. I quite think the dress would be the lesser of two evils, but I am not sure which it shall be." Sophie giggled.

Victor walked over and untangled her skirts, just as Keene hit the door.

His half-brother leaned against the doorframe and glowered at his wife.

"Ah, now you will have to watch the children while I soothe his ruffled feathers," said Sophie as she slid down to the floor. "He will be quite angry that he was frightened only about the dollhouse chimney."

Sophie pressed a tin soldier in Victor's hand before she walked past her husband in the doorway. Only Victor noticed the heated glance she tossed her husband, who followed her without a word.

Victor wondered sometimes, if Sophie was not quite as feather-brained as she acted. Perhaps Keene had not been a dutiful husband lately. Sophie knew exactly how to fire her husband's blood.

Regina slipped her little hand in his. "You shall

have to help me with Richard," she said. "He can be very unruly."

"Yes, well, it is good to be unruly some of the time."

Reggie looked up at him skeptically. His heart twisted in his chest. He wanted to hold his daughter to him. Yet he knew he could never explain that Keene really was her uncle and Richard her cousin, and she should be more tolerant of family. But, unlike Victor, she would have more than ill-conceived, unacknowledged relationships in her life. She already had one half-sibling and another on the way.

"What would you like to do?" he asked her.

"I should like to have a tea party," said Regina primly. She gestured toward a small table in a corner where a doll slumped over a heartily disturbed tea set. "But he always knocks everything down." She frowned in the toddler's direction.

Victor's nephew sucked on a tin soldier.

"By all means let us take tea then, Miss Reggie. I'll see if I cannot restrain Master Richard's boisterousness." However, Victor had learned that channeling his nephew and godson's enthusiasm was easier than restraining him.

Victor had to drop his daughter's hand to remove the sticky little soldier from Richard's mouth. After wiping his hand and Richard's face on his handkerchief, Victor crossed the room to sit at the tiny table, his knees up to his ears. He helped Reggie arrange the miniature tea set.

He found he could distract Richard by rolling a ball across the floor for his nephew to retrieve.

How the *ton* would laugh to see him taking tea with a little girl, and rolling a ball across the floor and blocking his nephew from the tiny tea table.

But then the moment with family members, unacknowledged as they were, was precious to him.

He only had siblings through his father's nefarious activities, and he was always grateful for their acceptance of him. Keene's mother had been deeply hurt by what his father had done to her. The previous earl annihilated the friendship that had existed between his mother and Keene's since they were young girls. Victor did not doubt that Keene's mother's seduction and Keene's conception had been, at best, forced. The strain of bearing a son not her husband's had created wounds that still ached.

Yet, he had created almost the same situation when he fathered Reggie. Nothing he could do, not even coaxing a smile from Reggie as she served him imaginary tea, would make up for the harm he had wrought.

Lydia sat nervously on a gold brocade chair in the front drawing room of the Sheridans' home. In two days she had been moved from Victor's home and installed in a spare bedroom at Sophie and Keene's town home. Now she was to meet her brothers and fiancé. After a few discussions with her new guardians, they had decided that she would meet with her pursuers on neutral ground at the Sheridans'.

Felicity, Sophie, Keene, Tony, and Victor were all on hand, although Victor stood in the corner shadows just past the farthest window. Ever since that kiss on the street, where Millars had to interrupt them, Victor had kept well away from her, usually with several yards and a couple of pieces of furniture between them. His message was clear: Even if he wanted her, he did not want to want her, and saw his desire as only doomed for disaster.

First shown into the drawing room door and announced by the Sheridans' butler was her brother James, who did not wait for further introductions but crossed directly to her chair and loomed over her like a giant tree. "Do you know how worried we have been?"

She stood, knowing that James used his size to intimidate anyone who crossed him. "I am sorry for the worry I caused you, but I am fine."

She did a quick pirouette in front of him, knowing that he could not see the healing bullet wound through her high-necked, long-sleeved day dress. Nor could he see how much turmoil churned in her heart. On the surface, she was fine.

Oscar entered behind James, looked her over and said, "Why would you cut your hair?"

"Don't know too many boys with long hair," said Keene, stepping behind her chair.

"Oh, I much preferred short hair. If it were not that Keene hates it, I would keep mine short too. So much easier to care for," said Sophie. "Really, we do not need to be bound by archaic notions of fashion."

That Victor's friends were rallying around her, ready to protect her from the wrath of her own family felt odd, yet strangely comforting. She did not know that she needed protecting from her brothers, she just needed them to pay attention to what she said.

Trevor was the last to enter the room and he shouldered past James and Oscar and wrapped her in a bear hug. Mist clouded Lydia's eyes at the tight enfolding hold of his embrace.

She patted him on his broad shoulder and noticed his coat was new, tailored in tighter London fashion. A coat by Weston? Since when had Trevor been so enamored of style?

He leaned back and looked her over. "You look wonderful, Lydia." Although she noticed just the faintest of furrows between his brows. "Now, let us get your things and go home."

Trevor was the last one she would have expected to start ordering her about. Not that he listened to her any better than any of the other males in the family, he just usually left orders to the others. She had hoped he might be her best ally in selling her plans to stay in London.

"I'm not ready to go home." Lydia stumbled back from his embrace and found Oscar waiting his turn to embrace her, as if reminded he had the right of it as her fiancé. His rich mahogany hair glistened with bear grease, the reddish highlights darkened by the pomade. He looked as handsome as ever, his features chiseled like a fine Greek statue's, but Lydia thought that he looked almost too perfect, his hair too restrained.

As his arms came around her, she could not help but glance in Victor's direction. His hand blocked his face, his fingers on his scar as if he did not want to witness a happy reunion between her and her fiancé.

"Now, you must take tea, and I am sure that you have many things to discuss that cannot wait," said Felicity. "I assure you we will give you time alone with Lydia, but first let me introduce you."

As Oscar stepped back, Lydia felt relief, nothing

like the wrenching sense of loss she felt when Victor simply looked away from her.

Felicity led James by the arm. "This is Sophie Davies and her husband Keene; they are housing Lydia for her stay in London." She stopped in front of Victor. "And here is Lord Wedmont, who discovered our little Lydia and penetrated her disguise."

Trevor gasped and then glared in Victor's direction. Had he guessed that there was more than that? Did he know that she had been living in Victor's house, sleeping in his bed? How could Trevor suspect anything?

Victor bowed nonchalantly as if bored with the whole conversation.

"Exactly where did you find her?" asked Trevor, his tone belligerent.

Victor looked in his direction. "I discovered her in a gaming hell."

"What on earth were you doing in a gaming hell?" demanded Oscar.

"Winning," supplied Victor as he stepped out of the shadows. "I do believe you took home more than two monkeys in winnings that night, did you not, Miss Hamilton?"

"Yes," she answered. While he had told no lies, it was hardly an accurate representation of the night. She had not been winning because she could not get her bets on the table, and she had only won when he played her one-on-one.

"Good Lord!" said James. "Over a thousand pounds?"

"She's quite a good gambler," said Keene. "And her disguise as a boy was quite effective too."

"Yes, I am sure we would have been amazed to learn she was really a female," Sophie said.

"I did think, however, that *Leonard* was too young to be on the town alone and decided to take the young man under my patronage," said Victor.

"How, exactly, did you determine she was a girl if her disguise was so remarkable?" asked Trevor.

The amount of venom directed at Victor dismayed Lydia. Trevor was her sunny, too-indolent-to-be-bothered brother. The one who rarely, if ever, displayed his temper. Her stomach turned, thinking he disliked Victor.

Victor looked at Trevor questioningly as if he too wondered at the animosity. "Let us just say that her costume did not hold up to the light of day."

"It is one thing to trick people in the darkness of a gaming club at night, another to be so persuasive under closer scrutiny, during the day," Tony said. "Lydia, gentlemen, please have a seat."

Lydia sat so fast, the chair hitting her backside stung. Poor Tony, his shot leg had to be aching.

"And I never fooled anyone for a minute," said Sophie. "I believe Lydia's disguise was well thought out and executed."

Oscar looked around the room and said, "I am sure we are all mindful of the gratitude we owe you for looking after Lydia, but we must take our leave." Oscar reached under her left arm and pulled her to a standing position. "We shall book passage for Boston immediately."

Lydia bit back a cry of pain. If it were not for her wounded shoulder, Oscar's lifting her up would not have been uncomfortable, except it was the way one would treat a recalcitrant child. She closed her eyes. The room was spinning and she felt decidedly queasy.

"Unhand her!" Victor's voice was laced with low fury.

He was just behind her chair. He must have dashed across the room the minute Oscar reached for her.

"Sir, she is to be my wife and she needs to learn some obedience."

Obedience? Lydia doubted if she would ever be obedient again. Running away to London had taught her more about independence than compliance.

"Sir, I will allow no man to mistreat a lady so in my presence." Victor jerked Oscar's hand from under her arm. "You have no right to yank her about, no matter what you may be to her."

Holding her shoulder, Lydia sank back down to the chair. Her heart pounded furiously as she feared that Victor's face was pale with rage. He had looked like this on that day at Tattersall's. She stared up at him and realized she had to stop him, before there was another duel.

She stood and reached for Victor's arm. "Do not interfere in my affairs," she warned in a low voice meant for him alone. Then she turned to the room at large and said, "If you please, might I have time alone to discuss my plans with my brothers . . . and Mr. Sullivan."

Oscar blinked at her, seeming surprised she had reverted back to using his surname.

Trevor looked sharply at her. "What is wrong with your shoulder?"

Victor's arm stiffened under her hand. She gave a soothing rub of her hand before she moved away from him.

Victor paced the rose drawing room as they all waited for Lydia to talk privately with her fiancé, then call in her brothers. Emotions boiled in his blood and Keene stood beside his path.

Lydia had asked him to step aside, and he had, but not without feeling as if he had abandoned his duty. He had caused her more pain than anyone, yet he could barely restrain himself from hanging over her to protect her from her own family. How could she have wanted to marry that overbearing lout?

Victor wanted to smash Oscar's—unfortunately handsome—face in. Yet she had called him off. And he was worried that Oscar's yanking on her arm had reopened her wounds.

"What is taking her so long?" Victor demanded.

Keene gave a tiny shake of his head. "I daresay they have much to catch up on. It has been months since they have seen each other."

Her brother Trevor narrowed his blue eyes so very similar to Lydia's and glared at Victor.

Victor raked a hand through his hair. This was what he wanted, for her to be settled with a man who would marry her and offer her every chance at happiness, a man who would not destroy her with his own needs, a man she had thought she loved and might yet still. But bloody hell, it felt wrong.

In the space of just a few minutes, Victor was sure that Oscar was all wrong for Lydia. He was not a man who could make her happy, not a man who would understand her need to be in control of her own destiny, not a man who would tolerate her stubborn pigheadedness.

Nor would Oscar understand there were moments when Lydia was fragile and unsure of her femininity and needed just the right word or touch to restore her confidence. Would the lout even be aware of such moments? Or would he just resent the moments when she was headstrong and in control?

Victor grabbed Keene's sleeve and dragged him to the door. "Tony, I need to view your library."

Tony waved him off. "Stay away from my guns, but help yourself to the brandy."

Lydia's older brother eyed him speculatively as he left the room.

Lydia was having a devil of a time convincing Oscar that she wanted to terminate their engagement.

"Your father will not approve."

"Yes, I know, but I will not be forced to marry."

"No one is forcing you, Lydia. But it is time for you to stop playing. Now have I ever done anything that offends you?" He did not wait for her to answer, but answered for himself. "I always treat you with the greatest of care and respect."

"But I do not love you," said Lydia.

"I would not expect you to until after the marriage. You are putting the cart before the horse, Lydia. A woman cannot help but love her husband if he is kind and keeps her well." His tone added, especially if he was the husband.

Lydia wanted to roll her eyes. Her shoulder hurt. She just wanted this interview to be over, before it had gone on so long that Oscar would tell her she had to marry him because she was compromised. "Am I to understand that you do not love me either?"

She knew he did not.

"Of course I love you. My affection for you has always been steadfast," he said earnestly, but he looked away.

"I think you love the idea of running my father's company, more than you love me." She should have confronted him before ever leaving Boston.

Oscar scowled. "I fear my restraint around you has led you to believe that my feelings are not deep." He clasped her hands in his and knelt down before her chair. "I am quite prepared to offer physical demonstrations of my affection, if I were not afraid of offending your sensibilities."

He leaned toward her, and she averted her head just in time for his kiss to land on her cheek. "Oscar, please stop."

"See there, you are calling me by name again."

"Mr. Sullivan, I am quite aware of the honor you do me, but I will not marry you. I heard you talking about your plans to usurp my brothers and take over my father's company when he passes."

He stood and paced. "Well, why shouldn't I? I am best qualified. I would be running my father's company if the war had not forced him into bankruptcy. Your brothers are not the best of managers. Trevor is lazy, James glowers at everyone and is too gruff, Robert would rather captain his own ship and—"

"Mr. Sullivan, I will not marry you and that is that."

His tirade ended as abruptly as it began. He stared at her. "You have obviously been through a lot. I will be waiting to marry you when you come to your senses. When we get back to Boston, you will be over all this nonsense."

What she felt for Victor was anything but nonsense, and she suspected she would never be over it.

In any case she had to stay here now, because this was where her heart was, even if Victor did not want it.

"I am not returning to Boston."

Half an hour later, she was repeating the same line to James, with as little effect. "At least not right away."

"You cannot stay here. You have to come home."

"Yes, I can stay here. Sophie and Keene will house Jenny and me for the next few months."

James let out a big sigh. "You cannot stay with strangers. How long have you known them?"

Lydia did not think James would be satisfied if she said a mere fortnight. "Victor—Lord Wedmont, that is—knows them and trusts them. He would not entrust my care to just anyone. He is ever so mindful of my reputation or I would just stay in the rooms I rented."

James gave her an odd look, then leaned over and planted his hands on her shoulders. "Did he ruin you?"

Tears welled in her eyes at the pain from his pressure on her injury. "No." *Not yet.* She stared down at the floor. "He has been most mindful of my virtue."

"Lydia, as much as you fancy yourself in love with this man, nothing will come of it."

James thought she was in love with Victor? Were her feelings so transparent? Or perhaps Victor had not ruined her in the traditional sense, but she could not abide by the thought of letting any other man touch her. She could not go home to Boston, where the pressure to marry would seem relentless. At least here no one was making such demands of her. She shook her head.

"We cannot leave you here."

"Then stay in London. I don't mind, but I'm not going back right now."

"Lydia, you have to let us take you home. Oscar has come halfway around the world in pursuit of you. You need to appreciate that, return home and get this wedding over with."

"Have you heard a word I've said? I am not returning to Boston, I'm not marrying Oscar, not now, not ever, and I'm staying with the Davieses for the social season."

"How are we to repay them? It takes money for a London season."

"I have money."

"Lydia, you have no idea how much money it takes."

"Actually, I do." Just as always, her brother was not listening to her. Although she had scored a small victory when she persuaded Trevor to take Oscar back to the hotel, she felt as desperate as ever to be heard.

"And then what? Even if we stay for the season and have ourselves a grand old time, what then? What will Father think? That we are a bunch of ungrateful, irresponsible, pleasure-seeking whelps? We cannot afford this." James took long, angry strides around the carpet, reminding her of the *Catch-me-who-can* steam locomotive that ran on a circular track in Torrington Square.

"I am staying in London."

He stopped, turned and glared at her. How could a blond, blue-eyed giant of a man manage to look so menacing? "We are taking you home, even if I have to drag you through the streets, kicking and screaming. I do not care if we raise a scandal in spite of Trevor's objections."

"No, I am of age; you cannot treat me as if I am just a belonging."

"You are chattel and you belong to Father. I cannot think anything good might come of your being enamored of that earl. I am taking you home before you commit any more foolish acts."

Her hopes and dreams were slipping away like the fog burned off in the morning sun. How could anything come of her feelings for Victor if she were across the ocean in America?

"He means to marry me, you know," she heard herself say. She closed her eyes. That was the one thing Victor had been quite clear about: he had no intention of marrying her.

"What?" boomed James. "He does not!"

The path opened before her like the jaws of hell and she stumbled along it. The only way she could convince her brother to let her stay in London was to mislead him. She did not know if she even wanted to marry Victor. She only knew she wanted to be with him, to calm him when his emotions were stormy, to touch him and be touched by him, and when night closed in to share his bed.

"He made me an offer." It was not that kind of offer, and an admission to the kind of offer he had made would have James scooping her up and carrying her out of the room, bound and gagged if necessary. "But, but . . ."

How could she convince her brother she was engaged to Victor, without him confronting Victor and demanding the truth from him?

"Well?"

"But he cannot acknowledge his intentions because he is in first mourning for his wife. It would create a huge scandal, especially since I was until a few minutes ago still engaged to Mr. Sullivan."

"Then, as I am Father's representative, I expect he will make a formal application to me for your hand no later than the end of next week."

Fiddlesticks! She had ten days. Oh, lord, what had she done? Victor would be furious, James would be furious, and her life would be over . . . "Of course he will."

Lydia sat at the dressing table in her bedroom at Sophie and Keene's house and rolled on her stockings. What would her brothers say when they saw her wounded shoulder? Her scars were not horrendous, and she suspected they would be inconspicuous in a year or so, but they had not completely healed. The best she could hope was that a dusting of rice powder would temper the appearance of the scabs.

Tonight was the Sheridans' dinner party and ball, the start of the season, and nearly the end for Lydia.

A soft tap on her door prompted her to bid the tapper to enter. Jenny was due to help her dress any minute.

Sophie swung around the door. "Are you excited? Lud, I swear I am all aflutter and I am not even hosting this event and I have been through quite a few seasons now. But the first real ball is always a lark."

Lydia nodded. Sophie did not require much participation from others to keep a conversation going.

"I came to talk to you about dancing. Or, well,

specifically the waltz." Sophie plopped on the bed beside Lydia's new dress. "I was already married when I first came to London, so I never had to worry about it. But if we are to take you to Almack's, you must not waltz until you have approval by the lady patronesses."

"I'm sure it will not matter." Lydia would not be around long enough to go to Almack's if they even would let her.

"Of course it will. I know that you are not newly out, but we have a peck of silly rules we must follow in London society. An unmarried young lady must behave with the utmost propriety. No more than two dances with any gentleman or you will be thought fast. I should have Amelia talk to you about the rules. She is more versed in them than I, and she, of course, was presented to the old queen and had a season before she married George." Sophie clapped her fingers to her lips. "Oh, Lud, I do not believe we told her about you."

Another tap was followed by Jenny swinging around the door in flurry. "Miss, I did not mean to be late, but Mr. Millars just dropped this off for you."

Lydia looked at the large pasteboard box with trepidation.

"Open it, do," said Sophie, clapping her hands together like a child.

Jenny glanced at Lydia, set the box on the bed and pulled off the top. Sophie leaned over and folded back the tissue.

"Oooo, look at that," said Jenny.

Yards and yards of white silk draped with Brussels lace and swags of tulle gathered with embroidered forget-me-nots met Lydia's watery gaze. Jenny pulled up the bodice. There were tiny capped sleeves and an inverted heart neckline banded at the top by a diamond-studded collar of lace.

"Oh, what an interesting neckline," said Sophie.

Interesting, yes, especially if a woman liked her breasts exposed, but oddly enough, the collared band around the neck gave the gown shoulders, unlike most ball gowns that had completely open necklines. More important, the material would cover her injuries. "I cannot wear that."

The gown was beautiful and far more expensive than the ball gown she and Sophie had ordered at a fashionable modiste and Lydia had paid for herself.

"Jenny, would you see if my maid has my gown pressed?" said Sophie.

When they were alone, Sophie said, "He does not mean it like you think."

"Yes, he does," said Lydia, bending down to fasten her garter over her pink silk stocking. Her stomach felt unsteady. "Even in America, men do not buy a woman clothing unless they mean to keep her as their mistress."

"Did he make you his mistress when you were staying in his home?"

"No, but—"

"He would have, if that was all he wanted from you." Sophie suddenly looked mature and thoughtful. "Wear the dress and make him pay. Men can be so ridiculous when it comes to such matters. I had to seduce Keene before he could figure it out, and we were married."

Yes, but Victor did not intend to marry her, Lydia thought.

Sophie reached over and squeezed Lydia's hand.

"Victor has been through many painful experiences. Give him time."

Time was one thing Lydia did not have.

Sophie bounced to her feet and held out the dress. "Oh, Ludcakes, you shall be unable to wear a shift underneath. You should tell him that, it will make him mad with desire."

CHAPTER 16

It did not look as if she would be able to tell Victor anything, thought Lydia as she sank down in one of the chairs lining the ballroom.

Two beautiful women had flanked him at dinner. One was a redheaded beauty with skin like alabaster and emerald green eyes that hardly wavered from Victor. The other was a slender woman, with hair so dark it reflected blue and skin so translucent that one could see how very blue her blood really was. She kept touching her gloved hand to Victor's sleeve. Lydia would not have been surprised if other touches occurred below the tablecloth.

Lydia imagined the press of a knee, the accidental brush of a shoulder. Victor had seemed totally absorbed in the attentions of both women, although he never offered either a smile, at least not in the time Lydia watched, but then the red-haired lady looked down the table several times and Lydia concentrated on her dinner, rather than be caught staring.

Lydia had tried not to slouch to compensate for the very short stature of the man seated to her left and worried too much about spilling anything on her beautiful gown. And even though Sophie had made her twist, shake, and hunch her shoulders while bending over without accident, Lydia still felt as if she might spill out of her low-cut neckline. A more generously proportioned woman would have looked like a tart, and Lydia wondered if that had been the message she was to convey.

Instead, James blinked as if he had never seen her before, Oscar actually looked at her when he complimented her appearance and Trevor had said she looked too grown-up. Even Keene had given her a second look before he said to his wife, "How could we have ever believed she was a boy?"

Trevor sat down beside her. "Are you enjoying yourself?"

The question sounded like an accusation, so Lydia answered, "Tremendously. London does not agree with you?"

Trevor snorted and sprawled in his chair, in the manner she had tried so hard to emulate as Leonard. He glared across the ballroom and Lydia followed the line of his sight to Victor.

He had the redhead on his arm, but it seemed he had been passed between the brunette and the redhead with Sophie, Amelia, and Felicity all taking a turn about the floor with him in between. Not that Lydia had been without partners. Sophie and Felicity showed up at her elbow with introductions to a new gentleman anytime she stood alone for more than half a second.

But the musicians were beginning a waltz. She had not wanted to heed Sophie's advice to sit out the waltzes, but she was tired and her shoulder ached. She studied Trevor's gaze and it did not waver as Victor led the redhead onto the floor.

"Do you know who that is, dancing with Lord Wedmont?"

"Lady Helena," said Trevor, the name coming out on a sigh. He looked away.

"Do you know her well? She is quite beautiful."

Trevor looked sharply at Lydia. He leaned forward and spoke in a low voice, "As well as any common man could know her, but I am not good enough for her."

The low fury radiating from Trevor's voice surprised Lydia. "Don't say that."

"It's true. They make a handsome couple, do they not? Lady Helena and Lord Wedmont. Their pedigrees are on par. They would make lovely little lords and ladies together."

Did he suspect Victor would marry Lady Helena? Did Trevor know something? "What . . . what are you trying to say, Trevor?"

"She would never marry me in a thousand years. People of their rank don't marry outside of it. She won't and he won't. The sooner you realize that, the less heartache you'll suffer. Oscar has his faults, but he does care for you and will not marry you with a mistress already in mind."

Lydia swallowed hard. Victor had never promised her marriage, but would he marry one of the women of his world and expect Lydia to be there on the side? That is, if she accepted his offer to be his mistress.

"Indian blood runs in our veins, and we come from trade. No one will ever let us forget that. We will never be good enough to marry the cream of the *ton*. We'd be lucky if the dregs of society considered us worthwhile. Although they will include us in their amusements. I suppose because we entertain them with our views on equality and liberty for all men."

"You met her when you were here five years ago," Lydia said. Lady Helena must be the woman who had broken Trevor's heart. Up until this moment, she had seemed a vague thing, hardly real, but Lady Helena was real, flesh and blood and dancing with Victor.

"Why are we here, Lydia, and how long are we staying? I've asked James but he keeps putting me off."

"You are in love with her," whispered Lydia.

Trevor closed his eyes, and she put a hand on his shoulder and leaned toward him. When Lady Helena had looked down the table several times during dinner, she must have been watching Trevor. As Lydia looked across the dance floor, Lady Helena's gaze was on Trevor. She was not indifferent.

"What are we staying for, Lydia?" he asked.

"Odd—I thought I was the only one who sought solution in running away from my problems."

Victor was having a hell of a time. When he first saw Lydia in the ballgown he'd had made for her, he nearly came unhinged. He wanted to scoop her up and carry her to a dark corner and inch down that delicious neckline that barely left her decent and lave her nipples until she begged for more, then kiss her senseless and then . . . he had to stop thinking of her in his arms, in his bed, making love to him.

Even with the yards of material, the skirt still managed to cling and reveal her long legs and she walked as if she had nothing on underneath. He had to turn away before his growing hardness became apparent to all.

At dinner he only glanced at her a time or two when he was sure he could control his lust, or at least that the table would conceal his response, but he feared calling attention to the way he felt about her. He was under too much scrutiny himself.

He'd been set upon by every marriageable lady.

Lady Helena had homed in on him the minute he walked through the door. That had surprised him, because in all the years she had been out, she never paid any gentleman singular attention. With her coppery hair and skin that rivaled her pearls for glow, she was a beauty, but he had never sensed any depth of feeling in her, as if milk flowed through her veins rather than blood. He always had the sense that she would be exactly what she appeared to be, a perfect lady who never, ever had an improper thought.

Her main attraction now was that he preferred her to Countess Beauly. Lady Penelope, with her elaborately styled black hair and her blood-red dress, reminded him of death. Of course, she was a widow fresh out of her weeds.

Although she had married for love, or at least whom she thought loved her best, her affection had not survived the honeymoon. She had gone running back to her parents, the duke and duchess, who had to be tired of their precious daughter. He supposed this time she meant to marry a man who could drape her in diamonds.

Now unencumbered by a mad wife, he seemed to have grown tenfold in attractiveness. What should have made him the envy of every man, was driving him insane. He wanted to spend ten minutes with Lydia without every mama remarking on his unfortunate attention to a woman not of noble birth.

Through the throngs of waltzers he saw Lydia put her hand on a man's shoulder and lean toward him. Without another thought, he steered Lady Helena in that direction and then stopped dancing before the music was complete.

"Come meet the Davies' houseguest," he said.

Lady Helena measured him with her green eyes and slid alongside him, putting her arm through his. It was unpardonably rude of him to end their dance before the music, but he could wait no longer to talk to Lydia.

Relief at seeing her with her youngest brother weakened his knees. He realized jealousy had driven him to her. But he kept moving forward toward the large man sitting with his elbows on his knees and Lydia leaning over him, engaged in an intense conversation.

"Lady Helena, this is Miss Lydia Hamilton and—"

"Ah, Trevor's sister, are you not? Mr. Hamilton and I are old friends. I am so glad to finally meet you, I have heard so much about you," said Lady Helena, with more animation than he had seen from her in a month of Sundays.

What had she heard? And she had called Lydia's brother by his given name? Very odd. Lady Helena was always correct and never familiar.

Lady Helena gave a curtsy without letting go of his arm. In fact, she tightened her grip.

Trevor slowly rose to his full height, animosity barely concealed in his slight bow. Of all the people around her, her brothers and fiancé, this man seemed to be the only one who realized how dangerous Victor was to Lydia, and let him know.

"Lydia, I beg you will allow me to dance the supper dance with you, if no gentleman has already claimed it," said Victor.

"Oh, and I thought you would promise it to me," said Lady Helena.

Lydia watched him without giving him an answer. He had led Lady Helena to dinner, but precedence was not so important during the buffet supper. "I never thought you would accept. You are never known to dance with one man more than twice in an evening. My apologies."

"I once danced three times with the same gentleman, but it was many years ago and the company was sparse, so I doubt if anyone remarked upon it." She looked up at the blond giant. "Ah, well, Mr. Hamilton, if you will be so kind as to escort me to supper, we can all make one happy group."

Trevor looked at Lady Helena and said, "No." He turned and walked away.

Lydia turned to Lady Helena and said, "I must apologize for my brother's rudeness. He is upset with me."

Victor could feel Lady Helena tremble on his arm.

"No, it is quite all right. It was not well done of me to force his hand," Lady Helena said.

Lydia looked between them. "I am sure you should escort Lady Helena to supper, my lord."

"You hardly ate any dinner," blurted Victor.

"I would not want to spill anything on this dress," Lydia answered. Had he been watching her during dinner?

Lady Helena's color rose. "Truly, it is a stunning gown, Miss Hamilton. Where did you have it made?"

Victor winced, praying Lydia did not answer. And

if she resented his buying her a ball gown, why had she worn it?

"I am sorry, I do not know. The dress is borrowed. I will have to return it to its rightful owner."

Lady Helena looked stunned and gave a tiny shake of her head. Then her green eyes narrowed as she took in Lydia's height. With the way the gown fit and the length needed, there could be no real doubt that it was made for her.

What the bloody hell did Lydia mean? Victor thought. She would wear his dress for the evening and reject it later? Was it a clear signal that she would not become his mistress? Lord, he knew that. He did not want her to take his impulsive reckless offer.

"You are beautiful," Victor said on a low note. Then as both Lydia and Helena stared at him, he realized he'd revealed far too much.

Both women dropped their eyes. A tapping on his free arm made him swivel, dragging Lady Helena, who seemed to be holding his arm as if it were a lifeline.

Lady Penelope looked him straight in the eye and said, "Did you not promise me this dance?"

No, he had not. "I'm sorry, I promised Miss Hamilton this dance."

"Oh, by all means, I free you from any claim I might have," Lydia said.

"The next, then," he said to Lydia, and held her gaze long enough that she had to know he would not accept a refusal. Hell, she and everyone around them could probably tell that he wanted so much more than a dance. "Shall I lead you back to your mother, Lady Helena?"

Lady Penelope slid her arm into his.

"What is this, Wedmont? A blond, a brunette and a redhead, must you hoard all the beautiful women?" A nattily dressed, slender man sidled up to the group.

Victor looked at his half-sister's husband. "Where is my . . . your wife, Margaret?"

"Meggie?" William Bedford colored and then shrugged. "Downstairs somewhere. She brought eggs," he said as if that explained everything.

Actually, it explained a lot. "Dance with one of them, Will. If you will excuse me, ladies, I must attend to a small matter."

He freed his arms and left the growing group. Where the diamonds alit, the moths soon followed. With three gorgeous women around him, the bucks and blades had unobtrusively made their way to his side.

Oscar stepped up and bowed to Lady Penelope, "It appears you are abandoned, my lady. Will you allow me to substitute as dance partner?"

Victor cast one desperate look at Lydia and then knew he had to leave the room. He would not be allowed to talk to her without interruption. But as gentlemen closed in around them, he knew it wasn't talk that he wanted.

Lydia watched Victor walk to the doors. Did his long look mean she should follow him? She looked at Lady Helena, who returned her interest.

Did these women always flock around him? And who was this Margaret person? Every time Lydia turned around, Victor's name was coupled with another woman's. He had been about to claim Margaret in some way.

From the corner of her eye Lydia saw that Amelia had waylaid him by the door. She had her hand on Victor's arm, her white glove a stark contrast against his black sleeve. Was he a magnet for every female in the room?

"Miss Hamilton," Lady Helena said, "would you give your brother a message for me?"

Lydia nodded.

Lady Helena nodded her head to the side and stepped away from the growing group of young men and women. Lydia fell in step beside her.

"Would you tell him—" Helena bit her lip. "Tell him, I need him. I need *to speak* with him."

Lydia stared at Helena. Did she need him? Or just need to speak to him? In any case, Lydia was disappointed. "If all you mean to do is break his heart, then do not speak to him."

Lydia brushed past the woman, knowing that part of her animosity was fueled by the way Helena had clung to Victor and danced the waltz with him, held in his arms. It was acceptable for her to do so, but it was not proper for Lydia who could be no more than his mistress.

She realized Victor had only to look at her and her heart beat faster, her skin heated and air to breathe was in short supply. Oh Lord, Trevor's warning had come too late.

The way her whole world brightened when he smiled at her as if she had been given a gift of the sun and the moon and all the stars in the heavens told the story.

She had fallen in love with Victor.

* * *

Chastened by Lydia's sharp rebuke, Lady Helena closed her eyes and gathered her composure. As a disobedient daughter, she deserved to feel chastised, especially as she contemplated her plans. She just could not let Trevor walk away from her and England again without letting him know how she felt about him.

She scanned the ballroom; Lord Wedmont was nowhere to be seen and she shuddered. Standing beside him and encouraging him had taken every ounce of will she possessed. He looked at her as if she was wanting in wit or understanding, and she felt blank and dull and could think of little to say to interest him.

She had to hang on to his arm to keep herself from running away.

Only around Trevor did she feel awake, alive and safe.

He stood on the far side of the room, near the musicians. With his broad shoulders and looming height he was unmistakable. She just wanted to press against him and soak in his strength, although it wasn't the sort of thing one could do in a ballroom. Most of the things she wanted to do couldn't be done in a ballroom.

She skirted around the edge of the dance floor, greeting people she knew, until she reached his side. Her body reacted as she grew near. Fear and anticipation clogged her throat. Finally she managed to whisper, "Trevor."

He turned around and looked her over, while she chewed her lip. Only his gaze on her mouth made her realize what she was doing. She never fidgeted or made faces. She forced herself to stop, but with her thoughts on her lips she remembered his kisses in the pouring rain. Everything about her turned liquid at the memory.

"Come to badger me into escorting you to supper?"

"No, I had . . . another thing on my mind." How could she ask him to . . . fix how she felt, to share the glow of her awakening, to repeat what had happened under the tree and take it farther. She looked down, struggling to find words to entice him to her bed, words that were safe to say out loud.

"I would be happy to take you down to supper, if we do not sit with Wedmont."

Helena looked over her shoulder. "I do not know where he went."

Trevor's expression went flat. "I see."

What did he see?

"I do not know why I thought things would be any different this time." He turned his shoulder to her, giving her a cut direct.

She stared at his back, wanting to reach out and smooth her hands over his evening coat, under it, under his shirt. Hurt burned in her heart, yet she knew she had upset him.

"Oh, by the stars, I miss the rain," she said.

He slowly turned back around, his expression intense. "There's more to life than rain."

"Yes, I am aware." Her face flushed as she thought of what had happened in the downpour. "Could we just have a civil conversation? There are things I want to say to you."

"What things?"

"I cannot speak so forthrightly here." She glanced around looking to see if anyone was close enough to overhear her. Her conversation thus far was dangerous enough.

He touched her forearm, causing pleasure to streak up her arm. "Stop. You look as if you plan to steal a loaf of bread in the baker's shop."

"I have never been inside a baker's shop," she said.

"Yes, I know, and you are immensely proud of that fact."

She frowned. He thought her too proud, simply because she had never been inside a bakery? "Since we are all here, I trust Major Sheridan was helpful. I met your sister earlier. She looks much like you. Quite a lovely girl."

"Major Sheridan brought us together, yes, but he refused compensation."

Helena winced, thinking how much disdain her mother would have for anyone who mentioned money. Her parents would have thought it vulgar to discuss such matters at a ball. "I do not think he does it for the remuneration. I am glad that all has worked out without incident." Without scandal was what she meant.

"And how is your father's health?"

"Much the same, but at least no worse." Helena swiveled, looking for her mother.

"Are you afraid to be seen talking to me?"

She turned back to him. He folded his arms across his chest. Her mother could hardly fault her for talking to Trevor, but she would not like it. "Yes. No."

Helena dropped her gaze to the floor, feeling her cheeks burn. His sister's admonition to not break his heart leapt into her head as encouragement to go forward with her plan. "Will you call on me tonight? After the servants are abed, I will put a candle in the library window when it shall be safe for you to knock. I shall let you in, so we may talk in private."

He made a noise of protest, and she lifted her eyes just in time to see horror cross his face. He mouthed a "No."

Hope drained out of her, leaving her limp, exhausted and humiliated. Had she shocked him? Horrified him? Did he not want to speak to her in private? Did he not enjoy what had happened in the park? She wished for the floor to open up and swallow her whole if she had mistaken his intent.

She realized he was looking past her. Could he not even stand to look upon her?

"Helena!" said her mother sharply.

She spun around and encountered her mother's pinched expression. Oh, God, had Mama heard everything?

Victor found his way down to the basement of the house, where his half-sister toiled in the kitchen with an apron over her ball gown. He grabbed her arm and led her out of the room, untying the apron strings as he went.

"What are you about?" he asked.

"I . . . brought eggs for soufflés and they needed help." She gestured back toward the kitchen.

Felicity would probably resent the implication that her exemplary staff needed help. No doubt her excellent chef, stolen away from Watier's gentlemen's club, could manage soufflés.

He pulled the apron over Margaret's head and tossed it to a footman. He marched her up the first flight of stairs, then the second, all the way to the top floor of the house, where the music was played. "Your place is in the ballroom."

Her disheveled state provoked his frown. He detoured down the passage way to the bedroom that had once been hers. He opened the door and pushed her inside. She yanked her arm out of his grasp.

"Sit down, I shall repair your hair." He pulled out a handkerchief and mopped the kitchen steam from her face, none too gently.

She stared at him as if he had gone mad. Perhaps he had. "What are you doing?"

"I'll be damned if I let my only sister—or at least the only sister I know—labor away in the kitchen because she does not think she is good enough to dance in the ballroom."

She stared at him, shocked, as she sank down to a chair by the dressing table. "I don't belong."

"It's one thing that you raise poultry and sell eggs to keep yourself out of the poorhouse. I do not care who your mother was or what you have done, but you have the blood of twelve earls running in your veins, and a husband who is a gentleman. You do not need to be found among your chickens with a kerchief on your head. Hire laborers."

He proceeded to lecture her as he repinned her hair in a more elaborate style. Her rich dark hair with its own luxurious waves did not require more than his wrapping it around his finger to train a curl. So like his own and Keene's and, for that matter, Regina's. In fact, she and his daughter looked so much alike with their dark eyes and winged eyebrows, he had only to look at Margaret to get a glimpse of his daughter's future beauty.

"You chose this life, Diana Margaret Bartlett Bedford. You wanted to be a lady. So be a lady and for God's sake tell your husband to stop calling you Meggie."

He looked at her simple ball gown and shook his head. He should have bought her better clothes, or at least shamed her fashionably dressed husband into taking a greater interest in his wife's wardrobe.

She stared up at him, made meek by his sudden attention.

He leaned down next to her. "You have only to look to Keene or me for guidance if you are ever in need. I know we cannot acknowledge you publicly, but we are there as your brothers and champions if you need us."

She turned around and hugged him tight.

He patted her awkwardly on the back. "Go now, before you wrinkle your gown."

"See, I am so bad at this," she whispered.

He led her out of the bedroom and toward the ballroom. He tucked one last curl into place and decided he had done a satisfactory job, then looked toward the open doors of the ballroom where Lydia stood still as a deer in the forest after a twig snap. Her blue eyes were wide and wounded as she stared at him and his sister.

He drew up stiff. Bloody hell, he could wound Lydia just by assisting his sister.

Lydia put a hand to her left shoulder. And agony wrenched through him as he realized that was where he had shot her. Dragging her into his world had brought her nothing but pain. As surely as he stood there, he was destroying her. He knew the only decent thing to do was to cut her out of his life.

Yet he continued toward her as if there were no other destination he would rather meet.

As he neared the ballroom doors and Lydia, Amelia glided toward them from inside the ballroom.

Lydia jerked her head away and turned to go back toward the dancing. Amelia stood just in her path.

"Leonard?" said Amelia, shock and surprise draining the color from her face. "Oh, my, you are Leonard!"

Bloody hell, how many people had heard her?

CHAPTER 17

Lydia stared at Amelia, wondering what else could go wrong this night. A few heads had turned in their direction after hearing her call out, "Leonard."

"Sophie did not warn you?" asked Lydia softly, but it was as much statement as question. Obviously Amelia had been startled when she recognized her.

Her hand over her heart, Amelia stared at Lydia, making her feel like a freak.

"Perhaps we should go downstairs," said Victor.

Amelia shifted her attention from Lydia to Victor. "Why did you not tell me?" she demanded of him. She no longer seemed interested in Lydia, but her voice carried an undercurrent of hurt and betrayal.

He grabbed Amelia's arm and pulled her away from the ballroom doors out into the passageway. "It did not occur to me that you of all people would create a scene, and you know I keep any secret that might lead to scandal."

Then their voices dropped lower as they walked down the passageway. Victor had his arm around Amelia's shoulders and their heads were close.

Lydia pressed her hand against her shoulder, the wound no doubt aggravated by the motion of dancing. The sight of Victor with Amelia caused another ache to start nearer to her breastbone. He had all these beautiful women flitting around him—whatever made her think he would see her as special? She was too tall, too slender and too radical in her thinking.

If she was lucky, he might remember she existed at the end of the evening. Although he had a way of making her feel as if she were the center of the world when he stood in front of her. She looked in on the revelers, few of whom she knew.

She was an outsider, not only an American, but one who did not understand their ways. Across the floor, Trevor talked with Lady Helena. Oscar danced, partnering Lady Penelope. She studied her former fiancé and watched as he flattered the English widow, and smiled and preened as he had once done with her.

If he was the least bit brokenhearted by Lydia's refusal to marry him, he did not let it show. Of course, she knew that he still thought they would marry each other, when she came to her senses, and he would think that until he had satisfactorily replaced Lydia or wed her.

Watching his antics with the English beauty, Lydia almost felt sorry for him. If he thought to wiggle his way into Lady Penelope's good graces, it would not happen. She might be amused by Oscar and his fulsome compliments, but she clearly wanted Victor's ring on her finger, and no one else's.

James appeared cornered by an older woman with a towering ostrich feather bobbing out of her turban, nearly tickling James in the nose every time she nodded her head. Lydia had been avoiding her older brother, because his looks in her direction seemed to indicate he did not think Victor behaved like a future husband to her.

The musicians finished the strains of the piece and the dancers drew to a halt. Lydia glanced over her shoulder to see Victor press a kiss on Amelia's forehead. It was not the kind of kiss that should prompt jealousy, but Lydia's eyes watered all the same.

Did Victor feel any affection toward her at all, or did he just want to seduce her when she slept in his bed?

Lydia ducked behind the potted palm, next to the ballroom doors. Squeezing her eyes shut, she wanted to run, but to where? To what end? Running from her problems did not make them go away. They just followed her, while she created bigger problems.

"Waiting for me, pet?"

She opened her eyes. Victor held back one of the fronds of the palm tree, an amused look on his face.

In for a penny, in for a pound. "I believe I am hiding."

"This tree does not conceal you very well. Besides, I am the one who should be hiding." He held out his hand. "I believe this is my dance."

Lydia stared at him, realizing she was hiding from the truth. Her vow to stop running away had little meaning if she meant to hide from it. She shook her head, and folded her arms behind her back.

"You will not take my arm, pet?"

"Every woman here tonight has taken your arm. I thought I should be different," she answered.

"You are different." He stepped closer between the tree and the wall. "You do not wish to dance, or is it just me?"

"Never you," she whispered.

He was so close to her, she could breathe in his scent, just a trace of sandalwood and spice of his cologne along with the hint of soap and him. She pressed back against the wall, feeling weak-kneed.

His searching dark gaze met hers, and he placed his hand to her shoulder, over her wound. "Is this bothering you? Should I find a place for you to rest quietly?"

Every grievance she had melted away to nothing. "No, I'm fine."

His gaze shifted lower to the swags of material that draped her breasts. "Exceptionally fine."

He ripped off his right glove with his strong white teeth, and gathered it in his other hand. His bared fingertips slid against her skin, just below the diamond-studded neckband.

Her breath caught in her throat.

"We should go back into the ballroom," he said.

"Do not let me detain you."

"Ah, pet, the room is empty without you."

"Hardly so."

His fingers slid lower, along the edge of her dress. "Yes, so. You are the sight I seek after every moment apart, yet I cannot look too much because I am intoxicated at seeing this perfection."

His touch left a riot of sensation. Tingles danced across her skin, under the edge of her dress that barely covered her tightening nipples. Would his touch reach there? She drew a deep breath as his fingers reached the upper curve of her breast.

His hand trembled and she too quivered inside, wanting him to touch her, to do wicked things to her.

"Say me nay, this is dangerous," he whispered.

"I have no fear."

He leaned forward and kissed her, both his hands coming up to her neck as he gently pressed his lips to hers. She answered back by touching her tongue to his upper lip. His attempt at a sweet civilized kiss faded into a hungry coming together of their mouths.

He pressed against her, his hard, lean length a wondrous thing. She had yearned for this moment for so long, that she did not care that it was only a stolen embrace behind a door and a potted palm.

Yet, he managed a measure of restraint that made her want to scream. His hands stayed at her neck, the left hand still gloved and holding his other glove, and his bare fingers of his right hand stroking her skin, threading through the blond curls at her nape, sending molten pleasure flooding through her body. She willed his hands lower to her daring décolletage, and lower still.

He ended the kiss and pulled back. He breathed in heavy quick bursts, his dark eyes hungrily searching hers.

She put her palms on his chest, feeling the rise and fall, mesmerized by the rhythm of his body, his thundering heart, his slowing breathing.

He looked over his shoulder and then back at her. "Bloody hell, I have kept away from you tonight so nothing of scandal will attach to your name. Yet, I am near to destroying all."

"A stolen kiss can hardly have so much significance."

"I should have made sure that Amelia knew about you."

A chill ran through Lydia's blood. Was he even now thinking of Amelia?

"She could have exposed your charade and ruined everything." He raked his bare hand through his hair. "I do not know if anyone overheard her call you . . ."

"Leonard?"

"Hush."

A reputation shattered could always be redeemed by a marriage, yet he was too mindful of her good name.

She dropped her hands from his chest and pressed her palms back against the wall. "None of this will matter when I return to Boston."

His expression went flat. "Is that what you mean to do?"

She had no choice. She did not doubt James's threat to carry her kicking and screaming through the streets. He had done it before.

Besides, what did she have to stay for? To be Victor's mistress while he married Lady Helena or Lady Penelope? If Trevor was right, Victor would never marry a commoner like her. She might be willing to be his mistress, but not if she had to share. She was too selfish for that. Just seeing him put his arm around Amelia was like putting a stake through her heart.

"Lydia," he put his hands on her shoulders. "Is that what you mean to do?"

She shrugged. "My brothers have come to take me home."

He searched her face, then removed his hands. His gaze dropped to his hands as he drew on his glove. "Perhaps that is best, then."

Did she meant so little to him? She loved him, but he would treat her leaving as unimportant. But when he could have his pick among Lady Helena,

Lady Penelope, that other dark-haired lady with whom he'd emerged from the room down the hall—what was that room? —or even Amelia whom he had threatened to make love to in that letter—why on earth would he choose too-tall, unfeminine Lydia?

Trevor had tried to stop Helena before she said so much. He should have been prepared for her words, she was acting so furtive, but she had shocked him just the same. Then when he saw her mother approach rapidly, he could not offer a verbal warning for fear the Countess Caine would overhear.

"My lady." He bowed.

Helena had turned, so he couldn't see her face, but she backed into him. He put his hand against the small of her back.

Helena trembled. "Is everything all right, Mother?"

"We must leave at once." The countess's face was so pinched and white, she looked ill.

Was she that angry? How much had she heard?

He pushed against the small of Helena's back, offering her comfort and steadiness. "Can I assist you by calling for your coach?"

The countess looked at him and at first her eyes were blank. Then they narrowed. "You." She slapped one hand over her mouth and the other against her stomach. "Oh, please," she managed in a muffled way.

"Helena, call for your carriage and wraps." He pushed Helena forward and then wrapped his arm around Lady Caine and with both his hands under her elbows he bore her weight as he walked her toward the double doors. "Please excuse my familiarity, ma'am."

She sagged against him and he knew she was ill. She never would have allowed him to help her otherwise. Any port in a storm.

Fearing she was about to lose her dinner, he swung her around the side of the door.

He whispered, "If you need to be ill, ma'am, I suggest the plant pot."

She had shut her eyes, so only he saw his sister and Wedmont, standing behind the palm, engaged in a passionate embrace. Good Lord, did the man have his hand on Lydia's breast?

"Lydia!"

She flattened against the wall and Wedmont sprang to the side, while Lady Caine leaned over the pot.

She rocked back and forth and swallowed several times. Beads of perspiration dotted her forehead. By some indomitable strength of will, she managed to defeat the urge to cast up her accounts and finally straightened. "I am all right now."

Trevor wasn't. He was ready to kill Wedmont. He glared at the man. But what could he do? He still had his hand under Lady Caine's elbow. He could not abandon Helena's mother even if she was an impediment to his relationship with Helena. He handed her his handkerchief.

Keene appeared by the door. Their host for the evening, Tony, limped toward them.

"Is there a problem?" asked Keene.

"Lady Caine does not feel well," said Trevor.

"Oh, please, all this fuss is not necessary," said Lady Caine. "Lord Wedmont, you may see us home."

Victor jerked his gaze from Lydia, who looked flushed but not terribly disheveled, to Lady Caine. Was insisting on his escort a ploy to get him alone with Lady Helena? The only woman he wanted to be alone with was Lydia. He had lost control after his pretense at nonchalance failed. He hated the idea that she would return to Boston, even though he knew it was the best thing for her.

Lady Helena appeared behind Trevor. "Our carriage will be round in a quarter hour. The servants are fetching our wraps."

Lady Caine nodded and dabbed the handkerchief to her upper lip. "Lord Wedmont, can your carriage be had sooner?"

"I am afraid I sent my coachman home with instructions to return for me after midnight. Didn't want my horses standing about," Victor answered.

Helena moved forward to take her mother's arm from Trevor. "Shall we find you a chair, Mother?"

"Whatever were you doing behind the tree, Wedmont?" asked Lady Caine.

"Avoiding the company, my lady."

She glared at him. Trevor glared at him, and Keene looked at him rather enigmatically. Lydia wouldn't look at him at all and Lady Helena kept looking between her mother and Trevor. How had Lady Caine come to be practically carried out of the ballroom by Trevor, to whom she would probably give the cut direct if he spoke to her?

"Not yourself or your lovely daughter, of course. You do know my American friends, do you not, Lady Caine? Miss Lydia Hamilton and Mr. Trevor Hamilton," asked Victor.

"I know Mr. Hamilton," said Lady Caine in such

a way as it was clear she wished she did not know
him. "We met years ago. How nice that you have
brought your sister to London this time." She nodded her head toward Lydia. "Miss Hamilton."

She did not even look long enough to see if Lydia
acknowledged her greeting.

"My carriage is close at hand," said Keene, stepping forward. "We arrived early and are first at the
corner. If you please, my lady, I would be honored
to see you home."

"You are the Baron of Whitley's oldest son, are
you not?" Lady Caine asked Keene.

"I daresay. His only son now," Keene answered
and gestured toward the stairs. "If you please."

Lady Caine moved to the stairs with her daughter
at her side. At the top she gripped the banister and
hesitated. Then she swayed and moaned a little.
Trevor, with one last glare over his shoulder,
scooped up the countess and carried her down the
three flights of stairs.

Victor reached out and took Lydia's hand. "Are
you all right?" he asked.

She looked at him and gave a slight shake of her
head. "I am fine. Is Lady Caine ill?"

"I would say so," said Victor, dismissing the sight
from his head.

"How odd. Being sick seems such a common
thing to do."

His lips twitched. "Although she is mighty high in
the instep, alas, we are all but flesh and blood."

Lydia flashed him a look that wiped away his
amusement and flooded him with yearning. Bloody
hell, he had been about to lower her dress in a pas-

sageway where anyone might have chanced by. How much had her brother seen?

Too much, if Trevor's expression meant anything. Victor tugged Lydia toward the ballroom. Too much time alone with her and he would ruin her. If he seduced her, he surely would kill any of her dreams for a life of independence. A fallen woman would never be taken seriously in the business world. A moral woman would have enough trouble. He would reduce her to the disreputable life of mistress or courtesan. Yet, in so many ways she was still an innocent.

All right, she no longer kissed like an innocent. She kissed like a siren, and he would willingly drown in her arms.

He tugged her along until he found Sophie. He told her that Keene had left to escort Lady Caine and her daughter home. Then Lady Penelope latched onto his arm. With her main rival gone, she monopolized him for the rest of the evening. The only silver lining in that cloud was that Lydia's brother never approached.

Lydia hardly spared him a glance. Sophie deftly kept her circulating among the available men.

A while after supper, Sophie approached Victor. "Have you seen Keene?"

"No."

"He has not returned." She stifled a yawn. "And Lydia and I are ready to return home."

Victor looked across the room at Trevor. "Perhaps Lydia's brothers could—"

Sophie rapped him on the arm with her fan. "They came in a hack. Besides, if Keene does not arrive home soon, I would have you go look for him."

"Very well, I shall call for my carriage." His coachman should have arrived by now.

"Thank you," said Sophie. "We'll take our leave of Felicity and meet you downstairs."

Lydia studiously looked away from him and Lady Penelope hung on to him as if she would never let him go.

"Must you leave?" said Lady Penelope, leaning her breast against his arm.

He felt nothing. He knew that even if she invited him to partake of her charms, he would be wasting his time. The only woman whose charms he desired was off limits.

"I am afraid so," said Victor. He would be glad to be rid of Penelope, but he had in mind that staying away from Lydia might be their best course. To consummate their passion would be ruin for her.

But how much could go wrong in a carriage with both Sophie and Lydia? Except when they arrived at the Davies' townhouse, Sophie insisted he come inside and wait for Keene.

She led them into the library. "The fire will still be banked in here," Sophie said as she opened the door to the soft glow from the fireplace.

While a footman lit a lamp for them, Lydia drifted off to the bookshelves and removed a book.

"I cannot imagine what is keeping Keene. I am starting to get worried." Sophie moved over to the brandy decanters and lifted a glass from the tray.

"You were not worried before?" Victor brushed off his sleeve and wondered if he could rid himself of the cloying scent of Lady Penelope's perfume. Had he ever found her attractive? She was thought a diamond of the first water during her first season, but he'd been married then and had hardly paid her any attention.

"Oh, you know I seldom worry about anything." She handed him a glass of brandy. "Poor Victor, you are the prize for all the matchmaking mamas this season, are you not?"

"Apparently not just the mamas," answered Victor. "For God's sake, Sophie, put out the word that I never mean to marry again."

Lydia stiffened to ramrod straightness. She flipped a page in her book. What had it been like for her to see all the women tripping over themselves to be his bride?

He had title, wealth, moderate youth and was not fubsy-faced; what more could an aspiring young gentlewoman want? Too bad none of them wanted him for himself. He sighed, supposing one ought to be glad to be valued for any reason.

"I was surprised at Lady Helena." Sophie looked over at her houseguest.

Victor took a sip of his brandy and avoided comment.

"All the royal dukes are married now, and she has been out five seasons." Sophie flounced onto a wing chair. "Besides, she may *need* to get married, now."

Victor looked askance at Sophie and moved closer to her. What did she know?

Sophie kicked off her slippers and in her inimitable style, curled up in the chair, her head against the side. "I do wish Keene would hurry."

"I should leave." Victor bowed. Why he bothered when Sophie's eyes were closed and Lydia had her back to him, was beyond him.

"No, sit," said Sophie, blinking at him. She looked about two seconds from falling asleep. "I am not used to these late hours yet. Our Lydia seems to be holding up well. How was your evening, Lydia? Come tell us your impression of our hedonistic world."

"Sophie," objected Victor. "You are her chaperone." Was everyone out to corrupt Lydia? Did no one but him see what a disastrous path she was on with him? Would no one save her?

"Lud, whosoever thinks it behooves a woman to be ignorant of the ways of the world, does us no favors. I would have been in much better stead if I was less innocent when I married Keene. It only made trouble between us."

Lydia glanced over her shoulder and he was lost, snared. Her blue eyes and the soft blond curls tempted him. He had to touch her, feel the curves of her hips, taste her ambrosia skin. He closed his eyes and was flooded with images of her naked legs in his bed. Damn it all. He never should have undressed her, because he knew how perfect she was.

He sat down hard on the sofa, cattycorner to Sophie, and took a big swig of brandy, while praying for Keene to return home quickly. How long could he be?

Lydia closed the book and drifted closer. The way the skirt of her dress outlined her form as she walked mesmerized him. All she had to do now was stand in front of the fire. Which was exactly where she stopped.

"I thought Lady Helena quite beautiful," said Lydia.

Victor swallowed hard, trying not to look at

Lydia's silhouette against the fire. But he found looking elsewhere impossible. "I find her personality flat."

"I think she is just very circumspect. I do not believe any of us really know her," said Sophie with a yawn.

"I would say our company is too fast for her," Victor said.

"Oh, I would not be so sure of that," said Sophie.

Lydia watched the conversation between Sophie and Victor, inching closer.

Victor tossed back the last of his brandy, feeling the burn of the alcohol sliding down his throat. Heat rose inside him and he watched Lydia, no longer trying to contain his desire. He tossed his arm along the back of the sofa and set his brandy on the side table.

"Still waters run deep." Sophie slurred her words. "Saw her at the midwife's house . . . trouble."

"What?" asked Lydia sharply.

Sophie blinked, clearly hanging onto the waking world by nothing but a thread. "She's not a good liar."

Lydia bit her lip. "You suspect she is with child?"

"Why else would she see a midwi . . . ?" murmured Sophie, just before she slipped into sleep.

Lydia sank down on the sofa beside Victor. Why was she concerned if Lady Helena was with child? He traced his fingers up her bare arm to the tiny cap sleeve and back down. Shivers ran up his spine as if she had touched him in the same way.

"You should consider that a cautionary tale," he warned. *Where the hell was Keene?*

She turned toward him and gathered his hands

in hers. "Come with me, I have something to give you." Her blue eyes met his with guileless beauty.

He rose and followed her out of the room. Just watching her walk in front of him, her hand extended back to him, was gift enough. When they started up the second flight of stairs, beyond the public rooms, he asked, "What do you mean to give me, pet?"

She turned and looked down at the floor. Her hesitation charmed him, and he reached out to lift her chin.

"The dress, Victor. I cannot keep it." She met and held his gaze.

His hand trembled as he feared she meant to remove the dress in front of him. As he stared at her, he realized she did understand the implications. "But—"

She pressed her bare fingertips against his lips. "I have thought about this and . . ." She looked away— "and this is what I want."

His heart pounded madly. "Lydia, if we go into your bedroom, I want everything, no holds barred."

She stepped closer and held his lapels. "And I want you."

Desire knifed through Victor, almost making him double over. Oh, God, he wanted to make love to her—he had never wanted anything so badly in his life. It had been so long, so desperately long. He had warned her of the consequences, but he could not fight her ruin when she welcomed it. A calmness and feeling of right settled over him. In this moment, making love to her could only be right.

CHAPTER 18

Lydia pulled the jeweled hairpins from her hair, not willing to risk their loss. Not that much could be done with her short tresses, but Sophie had loaned her the pins to add cachet.

Victor pulled loose his cravat and then removed his jacket and waistcoat.

She did not know precisely how to proceed, although standing apart undressing seemed coldly distant. She reached up to unhook the collar of her dress. The absence of her shift underneath made her feel exposed.

"Let me do that, pet," he said while toeing off his shoes.

She swallowed and dropped her hands. They fell uselessly at her sides. She sat on the edge of her dressing table stool, waiting for him to finish undressing. He drew his shirt over his head and then his undershirt.

She studied the floor and then realized belatedly that she could remove her shoes and stockings.

The black legs of his unmentionables came into her limited view and she did not know whether to be thankful or regretful he had not removed them. He knelt down and reached up under her skirt to the garters of her pink silk stockings and loosened one. He ever so slowly rolled her stocking down her leg.

She held onto the stool, not knowing what to do with herself. His dark head was practically in her lap, and the bare skin of his shoulders and back in front of her. She should touch him, yet she was unsure.

He lifted her newly bared foot and pressed a kiss to the sole. Her toes curled in response. He lowered her foot and reached for her other garter. Would he undress her completely with such reverent gentleness?

She touched his shoulder, the scarred one. His skin was warm and smooth. He stood, bringing her up with him.

Her eyes dropped to the smooth male contours of his chest and belly. His muscles showed through the skin and she was amazed at his visible strength. A dark line of hair that dipped down his stomach, below his waistband. He pulled her against him. The skin of her chest prickled where it came into the bare skin of his chest.

"Are you sure, Lydia?" he asked. "It is not too late to stop."

"I'm sure. Why cannot a woman choose to take a lover if a man can?" What she meant to sound brave came out squeaky and alarmed.

Victor's grip tightened around her. "You know why. I daresay you will hate me eventually, but I cannot fight this when I want you so much."

His words calmed her. Hardly a balm to her ego, but she understood. "I cannot imagine hating you," she whispered.

"But there is only this moment."

"This is all I want. Right here, right now. I expect no more of you."

He cradled her head with his hand. "Then do not be frightened. I will go slowly."

"And you must teach me how to do the things you like."

"No. I fear my pleasure will too easily be had. All I want is that you will like things well enough not to regret this disastrous choice."

She would never regret it. She loved him, and she wanted to show him. And in just a couple of days, James would force her to leave when he learned that Victor had no intention of marrying her.

Lydia did not know if Trevor had the truth of it or if Victor could not bear the thought of giving his heart again, but she knew that he needed this as much or more than she did.

He held her for the longest time, until she could hardly stand the wait for his kiss. Then his lips found hers and the mating dance began.

He kissed her until she was dizzy from lack of air, and she swayed against him, but he held her steady. He was her rock, while she flowed around him like the sea, her white skirts frothing around their legs like foam on a turbulent ocean.

He ran his hands along her back, over her hips with exquisite slowness and left ripples in their wake. Her skin heated and tingled. She breathed in deeply of him, exploring the lines of his back, the dips and hollows of muscle and bone. Every thing about him was perfection, from his lean muscles to his gentle caresses.

His lips left her mouth and trailed down her neck. He brought his hands slowly up her sides, while he bent pressing butterfly kisses along the edge of her neckline. His light guidance into the realms of passion made her feel treasured and just a bit impatient. Yet it warmed her soul that he took great care that she would not feel frightened or rushed. His patience was for her, not for himself.

"Ah, Lyddie, I have been dying to do this since I first saw you this evening," he murmured just before he pushed down her gown to bare her breasts.

She drew in a sharp breath as he touched the tip of his tongue to her nipple, then drew it into his mouth. He held her, supporting her weight as he treated her other breast to the same attention.

He ended it too soon, pulling her against his bare chest, then straightening to full height. She shuddered as her tight, wet nipples rubbed against his skin, and she arched to press closer.

Sensation after sensation racked her body and she wanted this moment never to end, but she wanted to be closer to him. Yet, his progression was maddeningly slow. He brought his hands up to cradle her face as he kissed her again, as if they would start at the beginning.

She made a sound of protest and his lips curled against hers. He drew back and stroked her cheek with his fingertips. She stared into his dark eyes and grew mesmerized by the smoky desire reflected there.

"Ready for more, pet?"

She nodded shakily. As cool air touched her skin, she realized he was unhooking the fasteners down her back. "I don't have on a shift."

"So I see," he said. "How divine. No shift, nor stays, and soon not much else."

A burst of panic made her clutch at his shoulders. "Should we not move to the bed?"

"Not yet, sweetheart." He brushed a kiss across her nose and turned her back to him.

The underpinnings of the dress had a complicated set of tapes that held the bodice tight and had kept everything in place. Lydia squeezed her eyes shut, thinking how long it had taken her and Jenny and Sophie to get them laced and fastened correctly.

He unhooked the diamond-studded collar and pulled it down in front, brushing the back of his hands against her skin, across her breasts. Sparkles danced down her front as if the diamonds had given her their luster through his hands.

She shuddered. He pressed his lips against her neck and moved lower; each tape that came undone was followed by his lips, lighting her skin with passion's fire, until she was panting. He slid the sleeves down her arms and the dress dropped to her hips, then to the floor.

His hands at her waist found the ties to her pantalets and had them undone, and the last of her clothing dropped to the pile at her feet.

Her eyes flew open and she realized he watched her in the mirror above her dressing table. The urge to cover her nakedness brought her elbows in.

"Do not cover yourself. You are lovely." He gently eased her elbow out and up. "I could look upon your beauty forever."

Just the hint of deep breathlessness and rough burr to his voice made her believe he spoke sincerely.

"I do not imagine I should look so forever." Heat flooded her cheeks and her flush spread down her chest. She fought her fears and embarrassments, wanting to give him whatever he wanted. If he wanted to look upon her naked, then she would stand here naked.

"But this is how I would see you, unless you managed to grow more beautiful." He held her hands back and trailed his hand down her inner arm, over her breast, across her ribs, and down to the nest of tan curls. "Truly, you could have been a model for a statue of Aphrodite, but no sculptor could do you complete justice."

She was caught between how telling his words were and that he touched her where she had never been touched. Then he pressed his fingers against her. A wave of pleasure broke over her.

How could he know to touch her like that?

With his shoulder he tipped her back. His palm against her spine supported her weight and he kissed her as he rotated his fingers against the hidden bud of delight. Oh, she was coming undone.

She moaned into his mouth.

He tipped her farther back and then lifted her. She was breathless and her body was thrumming with need that she could not name. Yet, she understood he would start at the beginning, repeating each kiss and caress and then finally when she was too eager to be fearful, he would add a new facet to this magical encounter.

He set her in the center of her turned-down bed and bent over to kiss her. She mourned the absence of his touch, but then the mattress shifted as his weight joined hers. She ran her hand down his back and she met no barrier at his waist. She slid her hand down over his firm flank. She wished she could employ such magical seduction on him, but she did not have his skill or fortitude. She only hoped that her touches gave him one-tenth the delight he gave her.

He moaned and dipped his head. She pressed kisses to his shoulder and neck and wiggled lower to taste his skin. She explored the ripples on his stomach and ran her index finger down the dark arrow of hair into the thatch of springy curls surrounding his male member.

He held himself still, poised over her as she touched the erect shaft. She wrapped her fingers around him and he groaned low in his throat. Oh, that she could please him. She wanted to make him to feel her pleasure.

"Lyddie, I cannot take this for long. I want to do so much more for you."

She trailed her kisses down, twisting to reach until she touched her lips to the velvety pink skin of his shaft.

Victor made an impatient groan as his member jerked in her grasp. Lydia stared as his hardened shaft throbbed.

He shifted, grabbing her under the arms and pulling her back up to the pillow. He nudged her thighs with his knee, and she opened her legs to him. He pulled her hands out of the way and settled his body against hers.

The long expanse of skin against skin made her shudder and arch up against his weight. He breathed harshly against her flesh and his growing tension fired her with a new sense of urgency. His mouth sought hers and his kiss exploded with passion and a hint of desperation.

A nudge at the core of her made her tighten with anticipation.

"Relax, do not fight me," he whispered against her lips. "I do not want to hurt you worse than I have to."

He eased the pressure and then pushed against her again. She could feel the resistance of her body and concentrated on staying limp. She fought her instinct to clench her muscles. She put her hand on his cheek and he turned to press a kiss in her palm.

His skin was damp to her touch and he was shaking, his restraint obvious. Yet when he pressed again, she folded her legs around his hips and added her own pressure.

Her body's resistance ended with a ripping pang that faded quickly. He was inside of her, stretching her, filling her, making her more complete than she had ever been before. She did not know where he ended and she began, but her heart was full of love. And she knew she would never again feel whole without him, because she had only ever been half.

He pressed gentle kisses on her face and held still. She wiggled, relishing the pressure of his body and sensing he needed to know she was not in any great throes of pain.

Holding her head still, he studied her face. She met his concerned look with a smile. His eyes glittered and emotions crashed through her.

"You did not cry out," he whispered.

"Was I supposed to? It was not so bad." She shifted her hips again, tightening her legs to deepen his penetration. There is more, is there not?"

Of course there was more. She loved him. His

heart beating against hers, his weight bearing down on her, his body and hers becoming one were all part of them together. In bed there were no countries, classes, or past hurts to prevent their union of bodies and souls. Did he understand how much they shared?

Yet he might resist if she spoke of her feelings. He would want to think this was just a physical act, but it wasn't. He was too tender and caring, too unwilling to cause her the slightest pain for this to just be about pleasure, although it was about that too. Because she loved him, she was able to open herself and give of herself in ways that she could not fathom before this moment.

He moved, sliding out and then slowly back in. A deeply erotic sensation of pleasure built and crested within her.

She whimpered and strained against him, until his long fingers found that place of intensity that had her writhing and twisting, seeking . . . seeking until she shattered, her center rhythmically pulsing around his shaft. And she heard the words leave her mouth, the words she had not meant to say aloud, words that came out on a sigh and a moan. "I love you."

Lady Helena peered out the library window and wondered if Trevor would come. She set the candle on the sill, holding her hair back so she did not singe it in the flame. She had allowed her maid to remover her ball gown and dress her for bed, although she had refused the rags for her hair that she normally slept with, and asked for lemon juice to treat her freckles instead. Her maid shook her head at the oddity of the nobility.

When the house grew quiet after the doctor had left, she had finally been able to prepare. She'd removed her stays and then retrieved the brown paper package from where she'd hid it on top of her wardrobe. Inserting the sponge was much harder than she would have dreamed.

Now as she paced the empty entry hall in her peignoir and slippers, she was sure her efforts were futile. He would not come. She had taken too long. Her heart thudded painfully in her chest.

Her mother's illness would put him off, although in truth it was not illness, but a combination of rich foods and a stomach made squeamish by pregnancy. Lady Caine had been put out that Helena insisted that Keene Davies fetch the doctor for them to tell her what she already knew.

She told herself she would wait until the candle burnt to a nub and no longer. Then there was a soft tap on the door.

Helena flew across the marble floor and flung open the door. A watchman stood there with his stave.

Disappointment made her limp. Then mortification plowed through her as she realized she was standing in her nightgown and a thin peignoir with the door open wide.

"You know this gent, milady?"

Helena looked over the watchman's shoulder and saw Trevor standing across the street, leaning against a lamppost. Relief surged through her but she bit her lip.

"Oh, yes, he is expected."

The watchman looked her up and down and shook his head.

"My cousin from America," lied Helena.

"Caught him skulking about, I did."

Stars above, if he was from London he would have known to avoid the watchman, but no, Trevor stood in the glow of lamplight. Or was he telling her he would not hide?

"Come in, Trevor, do," she said, trying to keep her voice low without being obvious. She pulled her peignoir tight across her front. "Thank you, good sir, for watching our house so closely. My mother is abed, but I will fetch my father to greet my cousin."

The watchman looked skeptical, but as Trevor made his way to the front door in no special hurry, the watchman shook his head and stepped back.

Trevor removed his hat and looked about for a place to set it down. She shut and locked the door. Now, he wears a hat, thought Helena, as she took it from his hands. She grabbed his hands and pulled him toward the stairs.

He tugged back.

"Helena, you should fetch your father."

"No!"

"He would shoot me, rather than accept me as your husband?"

"Do not speak so loud," she whispered and veered toward the library to retrieve the candlestick she'd set in the window.

She returned to his side after easing shut the library door, trying to hold his hat and the lit candle in one hand without causing a mishap.

"Then are we to elope?" he asked.

Her heart thundered in her chest. Why was he being so obtuse? "We shall talk in my room, please."

She nearly ran up the stairs, fearing any second his voice would bring out a servant or her parents. And she did not know what they would do, but allowing him to marry her would not even be on the list of solutions.

Without her stays, her breasts jiggled as she walked. She folded her arm across her middle, feeling uncertain, undone, undressed compared to him.

She tugged him into her room, his large stature at once rivaling the poster bed for domination of her pastel green room. She turned and locked the door, then set his hat on her nightstand.

She had left a lamp burning, but the light seemed too bright, although it was barely a soft wash of illumination.

"Pack what you need, and I'll help you get dressed."

Why was he insisting on a marriage this minute? Did he not understand that she could not marry him? "I cannot leave right now. My parents need me."

"Why did you ask me here, then?"

She backed away, feeling stupid and immoral and humiliated. She folded her arms tight across her midsection, trying to hold the ache inside. "Because I wanted . . ." She looked at the bed, then back at him. "You did not need so much encouragement at the park."

He took a step toward her, but she was suddenly frightened. His bulk cast a looming shadow on the wall and she could sense his anger.

"I was reminded tonight of how very wrong this kind of liaison could be. What does it mean to you,

Helena? Am I an experiment for you to learn how to use your womanly wiles? Practice for the lovers you will take after you are wed?"

"No." She backed until she was in a corner between her bed and dressing table. He followed her. This was not the soft gentle union that she had imagined. Her emotions were too unrestrained for that.

He grabbed her arms. "Don't you understand I want to marry you?"

"I know, but it is impossible."

He shook his head and turned around and took a step toward the door. He was leaving. Every doubt about herself crowded her mind. Her lack of passion, her inability to engage with anyone. Her emotions broke like a dam holding back floodwaters.

"Do not walk away from me again."

He stopped, but he still faced the door. "I don't care about your commands, Lady Helena. As an American, I am not impressed by your station in life."

"Trevor, please. I am frightened." Her heart ached with such ferocity that she thought she would have done better to stay in that sleepwalk that she had been in most of her life. Her knees buckled and she grabbed the bedpost to keep from collapsing. "I cannot stand for you to leave England again without understanding how I feel about you."

He turned and folded his arms across his chest, his broad chest that she wanted to be held against. "And how do you feel about me?"

"I would marry you if I could. Oh, God, I thought about you every night and day since you left. I walk around as though I am more asleep than awake. Only when you are near do I feel alive."

He gestured toward her bed. "And this serves what purpose?"

"I only want you as my lover. I cannot imagine intimacies with another man." A shudder of distaste rippled through her as she thought of having to allow any man other than Trevor access to that hidden part of her. "I thought after the park, that you would want it too."

"If you marry Wedmont, you will share his bed."

A shuddery breath left her. She gripped the bedpost with both hands. "I want you to be first. I did not think it would be so difficult to persuade you."

He took a step toward her, lifted a strand of her hair and rubbed it between his fingers and thumb. "I want you more than anything, my love, but I want to have you as my wife. Your virginity should be a wedding gift for your husband."

He shamed her with his words. "I would let you have it."

"Come away with me. If I cannot procure a marriage license for us here, I'll take you home. Any captain can perform a binding marriage at sea."

"Truly, I cannot, my parents . . . are not well. I cannot leave them. But if things are better in a few months . . ." If her mother gave birth to a healthy baby boy, would they care so much about her? Or would it be enough of a joy that they would not miss her overmuch?

"What? Do you wait their deaths so that you might be free of their influence?"

A wave of terror swept through Helena. "Do not jest about such things."

Trevor stepped closer and put his hand on the

back of her head and drew her close. "You mother's illness is long-standing, too?"

She shuddered as she put her head against his chest and his strong arms circled her.

"I am forbidden to speak of it."

He kissed her temple and smoothed his arms down her back. "Your hair is so long and glorious," he murmured. "And you smell of lemons."

She cringed.

"Helena?"

"The lemon juice is to prevent me from conceiving," she whispered and clenched her eyes shut.

"You do not want my babies?"

With the trouble her mother's pregnancy was giving her, the prospect of bearing babies did not thrill her. He pushed her away.

"Not at this moment. I was trying to be practical." She had given little thought to whether he might have a moral objection to preventing conception.

"Helena, I love you more than life itself, but if I start on this slippery path, I will never be free of it. I cannot bear to share you with another man. It would tear me apart to be only allowed into your bed in the dark of night. I want you as my wife, I will not accept anything less."

He backed away from her, his head down.

He was leaving her. In spite of everything he was walking away . . . again. Desolation ripped her in a thousand pieces. Her chest heaved as she fought back the crushing pain of emptiness. The only thing she had to fill the hole inside her was anger.

"Then you do not love me as I love you, for I would never ask you to abandon your family. I have only choices that lead to heartache. I lose you or I lose my parents, and God only knows what pain my leaving would cause them."

He swiveled and marched back toward her. She fought the urge to cower. His blue eyes were stormy and his jaw was thrust forward. What did he mean to do? Oh God, to share her bed when there was so much anger, what would that be like? Conflicting sensations of fear and anticipation coursed through her. She could feel her chest heave as her breathing was jagged.

Yet, as he crossed her room, she thought she would come apart when he touched her.

Victor heard Lydia's soft declaration of love and cringed. But somehow, with the soft waves of her climax gripping him and his release held too long in check, her claim broke free a torrent of emotions as he rocked into her and his body convulsed in spasms of pure rapture.

Had he ever felt such complete pleasure before? He could not remember ever feeling so intense a peak, nor such a perfect pursuit of it.

He groaned, trying to hold back so he would not hurt her, but the moment was not bound by any control. As his seed spurted into her, he poured everything he had of himself into her. She welcomed him, drawing him close with her long legs in a way he'd never experienced. Her eager reception and encouragement made him feel whole. Did she have any idea how much he needed her, needed this?

He buried his face in her shoulder, not trusting himself to look upon her. He buried one hand in her hair, her short fluffy blond curls, Lenny's hair, but Lydia's too.

It had been so long since he had been welcomed in a woman's arms. She stroked his back, gently, lovingly as if she understood his inability to talk, but he had to talk to her, convince her she did not mean what she said. She could not love him, because it would destroy her.

He kissed her shoulder and encountered the court plaster covering where he had shot her. Was there no end to the amount of pain he would cause her? He had wreaked havoc in her life from the first minute he saw her.

She rubbed her calf along the back of his thigh and shifted underneath him. Was he even now crushing her with his weight? He rolled, taking her with him.

A sweet moan of languorous pleasure came out of her. He held her head to his chest and wondered that she could sound so content. Did she not understand that he had ruined her?

She pressed her lips to his chest, and he felt he would burst from his concern over her. What would her future be like now? Would she dash pell-mell into another disastrous adventure or would she return to Boston and become some other man's wife?

Anguish bit through him. Better choices for her than to remain with him. If she was away from him, she still had a chance of happiness.

"That was a lark, can we do it again?" She raised up her chin, planting her arms across his chest.

Her blue eyes searched his, questing for finer emotions he no longer had to give. She deserved so much more than he could give her.

"No, you will be sore, Lyddie." He swallowed, realizing that he had been calling her Lyddie, a nickname that belonged to her mother and caused her pain to hear.

"Yes?" she said, her lips curling up in a knowing smile.

Bloody hell, he was destroying her innocence inch by inch. "Lydia, you do not love me."

She scrunched her nose. "I hoped you hadn't heard me."

Her reply gave him pause. How could he not have heard her? Two people could not be closer.

She wiggled her legs up to straddle him and lifted enough to rub her pert breasts across his chest. Yearning, passion and hunger washed across him. He could drown in her wicked blue eyes.

Was she gloating? Relishing her power to make him weak?

"I do not mind being sore," she said in her low, throaty voice.

He was lost and the lesson he meant to teach her was gone in trying to show her every pleasure he could give her. All he wanted was to keep her with him forever, but he could not bear the thought of what he would eventually do to her.

His temper, his past, his inability to love her back would win out over his intentions to make life perfect for her. He would not be able to protect her from the snubs and cuts of his peers. He had not been able to protect Mary Frances, he knew the *ton* would never forgive him for marrying below his station again. They would take it out on her, not on him. Yet that was nothing to the agony he could cause with his words.

In the aftermath she fell asleep. Long before he could control his anguish enough to talk to her, she had kissed his temple and settled down to sleep. Her hand curled around his scarred shoulder, and her head rested on his chest.

She seemed content to let the future work itself out, but he kept thinking there had to be a solution, a way for him to escape knowing he had destroyed her life. He felt restless and unable to sleep.

He did not want to leave her. And he could not be so inconsiderate to let Keene and Sophie learn that he had violated their trust and seduced their innocent houseguest. Even that thought confused him as he raked his hands through his hair.

He eased out from under her trusting body and carefully pulled the sheets and covers over her. He sat for a long time on the bed, moonlight streaming across the floor. His gut wrenched at the thought of leaving her.

After he gathered his clothes and hung her dress in the wardrobe, he pressed a kiss to her cheek. He half-hoped she would wake, but then his emotions were too tangled to face her. He was tired of facing people he had wounded.

He tiptoed to the door and eased out into the hall. He bent down to place his shoes on the floor so he could slip them on, and came face to face with Keene.

"Bloody hell!"

CHAPTER 19

Trevor stared at Helena. She looked like a Valkyrie, her red-gold hair streaming over her nightgown, fury and anguish on her face. She would lead him straight to hell on the path she had chosen. But, he could not entirely resist her.

There was enough anguish in her pleas that he wanted to comfort her. And she held the bedpost as if fearful the bed would fly away in the wind-storm of her emotions.

He put his hand on her shoulder, pushing back the masses of hair.

He caught her as her knees gave out on her. She stared at him, the emerald of her eyes only a tiny rim around huge black pupils. Her skin was flushed a beautiful peach and he could not resist her parted lips.

She clung to him and he held her, tormented with the memories of her response in the pouring rain. He kissed her and drank in her deep sighs and he fought back his need to make her his and concentrated on her arousal.

He ran his hands over her breasts, drinking in her moans. Leading her to the bed, he eased her back into the cradle of his arms. Her haughtiness disappeared as she became pliable in his embrace.

Still, when she reached for him, he shoved her hands away. "Just let me do this my way."

She untied his neck cloth and pushed his jacket from his shoulders. He allowed her that much. He caught her breast in his mouth along with the material of her nightgown. She moaned and arched into him, while he eased the hem of her nightgown up until he could see the dark red curls at the juncture of her thighs.

As he trailed his fingers to her slick wet core, she clenched her knees together. He laughed, she was not as ready for a lover as she would have him believe. But by the time he was through with her, she would be.

"Helena," he whispered, lifting her nightgown higher.

Her eyes were squeezed shut, and she tugged at the hem as if she would keep it down.

"Helena," he urged. "I want to look upon you."

"Oh, why?" she whispered.

"Because you are beautiful and I want to kiss every inch of you."

She blinked her eyes open. And he pulled her nightgown and wrapper up and off.

"Only kisses, love, you do not need to be afraid," he told her, and then he began.

He started at her forehead and kissed every inch of her that he could reach, moving down in a layer of sweet pecks and lingering, pulling nips. He paid special attention to the skin of her breasts, circling many times until the tips were beaded tightly and then he kissed her there. When he kissed below her navel, she twisted and reached, and he again shoved her hands away.

He moved up, pulled her and her pillows sideways on the bed and lifted her hands to the bedpost now above her head. "Hold here and do not let go."

"Or what?" she asked, staring at him with her eyes so dilated he could see straight through to her soul.

"Or I leave."

She wound her hands around the bedpost, and he kissed her honeyed lips. Then he drew down to the far corner of the bed and kissed her dimpled ankle. By the time he had made it to the soft flesh of her inner thigh, she was quivering like a unlashed sail in a gale. The sight of her slick woman's core, pink and dewing for him, made him swallow hard. He knew he could have her, but what he needed was her to believe her only option was to marry him.

He parted the damp red curls and pressed his lips to the swollen bud nestled there, and she screamed.

Christ, did she intend the whole house descend upon them?

"Ready for a brandy?" asked Keene from where he sat on the floor, his elbows on his folded knees, opposite Lydia's door. "I know I am. I have been sitting here forever. By the by, I sent your carriage home."

"No, I do not want a brandy," Victor told Keene. How could he have forgotten that his carriage was standing in the street? All his self-congratulation on being discreet was for naught.

Keene stood, stretching his arms above his head. Had he dozed as he sat on the floor of the passageway? "You are not leaving until we talk."

"I cannot." Anguish and desperate loneliness broke over Victor and he turned away. "I cannot talk."

Keene would expect him to marry Lydia and if Victor were any other man he would expect it too.

"Ah, she has left you speechless? Good for her."

If he could just get downstairs and out the door, mayhap this horrible ripping sensation in his chest would cease. "A state I am sure is most welcome to everyone."

Keene took his elbow and led him toward the stairs. "Brandy will help."

"Nothing will help. I have ruined her. Bloody hell, what is wrong with me?"

"If that was your intent, then you never would have passed her care to me."

Keene led him toward the library where he had once threatened to boil Victor in oil.

"It is never my intent to wound, but I do it all the same. You should have killed me when you had the chance."

"Shut up," said Keene.

Victor was almost affronted by the rude words. "We cannot very well talk if I am to shut up."

"Very well, talk then. Tell me why you do not want to marry her."

Keene opened the library and although Sophie was gone, the room still basked in the cozy glow of a banked fire. Keene shut the door behind him and folded his arms.

Victor stared at his empty brandy glass on the side table. How could this room look the same as it had a few hours ago? Everything was different, changed, ruined.

"At the very least, I will say things that will wound her. For God's sake, I already shot her."

"And I shot you, and it has never seemed to destroy your affection for me."

"You are my brother." Victor looked at Keene blocking the door. Did he mean to keep him here? It did not matter, because Victor wanted to be away from himself and no matter where he went, he could not manage that trick.

"And I have not been so loyal or kind to you."

"Yes, you have." Keene had not known they were brothers. He had not understood. He'd had a brother who was raised with him and shared his affection without strain or impediment.

Keene had been better than Victor had a right to expect.

Keene tilted his head to the side and said, "By the way, what did you say to our other half-sibling?"

"I told her to act like a lady," said Victor, moving through the room and picking up the book that Lydia had held earlier. He would rather talk about Margaret or his relationship with Keene. "Why?"

"She thanked me, and then Bedford thanked me. You said more than that."

Victor shrugged.

Keene looked at the book and then up at Victor. "You cannot follow just half my advice, you know. I told you to make love to Lydia, but then I also said you will have to marry her."

"Do not ask me to destroy another woman I care about again. I destroyed Mary Frances. I left her with no choice but death." The terror of watching his wife run back into a burning building still haunted him.

Keene shrugged. "Mary Frances was mad."

"She was not so, until I married her." He rubbed the scar on his forehead. Blackness ate at him. Only now did he understand what he had done. "She had been through horrors and I tried to coerce her into . . . bloody hell, every time she came out of the insanity, I forced her back into it."

Keene took his elbow and sat Victor on the sofa. After a trip to the sidebar, Keene squatted in front of the sofa and pushed a glass of brandy into Victor's hand. "You had better explain."

"What is the point? It is done."

"It is not done. Tell me what happened."

Victor took a deep breath and told him what he had learned from Sheridan. That when Mary Frances was a young girl, she had been attacked. She had been brutalized and not expected to survive. While Mary Frances had lived, it was believed that she would never be able to bear children.

Victor knew she could not even tolerate the act that would lead to children. Now he knew why.

Her mother had not been content with the monster's death sentence, but had visited him in his cell and poisoned him, leading to her own incarceration for manslaughter.

Victor had known nothing except Mary Frances's fears. He had spent years winning her trust and affection and then tried to persuade her into his bed so they might have a child—something that Mary Frances had known was impossible, even if she had been able to bear intimacy. Each time they made progress, she fell into madness.

"She should have told you." Keene moved onto the sofa and slid his arm around Victor's shoulders.

"I do not think she could, for fear I would divorce her for being barren." Victor leaned forward, wondering if he felt better, or just drained and empty.

"She did not understand who you are then."

Victor set down the full glass.

"Lydia has no such past to haunt her."

Victor shot to his feet and paced away. "There will be something else. I will destroy her. Like our father, that is my gift. I am just like him."

"You are not like that bastard. I am more like him than you. I have his ruthlessness, but you do not. You have a strength and loyalty that puts me to shame. You do more to hold our rag-tag family together than any of the rest of us." Keene picked up the brandy and drained it.

Because they were the only family Victor had. Except he now had Mary Frances's father treating him like a son, and that shamed him. His pressure and promises had forced her to burn herself to death. If he had not demanded Mary Frances be a real wife . . . but he had.

"It does not change anything. To keep her with me, may endager her very life. I know that. And I cannot bear to go through it again. Lydia is strong. She will be better off without me."

Keene slowly shook his head. "The only way you will destroy her is by refusing to do what is right."

He would do what was right; he would stay free of her so that she might find happiness.

Helena could not believe the sound that had come out of her mouth. Panic flooded through her, piling on top of the already overwhelming sensation.

Trevor did not miss a beat.

Belatedly, she realized she could let go of the bedpost. Of all the positions she had expected to be in during her lifetime, this was not one of them.

"Trevor," she hissed, as she struggled to sit. "You have to stop."

He pushed her down with a large hand against her chest. "Lie back and relax. You locked the door."

Then he went back to what he was doing. He did not care if they were caught. And why not? She was the naked one, he still had on most of his clothes. And he could not have made it all the way to her bedroom without her consent.

Heavens, when he said kiss her everywhere . . . he meant everywhere.

She wanted him to stop. She wanted him to continue. She grabbed the pillow and put it over her face and moaned into it. Then she was spiraling out of control, wound tighter than any longcase clock. Her tension broke, easing away into intense waves of pleasure, and she was sobbing with relief and desperation and amazement. He had given her a gift greater than all the world's gold could buy. She glowed, ridiculously happy, as if her heart would burst.

Stars above, she was capable of passion and it was all because of him. For no one else could she have bared herself so completely and trusted so thoroughly and fallen apart so wholeheartedly.

Trevor settled beside her and gathered her in his embrace. "Done chewing on the pillow?"

She shifted the pillow and buried her face in his shirt. He stroked her hair while she pondered what was next. She was sated and her body exhausted, but he was still fully clothed. Had she not brought him here so he might at least have the pleasure of making love to her? Albeit she had envisioned a more conventional encounter, one where she would seek his pleasure. She had not even believed she was capable of finding her own.

She put her hands against his chest, relishing the firm feel of his broad physique. Remembering the park, she reached down to his unmentionables and stroked her fingers along the hardness hidden there.

He grabbed her hands and pushed them over her head, turning her over and rolling on top of her in the same motion. Then he pinned her wrists to the bed. "Do not or I will tie you to the bedpost."

"But you are . . ." His breath was short and his body tense. She recognized the symptoms from her own fall into paradise. "You are not yet . . ." Her vocabulary was too limited in these matters.

"You have retained your virginity and I will not take it without the church's sanction."

His expression was savage and fierce, and oh, God, she had thought he was no longer angry.

Heat flooded her face. "But I would that you could feel as wondrous as I feel."

"You invited me for a talk."

She looked away, thinking he was draining her glow away. "We talk in circles."

"You know what I want."

"You want marriage, I know. But that is not how it works in my world. I cannot willy-nilly toss aside my upbringing. I would bring shame and embarrassment on my parents."

"Helena, in America a man takes a wife and he loves only her and she loves only him. We do not treat marriage as this disposition of property without love as you do here."

"Give me time," she whispered, feeling her world slip away.

"I've given you five years."

"You have been back for little more than a fortnight. I had no way of knowing if you would ever return."

"What will time help? You would make me your clandestine lover, but you will not accept my proposal."

Her head spun with possibilities. Could she marry him secretly? Could she walk away from her parents? Would she survive so far away? For all America had been a colony of England, it was a foreign place. "My parents—"

"Should want you to be happy. And I will do everything in my power to make you happy."

She stared at him, emotions swirling like a whirlpool. Her parents would hate her. They had come to London for the season because of her.

"No matter what you choose, love, I will never hate you, but I cannot be a secret lover."

A knock on the door nearly brought her out of her skin.

"Helena," her father called. "Are you all right, dearest? I thought I heard a scream."

"Hide," she whispered frantically.

"I will not." But, he lifted himself up and released her wrists.

"I am all right. I just had a nightmare, Papa." She rolled off the bed and stood frozen.

The door rattled. "Helena, are you alone in there?"

Oh, what was she to do? Trevor would not hide. Her father was suspicious.

CHAPTER 20

Victor was sure the madness of his wife had afflicted him as well. There was no other excuse for him showing up at the Earl of Caine's door. What Sophie had said before she fell asleep bothered him. Everything that happened with Lydia tormented him, and he tried to think about anything but her, although thoughts, memories, wishes of her intruded on his every waking thought and his dreams.

The Countess of Caine seemed to bear no lingering malaise from her illness of the night before. In fact, she greeted him with a beaming smile. When he asked for a moment alone with Lady Helena, he thought she might burst.

He was shown to a cozy library, and Lady Helena entered shortly afterward. Her forehead was crinkled in an expression between puzzlement and fear.

"Will you have a seat, my lady?"

She glanced over her shoulder as if she expected another to be listening. Then she sat down on the edge of a chair.

Victor searched for a less than blunt way of saying what he had come for, then shrugged. "I shan't ask you to marry me."

She blinked, and shook her head.

"My mother will be so disappointed," she murmured and folded her lips together as if to restrain a smile.

Perhaps she wasn't as insipid as he imagined. "You are probably wondering why I am here."

"Quite."

In for a penny, in for a pound. He might as well jump in headlong. "Lady Helena, are you in any trouble?"

"Trouble? No."

He sat down on a chair beside her. "Are you sure? I thought I might be of assistance if you are in a bad spot. I could talk to a gentleman for you, or defend your honor, if needed."

She smiled. "I am afraid to disappoint you. I do not need you to fight a duel in my name."

"That was not what I meant." Did everyone believe he fought duels for the fun of it? And did Lady Helena understand what he was trying to learn? "I assure you I meant to offer my assistance as a friend. Sophie saw you at the midwife's and I was concerned that you might be with child."

She smiled softly. "No, I wish I were. The only trouble I am in is that the man I wish to marry does not meet my parents' standards. I hate to defy them, but I cannot bear the thought of marrying another." Her expression was serene as she spoke.

"You do intend to marry this man? He has asked you?"

"My lord, he has all but begged me." She tilted her head sideways. "I do appreciate your concern though."

"So your attentions last night were to divert your mother?"

"I'm sorry," she blurted. Then she colored bright red. "I . . ."

"Never mind, then. You may count me as a friend if you are in need."

"I think I would have been in good stead if my answer were yes."

Helena made her way back to the drawing room, while Lord Wedmont was shown out.

Her mother leaned so far forward she nearly fell out of her chair. "Well?"

"He wanted to be sure I understood he would not marry me."

Lady Caine looked crestfallen. "Are you very sure you did not refuse him?"

"No, Mama. I am quite sure his affections are engaged elsewhere."

"Not Lady Penelope," wailed Lady Caine.

The butler entered the room with a calling card with the edge folded down. He carried the silver salver to Lady Caine. She picked it up and grimaced.

"Tell him we are not at home."

"Very good, my lady," said the butler with a bow.

"Tell him *I* am at home," said Lady Helena. "You should be ashamed of yourself, Mama. He was very kind to you last night when you were feeling poorly."

"How do you know who is calling, Helena?"

"I am expecting him." Helena felt near sick. Her father lowered his newspaper and stared at her.

The butler froze as if he did not know what to do with this turn of events. Helena could not recall countermanding her mother's instructions ever before.

She stood and went to the stair and called down to the entry hall. "Come up, please."

Helena watched Trevor, her qualms melted into a surety she was doing the right thing as he slowly climbed the stairs, his blue eyes trained on her. When he had refused to hide last night, she had finally agreed to marry him. He dived under the bed and she opened the door to her father, who had insisted upon entering her room and looking around to assure himself there was no intruder bent on harm.

Trevor entered the drawing room, his hat held in his hand. The footmen had not relieved him of either hat or coat. She winced but tried to ignore the set-down.

Trevor brushed through the doorway of the drawing room, his height imposing. "My lord, my lady," he said as he bowed.

"Trevor, this is my father, Lord Caine. Papa, this is Mr. Trevor Hamilton."

Her father stared at Trevor's hat. "Sit down, young man."

"I will not intrude on your hospitality long. Lady Caine, you are in good health today?"

Helena wrapped her arm in Trevor's. She could tell he was working very hard at being correct. He might have insisted on a marriage and might hate her parents' attitude toward him, but he would not do anything to raise their ire, for her sake.

Her mother gave a short nod.

"She's much better today," said Helena.

"My lord, I ask you for your daughter's hand in marriage."

Lady Caine stood. "Of course not. How dare you presume."

Helena closed her eyes. Trevor had insisted, although she told him they would be better off to elope and not bother with asking her parents, who would be furious.

Her father coughed.

She only hoped that Trevor's request had not startled him into a fit of apoplexy.

"Are you ready?" Trevor asked.

"I am packed. Let me get my valise," Helena dropped her grip on his arm and headed for her bedroom.

"Are you not stopping them?" asked Lady Caine, her voice rising. "Why could you not stay in the colonies where you belong?"

"Let them go, dear," said her father.

Helena stopped in her tracks. Had she heard her father correctly? Although what could he do to prevent a marriage, since she was of age? She slowly turned around.

"Let them go. Helena has made her choice." Her father turned and coughed again.

"How could you?" asked Lady Caine, staring at her daughter.

"Please do not distress yourself, Mama." Anguish welled up in Helena.

"I am sorry my birth does not meet your expectations, ma'am, but I will do everything I can to keep Helena happy. My country does not recognize titles and we are an old and venerated family in Boston."

"You have got the cart before the horse, young man," said her father. "If you mean to stay in England, I will see if I can stop the sale on the Coventry estate."

"Oh, Papa," whispered Helena her heart breaking and filling in the same moment.

"No!" said Lady Caine. "I will not have it. Helena, you will have no connections or respect."

"It is not too late for us to find a renter for the town house this season," said Lord Caine. "I presume you are in a hurry to be off."

"I am more than willing to stay in England if it will please you to have your daughter close," said Trevor.

"I never want to see you again. Helena, how could you squander such a good bloodline?" Lady Caine said.

Trevor lost his poise then. "Madam, I do think your blue blood would benefit from a drop or two of savage red." He shook his head. "Helena, let's go."

She ran and grabbed the valise in her room, shoved her bonnet on her head without bothering to tie the ribbons and scurried back down the stairs.

She returned to hear the tail end of Trevor's apology.

He took the bag from her and wrapped his arm around her waist. "I am sorry, love."

"I am sorry too," she whispered as they descended to the front door. "But my father took it much better than I expected."

"I don't know," said Trevor. "He kept staring at my hat."

Helena clapped a hand to her mouth. "Oh, goodness, we left it on the nightstand."

"So when your father tells your mother that, will it help or hurt my case?"

"The only thing that will help in my mother's eyes is powerful connections. Perhaps if one of your family was elected president?"

"I'll suggest it to my brothers."

Helena wrapped both her arms around his waist. "Being with you feels too right to be wrong."

Lydia leaned against a pillar and closed her eyes. She was so sleepy this last week. Her eyes jerked open. Just this morning she had been beset by a wave of nausea. A piece of dry toast had cured that, though. Perhaps these late nights were causing her to take ill.

She had not seen Victor in a week. She had expected that he would withdraw, but she had not expected a total defection. Sophie kept her busy, though. In fact, Sophie never let her be idle a minute. They had been to museums and academies and lectures and balloon ascensions until every waking minute was crammed with activity. Perhaps that was why she was so tired.

"Sleepy, pet?"

She smiled and blinked at Victor, half-wondering if she had slipped into a dream. Ah, but her world was brighter with him around. "Would you take me to bed if I said yes?"

He frowned at her and she wondered if he would always frown at her. "Lyddie, think where we are."

In a ballroom of a country house just outside

London. "Never mind, then. I shall simply lean against the pole, until your mob catches up with you."

"Dance with me."

She thought about protesting that it was a waltz, but what did it matter anyway? Given the studious way the Almack's patronesses avoided her, she would never be invited. Besides, she would be returning to Boston before very much longer. James was growing impatient.

Oh, but she wanted to be back in Victor's arms.

He held her closer than he should have and they moved to the music. He only looked at her and she at him. Their conversation was polite nothings.

"I have missed you so," he finally said.

For him to say that much, must have cost him. She made a caricature of a pout, as if she had not watched for him, waited for him, yearned for his touch. "You have not called."

His lips twisted. "I am banned from Keene's house as long as you are there."

"You are banned?" she asked, confused.

"Do not frown so," he said.

Lydia looked across the floor to where Sophie danced with Keene. "They do not know, do they?"

"They know."

Was that why they had been so solicitous of her care, yet never allowing her a moment alone? Sophie had treated her like a sister and Keene, well, he had played a brotherly role.

Tears burned at the back of her eyes. Were they sorry for her? Was that why they made her feel so much a part of their family?

"I am sorry, pet. I did not mean to be so indiscreet."

Indiscreet? She stared at him, at the concern in his dark eyes. "No matter," she said.

"I should stay away from you. I am no good for you."

No, he was the best thing for her. "I know. You made me go back to skirts."

"You look better in skirts." His voice dropped low. "You look best of all in nothing."

He swept her in a direction she did not expect. She stumbled, but he steadied her.

She looked around to see if anyone had noticed. Amelia stood with Lady Penelope and they both watched the dancers.

Victor took another turn and then led her out through French doors. The cool night air swirled around her. He pulled her to a dark corner of the stone balcony and gathered her in his arms.

His kiss was a heady reminder of the passion they had shared. Desire threaded through her and she could feel the answering call in him.

"I should not be doing this," he whispered, but he pulled her tighter against him. "But I cannot stay away from you."

All the sudden she felt she could not breathe. She was his mistress, and he meant to offer no more. What a fool she was to think he might come to love her as she loved him. She struggled back and he freed her.

"Are you to marry my sister, sir?"

Lydia spun around and saw Trevor and James standing behind her. Had they followed her outside?

"No. He does not intend to marry me," Lydia answered. She knew he would not, and as she stood in the cool night air with her heart filling with pain, she would not demand it of him. She had no right. He had never misled her about his intentions.

Trevor winced, but James stepped forward, his face a mask of anger.

Victor caught her arm.

"You said he had proposed to you. That is why we stayed in London," James accused.

Victor's grip on her arm tightened painfully.

Lydia could not look at him. "I lied."

He spun her to face him. She looked down at her toes. "Why? Did you mean to force my hand?"

"No. I did not want to return to Boston."

James growled.

"Lydia, I cannot marry you."

"I love you," she whispered. She looked up and saw his expression change from anguished to guarded. He thought she meant to trick him.

"Unhand her," threatened James.

"You have lied to me from the beginning," Victor said.

She jerked free of him, just as James lunged toward Victor. Not fair, as Victor was cornered by the balustrade and James had raised his fist. Lydia stepped between them as James swung. His fist connected with her left shoulder.

Pain burst through her and her knees buckled. Victor caught her going down to the cold stone, his legs under hers. She heard a moan, but it was not hers.

The bullet wound that had nearly healed seared with new pain deep inside. Had it burst open?

Victor held her half on his lap and he rocked her back and forth. "Are you all right, Lyddie?"

She would never be all right again. "My shoulder hurts," she mumbled.

He pressed a cloth to her shoulder and she was sure she was bleeding again, and the night spun around her.

"There—you have only to be close to me and you get hurt," whispered Victor.

Keene and Sophie shouldered through the growing throng around her and Keene picked her up, while Sophie pressed the handkerchief tight to her shoulder.

Trevor held back James.

She closed her eyes against the growing dizziness. She was vaguely aware of being carried down steps and across the lawn.

Then she was in the Davies' carriage with Sophie soothing her, and she slipped into the slumber she had craved.

Victor was not thankful Lydia's brothers had followed Keene and Sophie to their carriage. He rubbed his forehead. This was all his fault. He should have stayed away from her. And he would have relished some good fisticuffs, although he doubted he could return any of her brother's punches.

He was sick with anxiety that the punch had reinjured the wound he'd given her. She had never complained of pain before.

He would have followed too, but Keene gave him a harsh look of warning. Instead, he leaned against the balustrade and stared out into the dark of the night.

A slender hand on his shoulder prompted him to turn. Lady Penelope or Lady Helena or one of the others had found him.

"Are you all right?" asked Amelia.

He still had some friends, although he wondered if Keene would ever regard him warmly again. Keene did not understand.

"No."

Amelia leaned against his arm, her head coming against his shoulder. At first he thought she meant to offer comfort, but then her bare fingers smoothed his hair back from his temple. He closed his hand around hers and pushed her hand away. "Where is George?"

"I do not care."

He took a step away from Amelia, her fingers still in his grasp. "Where is George?" he repeated.

"I am tired of his games. Why is he the one who always is so histrionic? Why must I always be the one who apologizes?"

"Because you are the one who sleeps with others."

"Only you," she whispered.

"No more."

"Oh, for heaven's sake, she is just a child," said Amelia. "You cannot prefer a girl who would dress like a boy. You could have your pick of women."

"I only want her."

Amelia stepped back and looked at him strangely.

"Is that why you want me? Because I am coveted now?" he asked her.

"You always were coveted and your loyalty to a wife not worthy of you only made you more so." Amelia sounded bitter.

That was twice in a week that he was accused of

loyalty. Yet, he did not understand what had happened with Lydia. He had abused her and misused her and she came back for more. He did not even know what she wanted. All her plans of independence and freedom had nothing to do with marriage. Did she want to marry him?

If he told her of how he had torn down Mary Frances and destroyed her, would Lydia still profess to love him? If he told of the way he had ruined his friendship with George, would she understand? If she learned that Keene had wanted to kill Victor, would she understand how perilous a relationship with him was?

If she had any sense at all, she would run all the way back to Boston.

But for that moment in her bed he had felt whole, as if every mistake he made was behind him, just a distant memory. He had tried to believe it was just physical, just the long lonely stretch of his celibate marriage that made him so hungry for her. But it was her, not any woman, not Amelia or the lovely Penelope, but his Lydia whom he craved with pangs so strong they cut through him like knives.

When he had the chance to set it right, to declare before her brothers that he would marry her if that was what she wanted, he had balked. Because she whispered of love and he did not believe in love, not for himself. He did not believe her, and she had told her brothers he would marry her long before he considered the possibility. He did not know where the lies ended and the truth began.

He looked at Amelia, who had been watching him while his thoughts crashed about in his head. He knew what he needed to do now.

"Go back to George, or I will take you back to him."

Amelia whirled and went back to the ballroom.

After a decent interval, he reentered the house. He scanned the company for the host and hostess to take his leave.

Lady Penelope sidled up to him, lacing her arm through his. "Is it true?"

"What?" asked Victor.

"Is it true that the American girl was traipsing about London dressed as a boy?"

"Who told you that?" he asked.

Lady Penelope smiled unpleasantly. "Did you really keep her at your house? Did you grow tired of her and send her to the Davieses to keep? I assure you I would never behave so outrageously."

"Yes, and that is what makes you dull as ditchwater, my dear."

Penelope's smile vanished. "You do not deny it."

Hell, Lydia was ruined beyond repair. Her reputation was shattered forever and it was all his fault for introducing her to society. She had never cared to go beyond the gaming hells where she could eke out a living.

"You have a low mind to engage in such gossip."

"You, Lord Wedmont, are no gentleman." Lady Penelope marched off in a huff.

Victor agreed with her. In spite of his title and his descent from the long line of earls before him, he was lower than a polecat. No matter what he did, he would not be able to stop the besmirching of Lydia's good name.

* * *

Lydia stood looking at the crowded ships, their crisscrossing spars making a forest of masts. James had wasted no time in booking passage to Turkey where they could meet one of the Hamilton ships on a regular trade route.

Her shoulder ached and it was a mass of purple and black. The physician Sophie and Keene had fetched had pronounced her injury not serious. Lydia knew that James's punch had reopened half-healed wounds. Since she could move her shoulder, the damage was no worse, but telling James that she had been shot there and that was why she had been in so much pain was a mistake.

First thing in the morning, James had shown up and insisted that Jenny pack her trunks. When Lydia resisted, he threatened again to carry her over his shoulder if he must. Her brother was angry enough to do just that. So now she was here.

James paced angrily back and forth. "Where is Trevor? I told him to meet us here."

Lydia stared at the ship they would sail on for the first leg of their journey home. Nothing of the optimism and anticipation of the voyage she had taken to England months ago entered her. Instead, a sick dread filled her. Boston would be cold with the harsh winds coming in off the bay. She was born and raised there, but she did not want to return. Yet she had vowed never to run away again. Running away solved nothing.

As she was shown to her tiny cabin and her trunks shoved in with her, her heart ached at the idea of leaving England. She had not even said goodbye to Victor.

The worst thing was he had not been concerned

enough about her collapse to inquire after her health. She stared at the tiny berth where she would spend the next few nights sleeping, alone.

She had tried to give Victor what he needed and demanded nothing in return. She was a naïve fool. All she got for her troubles was a broken heart.

There was nothing for her in Boston but an existence that might as well be death. She would not be so foolish as to hope Victor would come after her. She knew he would not.

"She's not here," said Keene. "Her brother came for her this morning. He's taking her back to America. I sent messages for you, where have you been?"

Victor stared at his half-brother. "At the Archbishop of Canterbury's. Why did you not stop them?"

"I could not stop them without knowing that you would do the right thing." Keene shook his head sadly. "You took too long to come to your senses."

He had taken too long to realize that he had already done too much damage, whether he kept her with him or not.

Her reputation among the *ton* was shot. Rumors were likely to make their way across the Atlantic to her home. But a girl who would masquerade as a boy did not give a fig about reputation.

Alas, he had done what she hated; he had made the choice of her future for her, and he hated himself for it.

"Did she ask about me?"

"No. She went without a fuss. I asked if she

wanted me to send for you, but she said no. She doubted that you would have changed your mind."

Lydia knew what love was and she gave it freely without expecting his love or even his safekeeping in return. He had never deserved her, and he had deserted her when she asked nothing of him.

"Surely they have not sailed yet. I have to find her."

But by the time Victor had searched the manifests of all the ships sailing to America, the one bound for Turkey had already left.

CHAPTER 21

Victor sat on the low stone wall enclosing the park of his estate. Across the rolling green lawn stood the house his father-in-law had erected in Victor's absence. The keep that had loomed over the land with menacing power had a new slate roof that covered the crenellated battlements. The arrow slits had been broadened to contain wide mullioned windows.

The once gray and mighty keep now had a new façade of coquina. The new wings of the house jutted out on either side and were nothing like the harsh, forbidding structure that had stood on the spot for centuries.

The house looked warm and inviting. No reminder of the grimness that had marked his home for thirty years remained. Black-faced sheep dotted the rolling park, keeping the grass trim and neat. His estate was now bucolic and peaceful.

When he first saw the new house, he had been ready for the usual sense of heaviness and oppression that greeted him every time he came home, but he'd been shocked. It was if Mary Frances in her dementia had wiped away all the stains of the past and cleared the way for a new beginning.

The construction was ongoing. Scaffolding still stood against the exterior walls and a steady stream of carts and wagons went up and down the drive. Plasterers, carpenters and craftsmen busily worked at completing the interior. Tiled floors were being laid and wood planks sanded and planed for other surfaces. His house would soon be a home.

Perhaps if he sailed to America, by the time he returned, it would be ready for a family. If Lydia did not hate him too badly.

He'd been a complete idiot.

His carriage wound its way up the drive and one of the groomsmen hopped down and opened the gate. Barely high enough to keep the sheep inside, the low wall would not deter invaders. The carriage only contained Millars with Victor's trunks. Victor had ridden ahead on Waterloo, not wanting to inflict his bad company even on his servants.

Millars would probably not be happy to learn that they were leaving for the coast directly.

The carriage traveled a short distance up the drive and then came to a halt.

Victor watched as the door opened and a tall, blond-haired youth descended the steps.

He shook his head to clear it. He was seeing things.

But the youth in tan jacket and chocolate brown breeches, with boots to the knees, walked steadily toward him.

Bloody hell, it was Leonard.

Victor pushed off the wall. He took one step, then two and then he sprinted toward her. When he reached her, he grabbed her and swung her around, then kissed her thoroughly. A tradesman's cart passed and the occupants stared so much that one boy tumbled out onto the ground.

"Oh, does that mean you are glad to see me?" Lenny asked, her blue eyes bright in her face.

Emotions crashed one on top of each other. But his voice had never deserted him in times of desperation before, so he managed to say, "I daresay I am vastly relieved you have saved me a trip across the ocean to bring you home."

He pulled her against him, his heart pounding in his throat. Her long legs tangled with his and she slowly threaded her arms around his shoulders. She was what he needed to make his new estate a real home.

He touched her cheek, relishing her silken skin. Perhaps if he held her an hour or two he might believe she was real. "Ah, Lyddie, I have been a fool."

"Yes," she said. "Should we explain to yonder men that I am in disguise?"

Victor glanced over at the gawking workers and grinned. "No. If your reputation is destroyed, we might as well destroy mine too. But you have brought a dress or two, have you not?"

She nodded, her look distant.

He had so much to say to her, he did not know where to begin. "I hope you shall want to wear one tomorrow morning."

If she agreed, they could be wed in the village church. The special license burned in his pocket. Yet he had to explain his fears and make sure she understood the risks before he would let her decide. If she decided marriage was too dangerous, he would let her go. He wanted to carry her off and make love to her before he risked her refusal. Still,

she had come to him. He had not totally destroyed
her love for him.

She seemed distracted. "Is that your house?"

"The new one. The old was burned to the
ground. Only the shell of the keep remained standing, but it was built to withstand any assault. Would
you like to see it?"

She nodded.

"It is not ready to be lived in yet, but within a
twelve-month, it should be habitable."

He kept his arm around her shoulders as he
guided her across the lawn. If he could just show
her how magnificent everything would be, perhaps
that would counterbalance the real peril she faced
in marriage to him. Too many Wedmont brides
died young.

Lydia stared at the huge structure. Was that his
home? Few building in America were so big. Everything that Trevor had said about Victor's station in
life being superior to anything she knew was glar-
ingly clear. She had needed to see his country
estate to understand.

He was glad to see her, but he had said nothing of
their future. Nothing of his feelings. She wondered
if she had made the biggest mistake of her life.

When she left the ship, a pile of clothes stuffed in
her bunk to look as if she were sleeping, she had
been sure. Sure that she was doing the right thing,
that the only future for her lay right here.

As they strolled toward the steps leading to the
front door, her throat tightened. Would just being
here with him be enough? What if he never loved
her? Did he think being his mistress was all she had
come back for? If she told him of the weak stomach

she had experienced the last few mornings, would that change his mind?

Doubts crowded her thoughts as he explained the history of his estate, and that he owned little of the original land, but had decided to invest in businesses instead of concentrating on land stewardship. They had reached the portico leading to the open front door.

"We have much to talk about, pet. But I must do this." He bent, scooping her up in his arms and carried her over the threshold.

Her heart thudded in her chest and he kissed her gently before setting her down on the bare plank floor. She stared at him. Did his gesture mean what she thought it did?

He met her gaze with his own intensity, then he dropped to one knee, gathered her hands in his and said, "Lydia, would you do me the honor of becoming my wife, of sharing this home with me? I have done much to hurt you and I fear I may yet cause you more pain, but I love you and I cannot live without you. I was a fool to ever believe I could."

"You love me?" Just when she thought that she had made the biggest mistake of her life, he astounded her.

"You tie me in knots and I am half a man when you are not around, I presume that is love. I had thought I was not capable of such. Would you like to see the rest of the house before you give me an answer?"

She plunked down on his thigh and put her arms around him. "No."

"No, you do not want to see the rest of the house—or no, you will not marry me?"

"I thought you would never ask."

He twisted, digging at his pocket.

"Or at least I thought I would have to tell you about the baby. Of course I will marry you."

Victor jerked around, his expression startled, and they both tumbled to the unfinished floor.

She kissed him, pulling him down on her, relishing the weight and pressure of his long lean body, remembering the night in her bed. She hooked her leg around his, drawing his hips closer. He stroked her hair and feathered kisses all across her face. "Oh, Lyddie, are you sure?"

Two workmen entered the room and drew up short. One man dropped his tools with a loud clatter.

"No, not yet, but pretty sure." Lydia smiled and glanced at the workmen whom Victor seemed intent on ignoring. "I suppose if I am to be mistress of all this, I should not be romping on the floor with you."

He groaned. "The floor is all we have. I do not have any beds." He nonetheless moved to his feet and oh-so-gently pulled her up. "My future countess," he said to the workers and pointed at the open door. "Now leave."

"Lydia!"

"Who is that?" asked Victor, bewildered.

She winced. "Sounds like Trevor."

Just then her brother bounded through the door, followed by Millars and Lady Helena.

"My lord—" started Millars.

"I have better things to do then chase you all over England," Trevor said. "For the love of God, how did you run away from James?" He took one look at her apparel and rolled his eyes. "Oh, no!"

"I did not run away. I . . ." She squeezed Victor's hand. "I ran toward my future."

Trevor glared at Victor, his animosity making him look even bigger.

Victor scooped the piece of paper from the floor, the paper he had tugged from his pocket, and handed it to Trevor.

Trevor unfolded it, looked it over and then clasped Victor in a bear hug. He handed the paper to Lady Helena. "Might this help with your parents?"

She read it silently and passed the paper to Lydia, who had stepped forward, concerned that her brother might try to harm Victor.

"Perhaps. My lord, we have traveled quite a way. Would you be so kind as to put us up for the night?"

Victor looked bemused. "We would be happy to, Lady Helena, but there are no beds."

"Mrs. Hamilton, if you please. I am sure that we will make do."

Lydia read the marriage license and realized that Victor must have gone for it the morning after the confrontation with her brothers. Her doubts dissipated like morning fog burning off in the sun.

"Tomorrow morning too soon, pet?" Victor asked, reaching for her hand. "If you still want to after I tell you everything."

Lydia rolled her eyes. "My child would like a name. Even a black one."

Victor spent a good share of the night on a mattress on the unfinished floor of their future bedchamber, explaining every reason she should not marry him. After each new revelation she would say, "I don't care, now kiss me."

He started reaching far into his past for more

examples of the blackness of his soul, until he told her about the rock he threw through a window at the age of eight. To which she replied, "If you are done with all your confessions, we might move on to more interesting things."

He stopped trying to talk her out of marriage, eventually. And she told him in the morning that she was as good as indestructible. After all, she had been robbed, shot, and depended on her own wits to survive for quite long enough to prove she could.

He agreed. He also decided that he'd severely misjudged Lady Helena when she and Trevor had stayed outside in the pouring rain damn near making love under a tree in Victor's park. No milk and water miss was she.

So it was that two upstart Americans stole the best catches of the season before the festivities had gotten into full swing. And it was Helena who whispered to Victor after the ceremony that she had a message to him from Sheridan—she and Trevor had gone to him to locate Lydia once again. *By wedding your opponent, you have broken the curse of the dueling pistols.*

Which was beside the point, Victor thought, looking down at his new bride. He had found the greatest blessing of all: love.

ABOUT THE AUTHOR

Karen L. King fell in love with romance when her mother fed her voracious appetite for books with a romance novel. Sidetracked by real life, kids, husband and a career at a major Missouri newspaper where she authored a few incident reports and a system manual, she returned to her first love with her debut novel, *The Wedding Duel*, a HOLT Medallion finalist for best first book.

She lives in Kansas City, Missouri, with her family. She enjoys roller-skating, dancing and, of course, curling up with a good book. You can visit her on the web at www.karenlking.com.

More Historical Romance From
Jo Ann Ferguson

Available Wherever Books Are Sold!

Visit our website at **www.kensingtonbooks.com.**